The Quiet Dead

Niki Mackay studied Performing Arts at the BRIT School. She holds a BA (Hons) in English Literature and Drama, won a full scholarship for her MA in Journalism. Under Niki Mackay, she is the author of two books featuring Private Investigator Madison Attallee *I, Witness* and *The Lies We Tell*, as well as the gangland thrillers *Loaded* and *Taken*. Under NJ Mackay she has published two standalone psychological thrillers, *Found Her* and *The Girls Inside*.

THE
QUIET
DEAD

NJ MACKAY

hera

First published in the United Kingdom in 2023 by

Hera Books
Unit 9 (Canelo), 5th Floor
Cargo Works, 1-2 Hatfields
London SE1 9PG
United Kingdom

A CIP catalogue record for this book is available from the British Library.

Print ISBN 978 1 80436 492 5
Ebook ISBN 978 1 80436 493 2

Look for more great books at www.herabooks.com

Printed and bound in Great Britain by Clays Ltd, Elcograf S.p.A.

I

For Andrew, my mew, and the little mews too. Home really is where the heart is.

PROLOGUE

Fifteen years ago

The night is like a series of Polaroids. Still images, flashes of things she can't get hold of. Danny, his hand soft in hers; Cat dancing, the firelight making it look like sparks are flying from her hair as she spins; Matt, face screwed up, angry – a vague, unsubstantiated memory that is to haunt her for years to come.

Woodland everywhere, trees reaching overhead like hands joining in celebration. Her dancing, barefoot for a while, the feel of warm, baked earth beneath her free feet. Vodka sliding down her throat, sharp and slippery. She remembers walking, the sounds of the party distant. She remembers twigs from the trees pulling at her long hair, giggling, though what was funny she is unsure.

Then there is nothing nothing nothing until she steps into her house, into a scene so awful, so unthinkable, so surreal that she finds herself sobering up fast. Cortisol pushing through her veins, falling to her knees, her hands reaching out for Matt coming away thick and slippery, his eyes wide open and empty. She gasps for seconds, minutes? Fear making the hairs on the back of her neck stand up, she forces herself to her feet then she calls for Ethan, her little brother who is not here. She steps carefully on Bambi legs through the horror, managing

I

somehow to walk around the bodies of her mother, Ryan and Matt and up the stairs where it looks almost normal. Like any other day, like everything is fine even though it never will be. Never could be. She cannot look at them again, her mother and her twin, her best friend, sparring partner, confidant. Bodies now, corpses, faint parodies of what they had been just hours before. She cannot allow herself even for a second to contemplate how life without them will look. She must find Ethan.

Not here, not here and she is… running outside, the door slashed with red streaks from her hands slams shut behind her, a loud bang in the still woods; she runs so fast she loses her balance and goes down more than once, the drink and the horror combining to make her clumsy and desperate. She circles full speed around the whole of their odd little house, a place that she has hated since the day they arrived because she had never wanted to come here anyway.

She's fallen, more than once, face forwards, hands shunted out but still landing on her knees which feel sore and dented. The panic overtaking her as she looks down and sees her hands are smearing bright, thick red everywhere.

And, here she is. Just moments ago, she'd been surrounded by the deafening sound of her own screams, but now she sits, legs curled towards her, blood making her skin shiny and slick, waiting. For the police and for her brother. Little Ethan who must be here somewhere but has not responded to the cries of his name. She's shouted it so many times her voice is hoarse.

She's searched the inside of the house for him.

Hiding, she thinks, he'll be hiding. Anything else is too bad to even consider. Memories of him rush through her mind, his little body slipping into her bed after dark as her parents' cross words floated up the stairs hitting them both like slaps to the face. That's what he'll be doing, she thinks. He'll be hiding…

CHAPTER ONE

The call comes in just after lunchtime on a cold Friday. George Arnold is the one who dialled 999. He is the foreman. The men dragging the earth are his team. It is his responsibility.

There are bones, and unless he is very much mistaken, which he thinks he is not, they are human. They must have been buried deep, six feet almost if he has to hazard a guess. Jim Bryant pulled them up, a faint glimmer of white on the trowel of his digger. He'd paused, jumped off the machine, gone to look. Shouted for George.

George says to the telephone responder, 'They could be from an animal, perhaps?' The responder, of course, cannot answer. Cannot advise. And George knows really that that is not what has been unearthed here.

Peeking out from the ground are two large eye sockets. On Jim's digger is a long white bone with smaller bones attached, an arm perhaps? With broken bits of fingers hanging like loose teeth. Further beneath the skull and just about to be revealed is material of some sort. Brightly coloured.

He looks away.

They've all paused and men stand around the edges of the site smoking, sipping hot tea from metal flasks as other cars arrive. The help that had been promised on the phone. Too late for whoever was buried here on George's site.

There is a team of people now, a flurry of activity. Bright yellow tape is placed around the area which had been woodland and would soon be luxury flats. Though not as soon as expected perhaps.

A tall man with serious eyes heads over towards George. Next to him is a petite woman. Neither is in uniform, but George understands that they are police. The man introduces himself, solemn and respectful. George no longer feels quite so silly for being as shaken as he is.

The woman, 'Detective Constable Quinn', suggests that they go and she'll take his statement. George finds he is relieved to be getting away from the afternoon's gruesome discovery.

DI Sebastian Locke watches Lucy Quinn head off with the foreman and goes over to Dr Martina Mathewson who is instructing scenes of crime officers and scribbling on a pad. She holds up a hand as he approaches, and he stands waiting whilst she marks up what is where before the job of carefully excavating begins. Photos are being taken, but she always likes her own notes.

Seb looks down at the remains and knows, without having to be told, that the skeletal remnants belong to a child. Someone small and not fully grown. It is confirmed by Martina who murmurs, 'Maybe eight, nine.' In response to the question he hasn't yet asked. Her voice is slightly muffled under her mask, worn to protect evidence, though he understands there will be nothing of use left and that here, the back fields of a huge public park, may not have been the crime scene.

It is a bold place for a burial.

Where they stand, surrounded by uneasy workmen and half-erected scaffolding. Ahead of them is what appears to be deep woodland but actually is a thin circle, half a mile at most, which surrounds the park's central hub where there is a cafe, a play park full of shrieking little ones, and a skate ramp besieged by surly teenagers on scooters and skateboards, hoods up, eyes down.

Thames Park, the place for which this little town is named, is the community's heart and is well used by locals and visitors alike. There had been a battle raging for quite a while between developers and residents about the building of flats here on its outskirts. The developers had won but had to compromise on their specifications. It meant they couldn't build with the views they'd originally intended, but still, each dwelling would fetch over a quarter of a million pounds.

It is a desirable place to live. Direct links to London, green belt whichever way you turn. A much lower crime rate than the city itself, though, of course, not without its issues.

Seb forces himself to look away from the stark winter trees and back at the sad display half in and half out of tumbled earth.

Eight or nine years old.

He tries to make his mind scamper away from the thoughts it is feeding him, which are of his own child at that age. When she had a gap-toothed smile and round, puffy cheeks. When she was in between her baby years, which had passed so quickly, and before adolescence, which had just arrived: a rude and uninvited guest, as far as he was concerned. Transforming his daughter from the version he was familiar with into something entirely new. At least, he thinks, she is doing that, even as her growing up might sting. At least it is not her reduced to this small white heap, in a shallow grave.

He swallows thickly, asks Martina, 'How long have they been here?'

She sighs. 'Years, I'd say. I'll be able to tell you more when I get a proper look.'

He says, 'How quickly can you find out?'

She shrugs. 'I'll run some cross-checks, see if I can find anything in the system as soon as I'm back. There's a material here that might help me date it then I'll search for children within this age range. Hopefully, there'll be dental records to match against. But, it's the weekend.'

A historical case, which would likely be a headache. Just a collection of bones stashed in the earth, years ago at least.

A child. Someone's son or daughter, brother, sister or grandchild.

CHAPTER TWO

The restaurant is slick and shiny. The food here costs a fortune, and the drinks we've consumed with our meal would be into several hundreds of dollars by now. My husband, Sean, grins like a Cheshire cat, a wide, even smile exposing shiny white teeth. A beautiful smile, a charming smile, one that pulls you close with its promise. I smile too, playing my part brilliantly. I am Hayley Marriott, his glamorous, doting wife. I laugh at jokes that aren't funny, join in with conversations which don't interest me and pretend to be oblivious to the lechery of the old man Sean is reeling in for the kill. It is a big deal, huge, and Sean has to close it. This is what tonight is about, what this whole weekend has been for. He'd taken Murray around the city, shown him the sights that New York has in abundance. Last night a strip club and cocktails, today golf on the city outskirts, and now he is here, with us, and his long-suffering, disinterested wife who is quiet but drinking more than her fair share. Murray himself is half-cut and getting more so. I imagine drinks were had at the golf club earlier. It's too cold to be out for long. Sean is ramping it up now. He is close, we are a formidable team, and I can feel it like a glimmer in the air, heavy and pungent, as Murray relents to my and my husband's charm. They are discussing his portfolio, how to improve it, where to put his obscene amounts of capital for best return. Sean is fully armed. He has his silver tongue, his company's credit card, a file with paperwork longing for a signature, and me sitting pretty on his right-hand side, flashing just enough cleavage and my own super-bright smile.

Murray is dawdling, either playing at reluctance or still not quite convinced. His wife may as well not be here at all, her Botoxed face immoveable, bar the opening of her lips every time she raises her glass. I've been careful not to piss her off, but this needs to be finished, and I want to go home. I move closer to Murray. Sean slides the file over, opening it, signalling where he needs to sign. I press myself against the old man's arm and breathe out, 'I can't wait to see what you do here, Murray.'

And just like that he lifts the pen, signs and runs a celebratory hand across my shoulder, his rubbery fingers swishing past my left breast. I don't jump back as I would like to. I stay still, smiling, simpering.

The deal is done, and now, champagne.

Despite appearances to the contrary, Sean and I are not drunk. But now we can indulge, and as I press the flute to my lips, I let the warmth of the alcohol seep in. The triumph of the deal, my husband's latest achievement and what it means for us. His boss will be pleased; his next promotion will be in reach. We will be richer still.

By the time we get home, a cab ride through the city brightly lit with Christmas lights, the booze softening the hard lines of the skyscrapers, we are high on our own success. We fall through the door, his hands on me and mine on him before we've had a chance to close it behind us.

He takes me now, my back pressed to the wall in our hallway. It is quick and frantic. When he is done,

I murmur, 'Congratulations, baby.' And he kisses me full and hard.

'Maybe we'll have other congratulations soon.' He pulls back, rubs a hand across my flat belly exposed as my dress rides high above it.

I hold up my crossed fingers.

He says, 'I have to send some emails, let them know it's done.'

I say, 'Sure thing.' Pulling down my clothes, stepping out of my shoes, shaking off my underwear caught on one spiked heel. I say, 'I'll shower.'

In the en suite, I ferret in the cupboard at the back where my husband never goes. I pull out a box of Tampax, slide my hand inside and find the birth control pills I keep hidden there, popping one and swallowing it.

I shower and get into bed, exhausted from the evening. At some point Sean slides in behind me, pulling me close, his body pressed against mine.

CHAPTER THREE

Seb spends the weekend in a whirl of ferrying Tilly and her friends to the cinema, back to theirs for a sleepover and then depositing three tired teenage girls home on Sunday before an argument about homework erupts, ending in Tilly slamming her bedroom door and blasting godawful pop music from above. Val, his mother-in-law and steady voice of reason, says, 'Hormones.' Seb nods, smiles thinly. Maybe she is right. Maybe this is just par for the course, but, he thinks, it hurts like hell. They'd always been close, he and Tilly. Seb is the only parent Tilly knows, the only one she can remember, and he can feel her inch-by-inch shutting him out. He'd taken Tilly's love, her adoration, for granted; had never stopped to think it might change. Val is probably right. Hormones. Strong things that transform children into adults after all. It stings nonetheless and makes weekends tense at the moment.

Honestly, Seb feels something close to relief as he drives towards the morgue on Monday morning.

The relief is, of course, short-lived. It lasts for pretty much the car journey then comes to an abrupt end as his mind switches from home to work. He doesn't like cases involving kids. None of them do. Even so, there are dedicated teams at each station who delve into crimes involving children because, unfortunately, they are needed. Most cases involving children are now linked to online activity

-the internet is a paedophile's playground – resulting in nightmares it is hard to imagine but impossible to forget once you know.

Seb doesn't know how they manage their work, those dedicated child teams. He'd done a stint on one of them when he had first started in serious crimes, and he'd moved on as quickly as he could. Murder, homicide, is where he is now and where he plans to stay.

He stands, watching Martina Mathewson carefully lining up the too-small bones, and he feels that same little ache in his heart that he got watching predators using unicorn profiles to try and destroy young lives.

Death is indecent.

Grief, the one awful truth people have to live with.

It comes to everyone at some point, of course, the ultimate loss. If you've ever loved another soul, you aren't immune, but there is, usually, a natural order to it.

Most people died when they were old, and if they weren't just old, then you probably could have seen it coming. They smoked too much, drank too much, ate all the sweet things.

It is different for Seb, as it is for his colleagues. He knows that death finds other ways to seep in and that there are far worse things than dying.

Losing a child, for example.

Martina says, 'Good weekend?'

He sighs. 'Tilly had friends to sleep over.'

Martina laughs. 'What age is she now?'

'Thirteen.'

'Ha. Bet she was exhausted and pissy on Sunday.'

'Yes,' he says, glum at the memory.

She shrugs. 'It passes.'

'When?'

'By the time they leave home. Then you get to miss them like hell.'

'Great.' But he's smiling at the thought of adult Tilly. She is a good kid despite the mood swings and he is pretty certain she'll grow up to be a great woman.

Martina says, 'I have news for you,' waving at the bones. She pauses – for suspense, Seb suspects. She has a flair for dramatics.

'You have an ID?'

She nods. 'The material – pyjamas label still intact on the bottoms are from a batch that was sold for two years in M&S, so that helped speed it up. I cross-checked it with missing children in the area from then, very few as you'd imagine, and got you a name which I'm pretty sure of. We'll have an ID via dental records in a few hours.'

'Very clever.'

She nods, grinning, 'I reckon this is Ethan DaSilva. You may remember the name. His daddy Leonard DaSilva is the family annihilator.'

He frowns then. He remembers that case, or reading about it at least. Three dead, a mother and son, the son's friend who'd been spending the night, the youngest child missing.

Ethan.

Seb says, 'That was a while ago?'

Martina nods. 'Fifteen years.'

–

Fifteen years that little boy has lain there.

More than a decade unmourned. His eyes blur slightly as he scrolls through the newspaper articles from the time. Red-topped papers with lurid, screaming head-lines. Leonard DaSilva's face staring out from the front pages. Longish hair, dark eyes, every family's worst nightmare. He confessed straight away. He was a known drinker, had been seeing someone about his 'problem' – an alcohol counsellor. It was thought he had turned up in Thamespark, a reasonably sized Surrey suburb, to visit his soon-to-be ex-wife. Seemingly, the visit hadn't gone as planned. The couple had argued. Leonard had gone off, back to a local Travelodge. Seb can picture the place in his mind. He is often there at management's request to see off groups of teenagers smoking skunk in their cheap rooms, or to break up domestics, perhaps not dissimilar to the argument that occurred between the DaSilvas way back then.

The fair presumption was that he had gone back to his hotel, mulled over the argument with his dearly beloved, become enraged, started drinking – they'd found an empty bottle of vodka in his room – gone back, killed his wife, eldest son Matthew and Matthew's friend, Ryan Dudley, then Ethan. But Ethan had never been found, and that was a gaping hole in an otherwise neat and sadly not uncommon scenario. The notes say that Leonard went quietly, willingly. After his initial surprise at officers bursting into his room and waking him up at five a.m., he had stood and held his hands out to be cuffed. The mugshots show him straight-backed, that same intense stare as the image on the news reports. Officers on the scene noted that as well as appearing to be sober he was also calm. Seb lays out the photos now. Awful images of a violent act. Leonard doesn't have the look of a man at the end of a rampage, but then they didn't always. Seb had seen criminals with steadier hands than his when faced with their own depravity.

Leonard would have been drunk, and Seb knows that the darkness enveloping him would have been thick, complete. He knows from bitter experience that drink and drugs can turn decent people into monsters. There would have been fewer street lights then than now and very dark by one a.m., especially as much of that area was woodland. One a.m. is when it was agreed that Leonard entered the house picked up the knife that Anita had used earlier in the evening to cut onions for a stir-fry. There had been no forced entry, so she'd opened the door to him. He'd stabbed the knife once, hard into Anita's throat, then, startled by the teenage boys whom it is thought came in and interrupted him, he'd turned again, lunged first at Matthew then Ryan. Ryan was caught fast in an artery, would have gone down quickly. He had stabbed Matthew several times, but it was estimated to have taken minutes for him to bleed out. Seb tries to imagine the horror of the lad's last moments. Collapsed alongside his mother, blood spilling from holes up and down his body.

Had he spoken? Asked his father why? Had he tried to protect Anita and found it was too late?

Had he seen Ethan come down and slipped away with fear for the small boy lacing his last terrible moments?

Seb forces himself to look hard at the pictures of the victims from before that night. Matthew had been tall and gangly, but he still had much of the child in his face. The crime scene photos are obscene. The man boy's eyes open and wide. Shock looking out at an unfair world.

An open-and-shut case, or it would have been if not for Ethan. He scours pages, sees that officers searched surrounding areas, but by then, the crime scene was hours old. Ethan could have been anywhere.

Seb knows this town, he's lived here for most of his adult life and grew up a few towns over and it's his knowledge of timing and distance and the actual logistics that is bugging him now.

Seb grabs his car keys and steps out into the dim day.

He heads to the Travelodge, which is still there, probably not been decorated since that fateful night but now with a Toby Carvery attached.

He gets out of his car, walks from the car park to the DaSilvas' old house, the cold biting at his fingers and making his chest and throat feel clear and watery. It's mid-morning, but there'll be no real light today, and as Seb makes the journey on foot, he passes from the town out into fields and the housing estate, now sprawling. Back then it had consisted of five houses and only two had been occupied.

Ten minutes to the DaSilva house.

Ten minutes back.

He is back at the Travelodge.

They know that Leonard hadn't taken his rental, a bland Volvo, which remained on camera in the car park. He also had been seen on CCTV arriving back at the Travelodge after his first visit, but he hadn't been seen leaving a second time, nor coming back at, what, two, two thirty a.m.? Bundled Ethan alive, Dead, into his car? This niggles at Seb. In the notes it said Leonard could have walked under the camera and not been detected, and perhaps he could. Seb would be checking. That aside, it strikes Seb as highly unlikely that he could have walked out to the park's surrounding woodland, where Ethan's unmarked grave was, and back. Highly unlikely that he could have made it back by morning when the police thumped on his hotel room door, dragging him from

16

his bed, into cuffs, down to the local police station, on remand. To court. To prison, where he has remained to this day.

There was no way that Leonard made that journey on foot with Ethan alive holding his father's hand, or dead and slung over his shoulder like a rag doll.

Could he have taken another car? Driven on roads made empty by the hour?

Seb gets into his Golf now. Perhaps Leonard *had* used another vehicle? Unlikely, but certainly not impossible. Perhaps, Leonard had help. It said in the notes that they thought he had changed his clothes, and certainly, he had showered at the hotel room. Seb imagines him, off his head, naked in the moonlight, burying Ethan, walking back to the Travelodge, showering, falling into bed. If he had an accomplice, maybe they had buried Ethan. Maybe they had stashed Leonard's clothes somewhere never to be found? Possible, but he'd never mentioned an accomplice. Looking at his confession, he'd said very little.

Seb drives to the park, soon to be flats, now a crime scene.

Half an hour. How long to dig down six feet at least? A warm summer then, hard, heat-baked earth, cracked open in places, split by the pounding sunshine but solid nonetheless. Not a wet April to turn it to mush, not an easy nor a quick task, digging through that. An hour? More? Almost definitely more. Heavy work, sweaty work.

Four in the morning when the DaSilvas' only daughter arrived home. Walked into what must have been a living nightmare. Five a.m. by the time the officers had attended both the DaSilva house and the Travelodge picking up Leonard. Asleep in his bed, specks of Anita's blood on his long-sleeved white T-shirt. No mud. Not mentioned.

Not catalogued as evidence. The assumption had always been that he'd got changed. But why would he leave a T-shirt with blood on? Drunkenness perhaps? Carelessness, stupidity? Maybe he had it on underneath other clothes? Seb reimagines the walk back, maybe in underwear and a T-shirt. The items found next to his bed along with his shoes which definitely matched footprints inside the house, but then they knew he'd been there prior to the murders.

It is not likely, Seb thinks as he drives back to the station, that Leonard was the person who buried Ethan. Making it highly unlikely that he had killed the little boy, and if he didn't kill the boy, how likely was it really that he had killed the others? And, if he didn't kill them, why confess?

And who did?

CHAPTER FOUR

DSI Jackie Ferris glares at Seb as though he has intentionally brought this tricky case to her attention just to annoy her. Dragging it into her office like an unpleasant, unwanted smell.

'You want me to, what, reopen an old case?' He has expressed his doubts regarding Leonard and Ethan. In careful words that, whichever way he dresses them, are words she doesn't want to hear.

Seb says, 'I think that would be the best course of action.'

'So, you think Leonard probably killed him, but there is a slim, and I have to say unlikely, chance that someone else buried him?' Hope makes the question macabre and, somehow, darkly funny.

Seb smothers a smile, doesn't answer straight away. There's often a gallows humour to their days, he thinks. Jackie carries on staring daggers at him like a comic-book cross boss. Eventually, he relents ever so slightly. 'He might have buried him.' He does not think this but knows better than to say that outright with no hard evidence. 'He probably killed him, though I'd be open to questioning that as well, to be honest.'

'He confessed to killing him. He confessed to killing them all.'

'He didn't deny it, you mean.'

Jackie spits back, 'Semantics, he signed the confession.'

Seb nods. 'He did, yes.' That is undisputed. Clear as day in black and white. More than that, Leonard DaSilva is retained at Her Majesty's pleasure. Four counts of murder.

Case closed. The murder department likes closed cases. Not all loose ends can be tied up, of course, and there will always be a few bits that you can't cover entirely. A missing corpse though is one hell of a loose end. But it was fifteen years ago, before Jackie headed the squad, before Seb was a detective, before he was even a fully grown man, when he'd still been living unhappily with his adopted parents a few towns over. If mistakes had been made, it hadn't been on their watch.

That didn't matter now. The body, the white bones, accompanied by nylon Marvel pyjamas from Marks & Spencer, that once held the soul of a little nine-year-old boy, had been unearthed under their jurisdiction.

'And you've just said he could reasonably have buried the boy?'

'I said he *could* have. *Reasonably* may be a stretch.'

'Okay then.' Her face loosens ever so slightly.

'But I don't think he did. Bury him.'

'Shit.' The line of her mouth tightens again. The glare hardened on him. The messenger delivering bad news whom she may well shoot if she could.

'Another point, CCTV at the Travelodge showed him leaving and coming back from Anita's from his first visit but not leaving when the murders happened or coming back.'

'Could he have avoided them?'

'Maybe.'

'You don't think so?'

'I didn't manage to be completely unseen.'

He adds, 'Sorry.'

She sighs. 'You're willing to take this ball-ache on?'

He shrugs. 'Call came in on my shift.' Also, he's sick and tired of only being sent in to clean up drunken fights gone wrong and the odd domestic. That makes up most of murder, to be honest. Seb likes a puzzle. Already his mind is sifting through the scant information trying to get it to make sense.

'You don't want to hand it over? We could make an argument for cold cases to take it.' That hope again in her voice. Ned over in cold cases is a nice fella, but he'd been put there because they don't get a lot of action and this case, well, it isn't going to be your average unsolved burglary. Seb doesn't answer her. He doesn't need to. There are reasons Jackie is in charge, and she can see the facts of the situation even as she may wish they weren't so.

She sighs. 'I'm sure we'll get a lot of scrutiny.'

'Yes. It's been fifteen years, a nice number for a splash. It'll make a good front page.'

'I want you to understand that, at this stage, we are not officially reopening the case. We don't have enough evidence for that.'

'But—'

She holds up a hand, and he closes his mouth. 'I want you to partner up.'

Seb starts to protest. Whilst he's grateful to be on the murder squad, and he really is, he's under no illusions as to his popularity or lack thereof amongst the other detectives.

She holds up a hand again. 'Before you start moaning, I was going to suggest Lucy Quinn.'

Seb frowns. 'She's not on our squad.'

'No, but I'm considering her. Think of this as a trial run.' Seb knew this, and it was why Lucy had been out shadowing him lately. But partnering was different.

Seb would prefer to go it alone, but he'd worked with her on a case a while ago, just before she made it to detective and on to serious crimes, and she was diligent at least. She'd also dealt with the site manager well the other day, being the only other detective on shift. On the whole, she was all right, and like Seb when he started, she was young, ambitious and, as far as he could see, principled. Plus, murder, like most of the force, needed new blood.

Jackie says, 'You'll lead, obviously.'

He nods. 'Probably a lot of admin, six floaters?'

'You can have Harry when he's free, and as I have said, at this stage it is very much an informal investigation.'

'Come on.'

She continues to glare at him without saying anything. He sighs. That was as good as it was going to get, he supposes, and he nods agreement.

Jackie says, 'He could have had an accomplice. That ought to be your focus.'

Seb agrees. 'He could.'

'The daughter, she's still alive?'

'She is, yes. I mentioned her when I called the prison and I checked Leonard DaSilva's visitors.'

'Has she been in?' That hope again: maybe the girl had been in on it and, whilst they hadn't closed the case fully, they also didn't have an innocent man in jail.

Seb shakes his head. 'Not once in fifteen years. Married an American, relocated to New York over twelve years ago.'

Jackie says, 'Maybe they spoke on the phone or wrote letters?'

Seb nods. 'Maybe.'

'Call her first. Try and get the lay of the land there.'

'Okay.'

–

'Are we reopening this case then?' Lucy asks, eyes narrowed as harry comes into the room.

'Not reopening exactly,' Seb says, pondering it. 'Well, not officially. I think it will go to press as an ongoing investigation, tying up loose ends sort of thing.'

'Should it go to Ned?' Lucy asks.

'It's gone to me,' he says with a shrug, not willing to offer anything more. Including the thing he suspects are all thinking: that Ned, who runs the pretty much defunct cold crimes division, lovely though he is, would not be well equipped for what is likely to be quite a high-profile 'non-investigation'. It is also, Seb understands, a show of faith in him that he will deal with it correctly and discreetly.

'There's hardly any paperwork, is there, considering?' Harry says, looking at the thin file, which, when fully spread out takes up only a small foldable table in this tiny, airless room they've managed to get.

'No. Though they did have a confession, I suppose,' Seb relents, adding: 'They didn't document things the way we have to now.'

'For all the good it's done us,' Lucy says, screwing up her nose. There have been some awful cases in the press of late regarding criminal police officers. Public trust in the boys, and girls, in blue is at an all-time low, and honestly, who can blame them? There are officers in this very station whom Seb wouldn't want Tilly being carted off alone with. A wide, endemic problem brought about by flagging pay and lowered recruitment standards. Though he suspects you'd always get that type of person attracted to any role with power.

'Would he have had time, Leonard DaSilva, to bury him?'

'Funny you should mention that…' says Seb and tells Lucy and Harry about his drive.

There is silence for a moment. 'Could someone else have killed the boy?' Harry asks.

'Maybe,' says Seb.

Lucy makes a scoffing sound. 'Unlikely though, isn't it? Two murderers hit the same family on the same night.'

'It is unlikely, yes,' Seb agrees. 'Jackie suggested he may have had an accomplice.'

'Says here the daughter called it in, was sitting outside covered in blood and hysterical.'

'Yes. Hayley,' says Seb, who feels haunted by the image, the thought of a child, not much older than Tilly, walking into that. He wonders what she is like, how she has managed. 'Which I think is where we'll start.'

CHAPTER FIVE

I'm back in from a long run and yoga, showered and dressed, when our landline goes. I check my mobile to see if I have any missed calls.

No.

I contemplate not picking it up and remember that some of the older members of Sean's team still use it. As my hand reaches for it, it stops ringing, and I smile in small triumph. Then it rings again.

'Hello.'

'Hayley DaSilva?'

DaSilva. A wash of nausea rushes from my stomach to my head out into my newly stretched limbs. The relaxation of the class is gone in an instant. I am tight, tense, taut. My hand dampens on the handset, a fast, slick lick of fearful perspiration. My heart beats … *babadaboom* … *babadaboom*. 'Marriott, Mrs Hayley Marriott.' The words come out like a strangled choke. I say Marriott like a terribly rude curse word. Three syllables of fury. For the intrusion. The jarring sensation of hearing that name. Here.

'Sorry. Mrs Marriott, your maiden name was DaSilva?'

My eyes flick to our hallway as though my past might just swing open the door, clamour in, walk up to me and laugh hysterically in my face. I've changed my name twice, in fact. So DaSilva is my maiden name, but DaSilva is also a distant memory from a horror story I managed to escape.

'Mrs Marriott?'

My damp hand is holding the phone too tightly; my long, newly painted hot-pink nails dig around the receiver and into my palm. I loosen my grip, breathe in, breathe out. We spend half of every yoga class 'breathing'. The other women take it extremely seriously as though true spiritual enlightenment is there waiting to be found in an overpriced gym in Manhattan. 'Yes.'

'My name is Sebastian Locke. DI Sebastian Locke.'

Police. My blood seems to pulse extra hard; I imagine it coursing around me. My heart panicked and working to keep going, frantic and insistent.

It is a week before my sixteenth birthday. I am fifteen and scared. Police trample through the home that I'm never going to live in again.

But I'm not fifteen. I am thirty-one years old.

This isn't our run-down little house surrounded by a grim wire fence and set in isolated fields. This is my beautiful apartment owned by my handsome husband who comes from old money and is set to make a new, fresh pile of it just for us.

Hayley DaSilva.

'What do you want?' My voice is too quiet, a whisper although there's no one here to listen in.

He asks, 'Do you have anyone with you?'

'No.'

'When will your husband be back?'

'Detective, spit it out.'

'I'm a detective at Thamespark. Three days ago, Friday afternoon, a builder came across some remains on the edge of the park where the new development is going up.'

'Thames Park?' I ask stupidly, as though anyone there would refer to anywhere else as 'the park'.

'Yes.'

Remains.

My heart is racing. My mouth is dry. I wish I'd made coffee or at least had a glass of water.

I swallow and it's thick, a combination of not enough saliva and toothpaste.

Three days ago.

Fifteen years ago.

I know what he's going to say. Of course I do. It couldn't be anything else, and yet there is a pause. This stretching silence where I am still ignorant.

His voice soft now like velvet. 'They belong to your brother.' Words spoken gently but still sharp enough to cut.

Ethan.

I think of his little, smiling face. His small hand tucked into mine. I can almost feel the tiny weight of it. Hay Hay, he called me, because when he was a baby, he struggled with the whole word.

I nod, I think, even though the detective can't see me. I should be saying things. Asking questions.

Wailing even.

Remains.

He is dead.

Ethan is dead.

It shouldn't be a surprise. Logically, I'd not for a second thought he'd lived. But we are wired to hope. It is the hope, I think, that fells us, and I had hoped that he was alive somewhere and okay.

But that is not the case. Only I had carried on breathing, living, being forced to go about my business. Alone and without them.

No. That's not entirely true.

My father had lived too if you wanted to be pedantic about it.

'Are you all right?'

I don't dignify that with an answer. Instead, I bat it back with a question. 'You're sure…?'

'We are. We got a positive ID via dental records.'

I nod at no one, the gesture wasting into thin air. 'How… how long has he been there?' So close. Not far from home. My home. Our home.

'A long time.'

Shit.

Ethan.

'He's been buried all these years?'

'Yes. We think so.'

'Right.'

'We'll be going to speak to your father.'

I laugh then.

Daddy daddy. Dear daddy. Ethan adored our father, we all did, but he was also the most untainted by his terrible moods.

I shut my eyes. I can't catch my breath. It is tight in me. I imagine my ribs contracting, squeezing my organs. My heart like a small, fluttering bird trapped in a shrinking cage.

My little brother used to wake in the night calling out for him. I had hated him a bit by then, our dad. Mingled in with the complicated love were hard bits. Barbed wire cosseting the good memories.

Oh god.

Ethan.

Tears come then which I swipe at and try hard to sniff away. He can't see me, but a sob escapes and he, Locke, says, 'I'm sorry.'

I shake my head – at what, I don't know.

'We need to know, have you spoken to your father?'

'No, and I have no intention of doing so either.'

The detective suggests I cancel my plans for the day, reads out his number which I scrawl in shaky script on the notepad next to the phone.

I agree. Images of my mother's face, of Ethan's and Matthew's, assault me, reminding me of all I have lost. I could just ignore the call; I could pretend I never had it. I could stay here and keep being Hayley Marriott, but I won't though. My brain is already calculating how long it will take me to pack, the earliest flight I can get. What the hell I'm going to tell Sean.

CHAPTER SIX

'What did you think?' The call had been on speaker. Lucy is poised over the flat smartphone on the table between them; Harry has been sent back to desk duties.

'Generally?'

'Yes, and is she in cahoots with Leonard?'

Lucy says, 'No way of telling for sure yet, but I'd be surprised. I mean, she's obviously moved on, started a new life.'

Seb nods. He feels awful that he had to relay the information over a phone call rather than face to face. She had known he was dead, told them as much, but until there was a body…

She'd lost her entire family in one fell swoop. Seb knows from the case file that Anita DaSilva had moved her children here to the town she herself had grown up in. Her father had outlived her mother and had died, leaving their only daughter the small cottage in their will. Anita and Leonard had been having problems for a while, and he assumed, for Anita, it must have been the deciding factor. A fresh start, a step away from her often drunk and, according to the scant notes they have on him, occasionally violent husband.

Lucy says, 'Do you think she'll come back?'

'Maybe.' His phone rings. He picks it up, listens, murmurs an obscenity into it and hangs up with a face like thunder. 'How are you with the press?'

'I don't know.'

'Think you can cobble together a press release?'

'Should think so.'

'Say we've found the lad. Enquiries ongoing. Keep it low-key and get it sent out to locals.'

'All right.'

Lucy is disappointed not to accompany Seb to see the man himself, but she smiles and nods. This case is her chance. She knows that. Jackie likes her, and she's got a good solve rate, has assisted on some big investigations, but she's young and inexperienced. She was surprised when Seb approached her at all but pleased. She'd heard a lot of the olds bitching about him: 'smart alec' and 'know-it-all' were favourites. The problem with Seb is he is good-looking, clever and sounds a bit posh. He is also one of the youngest detectives of his rank and unapologetic about it.

She can see how he might rub people up the wrong way, but she likes him well enough. More so since he gave her this chance, and she isn't going to blow it sobbing about being left out of the good bits.

She suspects they will have to see Leonard DaSilva again and she is happy to bide her time.

He says, 'I'll make sure you're in on the next chat with him, but taking care of the comms is going to be equally as important. Sensitivity is needed.'

She blushes, feels as though he'd somehow been peering into her thoughts. His words do make her feel better though, and he's right, of course. It's not grunt work, she's not being palmed off, and as she heads into the station, she does so with a sense of purpose.

–

Leonard DaSilva is a good-looking man. Despite his years incarcerated, he looks like his mugshot, better even, his face leaner, the crinkled lines around his eyes and his forehead adding depth rather than age. Wiry without being thin, and very tall. He has olive skin and wide-set eyes. His dark hair, streaked at the front with the first hint of white, is long and pulled back in a ponytail. He has a surprisingly calm demeanour.

Certainly, he isn't what Seb was expecting. Though he knows well enough that monsters rarely look like what they are.

Leonard listens without interrupting whilst Seb outlines why he is here, though not in detail. Just that Ethan, his young son's body, has finally been found.

He waits, giving him space to respond. The man's mouth drops at the corners, shoulders sagging, but he keeps Seb's eye, unflinching, not looking away. The only thing he says is: 'Hayley?'

'Your daughter.'

He nods. His eyes sink to his hands, then: 'I figure you might have spoken to her? If you're here?'

Seb admits this is the case with a nod. 'It felt right to inform her first,' he says. He does not say that they were wondering if she was in cahoots with her dad. If it was she who'd buried Ethan, perhaps even before her mother and brother died.

She'd been with friends. The friends had been teenagers, out after curfew, drinking. Her alibi had been

32

checked though not in any depth. It hadn't been pushed and picked at. Nothing in this case had. They had a man with a motive who agreed it was him.

Leonard asks with raw hunger, 'How's she doing?'

'It was a brief call.' Seb imagines not seeing Tilly, not knowing about her life. How it must be for Charlie, who he supposes feels that pain somewhere beneath the fug of drugs and whatever disaster she's embroiled in now. He tells Leonard, the parent who'd failed, whether he was guilty of murder or not, 'I couldn't say. She lives in America now.'

He looks up and kind of smiles. 'Oh yeah?'

'Yes, she married a man from New York, helps out with his business, I think.' Seb shrugs. This is the scant information he could find on her and as much detail as he is willing to give away. He's also quite sure now that Hayley genuinely hasn't spoken to this man since the day he was arrested.

Leonard says, 'She was always clever.'

Seb doesn't respond.

'So, you found my boy?' *My boy*.

'Someone did.'

He nods, head bobbing up and down. His jaw chewing, perhaps on the inside of his mouth.

Seb realises he is fighting tears.

They come anyway, and Leonard moves big hands across his face, swiping at his sorrow. Seb looks at them, wondering if those hands slashed at his wife and child, wrapped around Ethan's little neck and applied sustained pressure until the life slipped away from him. Martina had found a break in the bones there that indicated manual strangulation.

A hard way to die.

A mean way to kill.

Up close and personal. It would have been difficult to look away as the life had drained out of the small child.

Leonard murmurs. 'God.'

Grieving parents are one thing, but this man has been charged with and tried for the boy's death.

He asks Seb, 'What do you want from me?'

'Information.'

Leonard laughs. 'If I had that...'

'You claim you were in blackout that night?' Seb's voice conveys doubt, but he knows that intoxicated people can lose large swathes of time. Understands what it's like to have a full-blown conversation with someone who is up, moving about, eyes wide open, only to realise the next day that they have no recollection of it whatsoever. He has always had the dubious upper hand over his estranged wife, Charlie, in that he gets to remember every single one of their bitter arguments.

Leonard looks up, meets his eye. 'Detective, half the people in here are missing years of their life. Now, in your line of work, I'm sure you know prisons are chock-full of idiots like me who blunder through years not knowing what they're doing.'

He does know that. He also knows that whatever state a person is in when they commit a crime, a crime is a crime. The law is the law.

You break it; you do the time.

Leonard seems to sense what he's thinking. 'I'm not saying I shouldn't be here. Shit, I deserve far worse than this.'

'But you don't remember killing them?'

He shakes his head. 'No, sir.'

'You don't think you did it?'

34

'That's not what I said.' He frowns.

Seb says, 'But you've contemplated it?'

Leonard pauses. 'No one wants to think they're capable of something so heinous, but I didn't think I had it in me to hit my wife.' He pulls himself up. 'That last week, before she left, brought the kids down here, I lost all control. We went ten tons at each other, and I laid punches on her little body like I would have a man.'

'But you remember that?'

'Not exactly, no, but I did it. What I'm saying is if you'd asked me before it happened, I'd have told you I wasn't capable.'

'So why not murder too?' Seb agrees.

He shrugs. 'When I'm in that state, my body is moving around, and my brain has no real idea.'

'You still drink, take drugs?' They both know it's easy to get what you want inside.

Leonard shakes his head. 'Haven't touched a drop since the police showed up and arrested me.'

Seb says, 'You've taken a degree in here?'

'Yup, criminology.' He grins.

Seb muses on the fact they'd studied the same subject, would have covered similar modules, evidently shared intellectual interests, and yet they sat on very different sides of the table between them now.

Leonard, still grinning, tells him, 'Hoping to understand mebetter.' It seems a well-rehearsed joke, and Seb thinks his smile is forced.

'And do you?'

'I'm not all that interesting.' That quick-fire put-down that Seb isn't buying one bit. He thinks Leonard understands himself just fine and has more self-awareness than most of the criminals he's picked up. 'What I learnt and what I do understand is that criminals breed criminals. My daddy was a violent drunk. I grew up to be the same. Didn't know better.'

'Hardly an excuse.'

'No. Just a reason. I see young ones come in here, try and work with them if they'll give me a bit of time. Tell them my truth, maybe save them from the same mistakes.'

'Did you love your family?'

'Oh yes. Me and my wife… god, we were young when we met, but from the first day she was all I could think of. She took over every thought I had. You know what I mean?'

Seb keeps his face blank while his brain is filled with images of Charlie, in a bar, dancing on the table. The most beautiful thing he'd ever seen. He sees flashes of her now imprinted on Tilly who looks more and more like her mother each day. He was obsessed with Charlie, she took up all of his thoughts, she nearly destroyed him. He gets what Leonard is saying. Gets how that kind of all-consuming love can rot and turn sour, like curdled milk giving off a stink.

Leonard sighs, eyes still damp from tears shed for Ethan, shining fresh again at the memory of his wife, all he has lost. 'Loved her, loved the little 'uns. Each one different to the last, all good kids. I had a life once, Detective, and I was a young man when responsibility knocked at my door. A child really when Hayley and Matt came along, and I never resented it, stepped up. I had a job I liked, prospects.' Seb feels a stab of understanding at that. He'd been a father before he was even fully grown and it remained, to this day, the absolute best thing that had ever happened to him.

'You got made redundant?'

He nods. 'I did, and it unhinged me. All of me was tied up in being Anita's husband, the kids' dad. The provider. I'm a musician at heart, but there's no money in that, and I accepted it. I played for pleasure, but my job was something I was proud of. It kept a roof over our heads, put food on the table. When it went, I couldn't handle it. I had some kind of a breakdown, I suppose, though I didn't know to call it that.'

'You couldn't find another job?'

'Nope, and the bills piled up. We had to choose between us eating and the kids. I failed them.'

He looks down at his hands.

Seb doesn't want to feel sympathy for this man but what he does feel is that glimmer of doubt growing and stretching. Picking at the pieces of the story that put Leonard here. Casting a doubtful hue upon it.

Leonard DaSilva had felt bad about all kinds of things when his family was killed. What was more guilt heaped on? He was, Seb realised, the perfect patsy.

He says, 'You'll never get out of here.'

'Nope.'

'You okay with that?'

Leonard nods.

Seb says, 'Some people don't think you did it.' There are endless Reddit threads claiming Leonard's innocence but not offering anything else in its place, though they have promised to do so soon. Leonard would probably be aware of them if he'd ever googled his name.

He says, 'No one would like proof of that more than me, but it isn't out there.' His voice is very certain for a man with no memory. It brooks no argument, claims no room for error.

37

'So why bother to study in here? Why bother to stay sober?'

He shrugs. 'I've done enough damage to others to last a lifetime. People in here are still people, a lot of them in pain. I try and help, especially the guys who'll be out. If I can change something tiny for them, their families.I don't know.'

Seb likes him, he realises. It almost pains him to say, 'Did you strangle him before or after Anita and Matthew died?'

And Leonard looks at him, startled. 'He wasn't stabbed?'

'Did you borrow a car?'

Leonard frowns. 'I had a car. It was at the Travelodge.'

'How did you get to Anita's?'

'When we fought?'

'The fight you remember.'

Leonard says, 'Drove. I was sober when I got in the car, sober for a month before then. That's why I'd come down, all ready to show I was a changed man, beg forgiveness.'

'What happened?'

Leonard laughs, 'She told me she'd heard it a hundred times before. That a month was nothing, we could talk in a year.'

'And that pissed you off?'

Leonard nods. 'It did. Real bad, but I wasn't drunk, not then. I shouted at her, and she jumped back, cut her hand on the kitchen knife.' He looks down at his own hands resting on the table. 'She jumped because she was frightened of me and I had never argued with her when I wasn't out of it before. I'd never really registered that fear. One of my last memories of her is her looking at me scared, me reaching out for her hand and her snatching it back.' Seb tries again not to feel sympathy. He may have slashed a knife across that scared woman's neck. Or he may not... and the tiny spots of blood found on his T-shirt were from that cut on her hand.

'Matthew?'

Leonard shakes his head. 'When we rowed, Matt was out, so was Hayley. Ethan in bed. That's half the reason I got so pissed at her.'

'Because the kids weren't there?'

He nods. 'I honestly thought I could sober up for a few weeks, show up like god almighty and she'd take me right back.' He shakes his head. 'Deluded.'

'Where did you go after the argument?'

'Stopped at a Tesco, bought a bottle of vodka. Drank a good deal of it in the car. Nursed it back at the hotel. Last thing I remember is drinking in that shitty little room and feeling nothing but sorry for myself.'

'And angry?'

'I guess I must have worked my way up to that while the booze settled in.'

Seb says, 'Guess so.' But the glimmer of doubt, the unease, is growing. Too many loose ends. Too many question marks. Leonard may well be guilty, but Seb would have made sure all of these other things would had been answered along the way.

Leonard says, 'Where was he? Ethan?'

'On the edge of Thames Park.'

Leonard frowns. 'Near Anita's place?'

'You don't know the park?'

'I'm not from around these parts, am I?'

'And that was your first visit? To Thamespark?'

Leonard nods. 'First and only.'

Seb has a million questions pinging around in his mind: unformed whispers bursting like fragile soap bubbles begging to be asked. But he will need to tread carefully, as though tiptoeing on glass-thin ice. Careful with this case that other detectives had signed off, put to rest. Careful of the hornet's nest he was poking ever so gently. Because if he had to take a stick to it and release stinging, buzzing bugs from inside of it, he'd need to be sure it was necessary. He stands now, needing to think about what has been said, what it all means. 'Thank you for your time.'

Leonard nods. 'If you do find anything…'

'I'll let you know.'

Seb heads to the prison office, collecting his belt, badge and wallet. He's almost signed out when a voice behind him says, 'Detective?'

He turns and finds himself face to face with a woman almost as tall as he is. She is in a sharp suit softened by bright white trainers, with auburn hair that stretches loose to her waist and the most beautiful deep-set eyes. He covers up the unexpected jolt of attraction with a frown. 'Yes?'

She holds out a hand to him, shuffling paper files beneath her arm. 'I'm Faye Doyle.'

He shakes her hand, which is soft and cool, still frowning. 'Okay.'

'Sorry.' She laughs then. Her whole face changes, brightens. Yes, he thinks, she's stunning. 'I'm the prison psychologist.'

'Right.'

'I wondered what you wanted with Leonard DaSilva?'

'He's a… patient?'

'Not exactly. I facilitate support groups mainly, along with far more paperwork than I'd like.'

'Right.'

'Leonard helps a lot of men I work closely with. He's especially good with addicts.'

'He mentioned that.'

'I like him,' she admits. 'He's also hard on himself and unlikely to reach out for help if he needs it, so I thought I'd ask you directly what's going on.'

He breathes in. The air is stale inside these places, the rankness of desperation pervading it. Faye Doyle looks impervious to it though it must get to you, the environment. He tells her, 'We found his son.'

'Ethan?' Her smile drops.

'Yes.'

'Dead, I presume?'

Seb nods.

She shakes her head. 'This'll be tough on him.'

'He's in here for the boy's murder.'

'Technically not.' She tilts her head and narrows her eyes at him. Her hair dances around her shoulders, held back by black-rimmed glasses. 'As Ethan's body was never recovered, he wasn't convicted for that one. Besides, even murderers have feelings, Detective.'

'Not all.'

'No, not all.'

There is a pause that Seb finds awkward though she seems perfectly relaxed. She also looks like she's gearing up to speak again.

He says, 'Well, nice to meet you.'

'Oh, well, you too. If I can help at all.' She digs around in an inside pocket of her jacket, hands him a card. Their fingers touch, and he looks away, sliding it into his own pocket and mumbling, 'Okay, thanks.'

41

CHAPTER SEVEN

I walk away from the phone in a kind of daze. I open my laptop and start googling flights. I book one, using the credit card Sean has put in my name. My house, my mother's house, is currently empty, ready to be shown to new tenants, but no one's in there yet. I have no desire to see it, let alone stay in it, but the only hotel in Thamespark is the Travelodge, and that seems like it might be even worse. I can figure it out when I arrive. I don't need to make any decisions yet. I start to pack, my body vibrating on a nervous frequency. Heart racing, hands damp. I have two hours before I need to be at the airport. I'll fly overnight their time and arrive at Heathrow in the early morning there, practically the middle of the night here. I feel an odd sort of splitting, a disconnect. I imagine myself existing in two different time zones simultaneously. Mrs Marriott in America, doing a few jobs around the apartment. Getting dinner ready for Sean. And Hayley DaSilva. Someone I've tried so hard to leave behind. Getting on an aeroplane. Crossing the ocean. Sad and petrified as if no time has passed at all.

I sink onto the edge of my bed, my packed wheelie suitcase at my feet. Designer handbag clutched in my lap. Inside, my passport, money, cards and phone which I slide out now. I call a cab and ask him to take me to Sean's office.

The air is cold, the wind whistling between tall build-ings as I step out of the cab and into the skyscraper where Sean's dad used to sit on the board, guaranteeing his son the same smooth transition through life that he himself had. I never met him, he died before I knew Sean, but he's revered here by his old colleagues and by his son who seeks to emulate him.

I'm waved through reception and make my way up to my husband's office on cotton wool legs. I pause at the door, to steady myself I suppose, and hear the faint tinkle of laughter, followed by the deep burr of my husband's voice. I think about just turning around, getting back in the cab, sending him a text, but I don't. Instead, I step in.

Sean is behind his desk, a broad grin now frozen on his face. Draped at the edge of it but now standing stiffly is his secretary, Sophie. She murmurs something and leaves, face red, whooshing past me, a trail of sweet perfume in her wake.

Now Sean is standing, stepping around, coming over to me, arms outstretched. 'So good to see you,' he lies, or maybe he doesn't. Maybe he is glad to see me.

I smile brightly, my role in the make-believe we like to keep intact. 'I have to fly to England.'

He's scowling now. 'What? Why?' We never go to England. We holiday everywhere but never there.

I wave a hand. 'A problem with the house.'

He sighs. 'Why you don't just sell it I'll never know.'

I shrug like I'm terribly stupid. I don't mention the prenup he had me sign, the fact that I have no career of my own and my sole income is the rent from that house. I say, 'Maybe I will if it proves more trouble than it's worth.'

That seems to cheer him up. 'Well, if you need any help...'

'Thanks.'

'How long will you be gone?'

'I'm not sure yet. I haven't booked a return flight; I'll see what needs doing.' I add, 'There's been a flood, downstairs. The damage is quite extensive, and they are going to have trouble letting it out again. I feel like I should go and oversee things. I'd prefer to talk to builders directly in this instance. Make sure we're getting the best deal.' I try to appeal to the financially astute part of him.

'Well, see how much repairs will cost. Then you can either let again or get rid, eh?'

I smile. It makes my cheeks ache.

He tells me, 'I'll miss you.' And he's close now, pulling me to him, a hand sliding up my denim-clad thigh. We are apart fairly often, but usually, it is him going. Me left to potter around the apartment with too many hours in each day and an ever-increasing feeling of suffocation. I realise I am almost looking forward to getting away. Though the circumstances are, of course, awful. He says, 'Call when you land?'

'Sure.'

I pause at the door, blow him a kiss which he mimes catching.

Back in the cab I pull out the scrap of paper on which I'd scrawled the detective's number and get out my mobile.

He picks up on the second ring. 'DI Locke.'

'Hello, Detective. It's me. Hayley.'

'I visited your father.'

I don't ask any questions. I don't want any information. At least, not yet. Just the word 'father' makes my heart contract. Things spring to the forefront of my mind that I can't stop in time. I say, 'I'm coming over there. To England.' I flinch at the word watching New York roll by outside, half-hidden behind my overlarge Chanel sunglasses.

'Okay. It would be good to meet in person.'

'Of course.'

'Just to prewarn you, we've issued a press release.'

My heart thumps, whisking me back in time.

I imagine who might read such an article with interest. The kind foster parents who took me in in the interim weeks whilst the authorities searched for my mum's second cousin who returned from her travels to take me in? That second cousin of my mum herself, Nancy? Danny?

The last person I saw before everything changed. The boy whose kiss lingered on my lips as I walked into a never-ending nightmare.

I ask the detective, 'When will the story run?'

'I'd say soon online. They'll try and get it into print in the locals tomorrow, and it might get picked up more widely.'

'Right.'

'This must be difficult.'

There will be a picture, I suppose, of Ethan. The school photo is the one they dragged out last time. His toothy grin. Goofy and lopsided.

I manage a strangled goodbye, and the phone slips from my fingers into my bag whilst my heart beats too fast, too loud. *Babadoombabadoom*.

–

At the airport I go straight through to the lounge, and I play a sorry little game with myself. I dare you not to check on your phone. I dare you not to check the Thamespark news, local Twitter, Facebook.

45

Wider, national perhaps. The missing boy from that sad affair fifteen years ago. People will say words that leave a bitter taste on the tongue.

Tragic.

Frightening.

Unthinkable.

Unimaginable.

And yet it is so.

I go to Cat's Facebook page, something I have always done intermittently. Cat Carter as she was then; Mrs Smart now. It is full of new-mum things. Multiple pictures of her with a baby. Her baby. Lots of posts on a local parenting page asking for tips along with pictures of the chubby infant captioned: *So we don't forget where we are*, which annoys me far more than it should. Why am I irritated? I have no right to it. It's not her fault my life was cut to the ground whilst hers carried on untroubled but for a minor blip.

Sean texts: *Have a safe flight my darling. Call soon all my love XX*.

Relief. That I am getting away. From him, from New York, from our beautiful Manhattan apartment and dream life. Though what I am going back to feels terrifying and sharp. A dangerous, familiar place of pain. One hot summer that ruined everything.

I've been vague with Sean about my past. I said both my parents were dead. Agreed with his sympathy – yes, it was terrible. No, I don't like to talk about it. He enjoyed the story I fed him, swallowing every word, enjoying his role of hero. He had whisked me away from my sad, lonely life to the bright lights of another country and I'd been happy to go. *Needed* to go, to believe I could be someone else.

In the end, I cave in further and check local headlines. There it is on the paper's home page already. The picture of Ethan *is* his last school one. He is sweet and smiling but shy. There are comments and I do manage to do myself the courtesy of not reading those now.

I know what they will say. *Little angel. Darling boy.* People claiming grief that does not belong to them, letting it lodge in their public hearts, sympathy splashed across social media, horror expressed and shared, before getting on with their unruined day.

You couldn't blame the papers. Nor the ghoulish journalists who'd been waiting, apparently, to hound me the day I turned eighteen and was considered fair game.

I was asked by my social worker, a year after it all happened, if I wanted to change my surname. I'd thought and thought about it and in the end I had. Along with my hair colour, the way I dressed and anything else I could manage.

I took Taylor, my mother's maiden name. Still a link to Matthew. Ethan. A name I had a right to.

Ours.

A reminder to me if no one else that I was once a daughter, a sister. I had a family. I was loved. In my darker moments, of which there were plenty, I clung to it as the only proof I had left that I existed at all.

My flight is announced and ready to board. I am flying business class, and getting on the plane is short and easy. Everything is easy with money, just as I'd thought it would be. Though I am learning the hard way, it cannot make you immune to pain, and I feel sharp stabs of it now as I settle into my seat, my small brother running through my mind.

CHAPTER EIGHT

Seb has the original file out now and is laying bits of paper across the table of the incident room. He and Lucy are putting together a board that lays out everything as it was, alongside the scant new information they have now.

Ethan is not missing any more. Ethan is in a morgue on a slide-out metal table, reduced to bones and scraps of material, cotton and polyester brightly coloured little-boy pyjamas.

Seb looks over what makes up the entirety of the action book from back then, where all the things that needed doing and by whom are laid out. Even that is flimsy. Then on to the statements, evidence gathered, pictures, etc. A quadruple murder – you'd expect files to be bursting at the seams, the action book to be worn and well-thumbed by many hands. This one looks almost new. He turns to Lucy. 'You were right. It is thin.'

She nods. 'Bloody hell though.'

He sighs. Sits and wipes a hand over his face.

Lucy says, 'I guess they had their man, so it was pretty cut and dried?'

But they can both see that things had been missed. Leads were not followed up. Even the search for Ethan had only lasted twenty-four short hours in earnest. He can picture the scene: dogs smelling the boy's clothes, Hayley in shock, watching it all unfold. He cannot imagine walking in on it, not much older than Tilly is now, the shards of pain and disbelief that would lodge within. Just contemplating the idea of it is appalling. How must Hayley, a girl of fifteen, have felt that day? Her mother, her twin. Little Ethan missing. She would have been frantic while they searched. Each passing minute stealing a thin sliver of delicate, unfulfilled hope.

Seb blinks at the computer screen, pushing thoughts of his daughter aside for the moment. 'Okay, now look at this.'

The Reddit thread. It lays out the day of the crime in forensic detail. Sensationalist, of course, but it gives close and accurate information in a more reasonable and full account than in the official files.

They both bristle when Lucy reads aloud a section that denigrates the original investigation. You can't help it in this job. Being a police officer is as much a way of life as it is a career. They go through stuff together. Things other people can't fully understand. They are like one big, often dysfunctional, family.

Seb says, 'Digging around in this is going to annoy some of the old boys.'

Lucy flinches. And Seb suspects she knows exactly which officers he means. The few left from the 'good old days', most of whom are in murder, which they consider the rock-star squad. They can often be found bemoaning 'political correctness' and telling others to 'man up'.

Seb smiles at her now and shrugs. 'We'll be doing it anyway.'

Harry arrives. They start the tedious task of building a timeline for the family in the twenty-four hours before the murder. Seb is determined he won'tmake the same careless mistakes as his predecessors here. Ethan had beenmissing

49

for fifteen years, and, as far as he could tell, no one was losing any sleep over it. Well, he will make sure he gets justice for the boy, his family and for Hayley too.

CHAPTER NINE

The plane touches down and I come to with a start. I must have drifted off. Perhaps my mind wore itself out so fully with the awful musings I couldn't quite push away that it shut down in response.

Either way. I am here. Home. England.

It takes a while for us all to disembark and there is a further wait for luggage. I spend it standing rigid, ramrod straight. A man next to me smiles and rolls his eyes. 'Always takes forever.'

By the time I realise I should say something back, it's been too long, and he turns away looking scolded. Even the accent feels jarring though it's the same as my own. I have become used to drawn-out American vowels and voices which are louder, even when they don't mean to be.

I am finally out of the airport. It is drizzling and grey. I have in my handbag my passport, credit cards and the keys to my mother's house.

I haven't been back to England for close to thirteen years. I haven't been back to Thamespark for almost fifteen, bar one visit to the house to meet decorators and an estate agent, which was brief and still more than I could bear. I sit in a taxi that makes its way through London at a maddeningly slow pace. Just half an hour from the city and we are well into the suburbs. As streets become familiar, my heart beats a tattoo.

'Sixty quid I'm afraid, love.'

I jump at the voice. 'Sorry.' For what, I'm not sure. 'Yes, that's fine.'

I give him seventy, and he perks up with a smile, pressing his card into my hand. I stand on the pavement with my bag at my feet and watch him drive away. This feels like a moment that doesn't need a witness. It's early in the morning but still dark. The cars parked on the drives have white frozen windscreens, and I guess people will be out to see to that soon. I turn, face the little house now surrounded by many others, and put the key in the door.

The first thing I feel is relief.

It is barely recognisable. The inside is so different it might never have been ours. I had the downstairs ripped out, made into a huge open–plan. Not because I ever thought I'd come back, but because that's what families want now and they are my rental market. The effect is almost, almost, of a place I have never been to before. I half convince myself of it before the memories shunt in, ludicrously full of love and pain in equal measures. I think about sitting in the front room listening to records with Matt, my mum singing along to Dolly Parton while she washed dishes at the sink, Ethan making his way down the stairs, his face soft and mussed with sleep. I think, staying here probably isn't the worst idea I've ever had. I stand in the neutrally decorated room, the last place my mother stood, the last place Matt said anything, and blink away tears.

I turn on light switches and almost have a heart attack when I catch a glimpse of a person, then realise it is myself reflected from the new bifold doors. My phone rings and for the second time I jump. I have been back here less than two hours. Already I am a nervous wreck.

'Hi.'

'Hey, babe.' The words drip like candy from his lips, reaching out across oceans and into my ear. He is good with words, Sean. He can string them together to make all kinds of feelings. In our early days, I walked around, heady and under his spell. I wanted him, needed him, could see a future with him different from anything I could have alone. Now 'babe' falls flat and seems out of place, his brash accent taking up the space in this small cottage in the damp grey Surrey suburbs.

'Okay there?' I ask, lifting the phone away from my ear to check the time. It must be the early hours of the morning. 'Did you wait up to call me?'

'Of course.'

'You'll be shattered at work.'

'It's fine. I'm in good books over the deal with Murray.' The shiny close that will bring millions into the company and create more work than they'll know what to do with. He asks, 'Are you all right?'

'Yes, fine.'

'And the house?'

'I'm here now.'

'What's the problem?'

My mind races, jet lag fogging it. I try and pull out what I've already said. 'Damp, I think. A few other things. I'm not sure exactly. I'll meet with the agent later today.'

'Maybe do just sell if it's hassle?'

'Maybe.'

We say our goodbyes and our love yous, and I hang up, the echo of those hollow words reverberating around my jangled mind.

I go upstairs where the layout is the same as it has always been, as it was that final summer the last time I slept under this roof. I try to avoid thinking too much as I unpack the clothes I brought and put them into the wardrobe. It's not until I go back down that I realise I have unpacked in my old room. Despite my mother's being slightly bigger.

I push these thoughts away. I need to focus – on what, I'm not sure exactly.

Why have I come?

Because Ethan has been left alone for long enough.

CHAPTER TEN

Seb's phone rings as he and Lucy get further away from Surrey, further from London. He waves at her to accept the call, and she picks up, putting it on speaker. Seb says, 'DI Locke.'

'Hello, Detective.'

'Mrs Marriott?'

'Hayley is fine.'

'Hayley then.'

'I'm here.'

He raises his eyebrows at Lucy. 'Here in the UK?'

'Yes. I landed this morning.'

'If you text me the details of where you'll be staying, my colleague and I would like to speak to you.'

'Today?'

'If that's possible, yes.'

'I'm at my mum's house.'

Lucy gestures surprise with comically raised eyebrows and an open O-shaped mouth. Seb nods whilst trying to keep his eye on the road though it's quiet out and getting more so as they hit the countryside. 'Okay. We are in Sussex, but I'll call in soon as we're back. It'll be a few hours, I'd say.'

'Thank you, Detective.'

Lucy puts the phone down. 'Staying at her mum's place?' Her voice is incredulous.

Seb shrugs. 'I guess she must have kept it.'

'Still.'

The satnav has taken them to an impressive house at the end of a long private drive. There are only four houses on it, and each one is detached with masses of land.

Lucy lets out a low whistle. 'Wouldn't get this on a copper's salary.'

'No, he said he'd left the force.'

'Onto something more lucrative I'd say.'

'Yes,' Seb agrees, 'looks that way.'

—

Nigel Baker opens the door before they get out of the car. He had been the first responder to Hayley's 999 call all those years ago, and the named officer on much of the paperwork that followed afterwards.

Seb tells him, 'Great place you've got here.'

He grins. 'Gorgeous, isn't it?' Then whispers almost conspiratorially as Lucy and Seb get closer, 'I married money.'

Lucy says, 'Nice.'

And he winks. 'She's also the love of my life which definitely helps.'

Seb says, 'Is she here?'

'Not today, out for lunch with girlfriends. Come in, come in.'

Inside is just as stunning as outside, and they settle into a room with breathtaking views. Rolling green hills as far as the eye can see. Seb and Lucy take a moment to appreciate England at its finest.

'Lovely.' Lucy says.

They all sit. Seb is mildly horrified to see Nigel's feet are clad in the same ugly sheepskin shoes that Tilly insists upon every Christmas. Cost a fortune can't handle the rain. Glorified slippers. Nigel follows his gaze. 'I know. My wife bought me a pair, and they are so comfortable.' He shrugs. 'They are ugly though.'

Seb smiles. 'My daughter likes them.'

Nigel says, 'You're not here to discuss my footwear though, eh?'

'Nope.'

He shakes his head. 'I read your email, of course, and heard it on the radio. Baffling.'

'You feel you got the right man?'

Nigel nods. 'Absolutely. No doubt in my mind.'

'You knew the family?' Seb had read it in the notes.

'Not well. I knew their neighbours. I grew up in Thamespark.' He shrugs. 'Everyone knows everyone a bit. I went to the same school as Diane. We even went on a few dates.' He makes quotation marks with his hands.

'Oh?'

'Yes, nothing serious. I took her to Pizza Hut twice.' Diane Smart lived next door to the DaSilvas. At that time, they were the only people on what is now a sprawling estate.

'Apparently, Anita was at our school at the same time, year below us, but I didn't know her.'

'And how did you like Nathan? Diane's husband.'

Nigel sighs. 'You've heard the rumours then?'

'That they were unstable? Yes, we read the files. I know the police were called out once.'

'By Anita, actually.'

'Oh really?'

'Yes. I attended that call. She'd overreacted, to be honest.'

'Had she?'

Nigel nods. 'Yes, with her history... understandable.'

'Because she and Leonard were separated?'

'He hit her. She called the police the night she took the kids and left London, I believe; he didn't deny it. Was on a course for anger management still when we picked him up.'

'And he had a drink problem?'

'He had a drink problem,' Nigel agrees.

'And their neighbour, Nathan Smart, had had some trouble. Did he have a drink or drug problem too?' This is one aspect that Seb couldn't believe hadn't been delved into a bit more. A drug dealer living next door struck him as headline news.

Nigel shrugs – a vague movement. 'He was a bit lively back then, but he's settled down somewhat I believe they've worked things out since. Maybe what happened was a wake-up call. I know it made me think about what I had.'

'You have kids?'

He nods. 'Two, both adults now, but they were small then.'

'Must have been an awful scene.'

'Dreadful. Never seen anything like it before or since.'

'And a missing child.'

'The worst part. I honestly thought we'd find him with his dad.' He shakes his head. Seb can imagine it. He'd have concluded the same thing. That Leonard had killed Anita, Matt and Ryan in a fit of rage, that perhaps he'd been pulled from it by his youngest son, still very much a child, grabbed the boy and run. But little Ethan had been strangled, driven forty minutes away, buried, covered over. Hidden for all this time. Seb wasn't even convinced the boy had been buried that night. Secluded though that spot would have been, and more so fifteen years ago, digging a grave isn't something you'd want to attempt in a rush. Anita, Matt and Ryan were killed sometime after one a.m. Hayley came back at four. When the scenes of crime officers arrived, the bodies were cooling, the spilled blood starting to congeal. Seb's mind flashes to Hayley now, sitting in that same house. Fifteen years is a long time, but no time at all to distance yourself from something so awful. So completely defining.

'Walk me through what happened from your point of view.'

Nigel says, 'Okay. I'll do my best.' He blinks rapidly, and it makes him look vulnerable somehow. Seb glimpses the young officer he would have been then. 'I was at the end of a night shift.'

'You were a sergeant?'

'I was, yeah.'

'Superior officer?'

'Wasn't due in until later.'

'So a 999 responder contacted the station?'

'Yep. Hayley DaSilva had called them.' He kind of shudders when he says her name, then he pauses, looks directly at Seb, 'Shit, this'll be tough on her.'

Seb nods. 'Go on.'

'Call comes in. I called the boss.'

'Mackenzie Arnold?'

He grins. 'Mac, yeah.'

'Good boss?'

Nigel nods. 'He passed away, you know.'

'I heard.'

Nigel tells Seb, 'He was a good boss. Good guy, well liked.'

'I'm sure.' Seb smiles. 'And you? Ambitious?'

Nigel shakes his head. 'I thought I was before I started. I signed up out of school, didn't know what else to do.'

'It's a tough job.'

'It really is. Much more so than I'd thought it would be, and that case. God.'

Not everyone is cut out for murder or even serious crime. That's the truth of it and plenty didn't make it up the ranks, didn't want to. 'You were still a sergeant; it must have been frightening trying to manage that scene.' Seb's view was that Mac or someone more senior should have been overseeing it and, whilst he had some vague sympathy for Nigel, he didn't love the plodders. There were plenty of them on the force. Joined because they thought it would be a job for life with good benefits and a decent pension. They wanted to progress but not too far. That was fine and they needed foot soldiers of course, but Seb felt the work mattered. More than your average nine-to-five. People's lives often depended on you doing it right and if it wasn't lives you were after saving there were families left who needed answers.

He thinks of Hayley fifteen years later – this, unre-solved, reaching out across the world to grab her back. She'd got on with her life. Tried to make some peace for herself. Now it was getting stirred up again, and he couldn't help feeling that if the man sitting in front of him had been a bit more on the ball, if Mac hadn't just been coasting towards retirement, maybe they wouldn't be here now having to tie up loose ends that were more than that. Glaring, gaping holes in this investigation.

The case had just petered out after Leonard went down. No body found. That would have nagged at Seb, chewed away in his brain at night. A little boy who never got to go home to anyone who loved him.

'So you went in?'

He nods. 'With Ben.'

Seb asks for his full name, Ben Green, checking it matches the one on file. It does. At least some basic admin had been done right. An email address, home address, and a landline. No mobile listed. Seb had left a message for him.

Nigel nods. 'We went in. It was, I mean...'

Seb and Lucy had seen the photos. But Seb wants to hear him talk. 'Who did you come to first?'

'Hayley was sat on the front doorstep and she... she looked like something from a horror film. Covered in blood. She'd touched them, her twin anyway, the boy, Matthew DaSilva. He was nearest the door. Anita was on the other side of the room.'

'And Hayley was covered in blood?'

'Yeah, she was the one who'd called it in. She'd puked up where she sat.'

'You questioned her?'

'Of course. She was out with mates. Gabe, the Smarts' son, Diane and Nate.' Seb nods, and makes a mental note of 'Nate'. 'Cat Carter and Danny Morgan. They were all pretty tight. Gabe and Cat are married now.' He smiles. 'Childhood sweethearts.' Seb thinks of Charlie, holding his hand, grinning up at him in the registry officer. Impossibly young, ludicrously hopeful.

'You're still in touch with them?' Seb asks him.

'I mean, vaguely on social media, with Diane.'

'They all backed it up, Hayley's version of events?'

'I didn't speak to them, but it was checked, as I recall she'd been at some sort of gathering in the woods behind her house.'

'She wasn't a suspect?'

'We fingerprinted her, treated her like she might be at first, but then Leonard confessed, and her alibi checked out. She was at that party.'

There were transcripts of interviews with Cat and Gabe. Dismally shortstatements. Effectively: 'Was Hayley in the woods with you?' 'Yes. End of.' More sloppiness and, whilst it may turn out not to matter, he would be going to see them himself. Whichever way he looked at it, any of them could have been involved. Bizarrely, there didn't seem to be an official statement from Danny Morgan.

He smiles at Nigel. 'Ben's out in Brighton now?'

Nigelsmiles. 'Think so. Last I heard he was running a boxing gym out that way.'

'He left the force too. Not long after you did.'

Nigel's smile dims a bit. 'Not for everyone, I guess.'

'No.' Seb's voice smooth, understanding, 'You were friends?'

Nigel shakes his head. 'I wouldn't say friends. He was older than me but new too. Ex-forces. Bit of a stickler for the rules. Could be difficult to work with.'

'Oh really?'

Nigel waves a hand like it doesn't matter much, but Seb feels the need to find and talk to Ben pressing even more urgently. He himself could, and has been, described as 'a stickler for the rules'. He finds that kind of thing is bandied about when other people aren't doing their jobs properly and resent you for not being the same way.

'Do you know the name of the gym?'

'No, sorry.'

Seb smiles. He'll find out. 'So, you called Mac at this point?'

Nigel nods. 'Yeah.'

'His reaction?'

'It'd be the husband.'

Seb raises an eyebrow.

Nigel shrugs. 'You know as well as I do that nine times out of ten that's the answer.'

A crime of passion. Terrible violence between spouses sadly wasn't uncommon. Seb does know as well as Nigel, as well as anyone, the things love can drive you to do. If he and Charlie hadn't had Tilly to consider he may well have gone down with his young wife, slipped into turmoil and ruin.

Such was the force of feeling he'd had for Charlotte Brady. So ridiculous and blind was his love. It was lucky for all of them that what he'd felt for Tilly had eclipsed everything else. Seb was adopted and had no siblings. Perhaps because of that, from the moment he held his baby daughter, the only other person he'd met who shared his blood, his genes, it was all-encompassing. Still, when he sent Charlie packing it had broken something in him. He understands how people can behave badly in light of feelings that strong.

'I do, yeah.' He would have gone in though if he was Mac. He would have walked the scene himself. Questioned everyone and looked for that little boy until he'd been found. Mac had decided on the phone then left well alone, showing up to get an easy confession and do a press conference where he claimed credit for a successful capture. He'd done the same during the trial: every news piece had a picture of Mac standing proud and well dressed. It was unforgivable, and yet a lot of the old boys at the station revered him. Seb says, 'So you went and got Leonard DaSilva?'

'Yeah, and he had blood on him. That's in the report, surely?'

'Yes, specks. Anita cut her hand earlier in the evening.'

Nigel shrugs. 'Didn't know that then, did we? It was thought he'd got changed, took off a top layer of clothes and discarded them, somewhere.'

'They were never found though?'

Nigel shrugs. 'Didn't matter anyway. He confessed.' This bothers Seb a lot. It also bothers him that Leonard's shoe prints were found in the house and used as evidence ignoring the fact that they weren't covered in blood. He could have sidestepped a lot of the mess, of course. The scenes of crime team said that that was completely plausible. If he'd been wearing a coat that would have had blood on it, the upper half of any trousers worn would, but his shoes only if he'd stepped in the blood and walked it through the house.

'He wasn't seen leaving the Travelodge again or coming back, and there was CCTV covering most of the entrance.'

'Most, not all, he could have walked close to the wall and slipped in just out of sight.' Seb had tried to do exactly that. In his best attempt, the side of his body had been visible, and Leonard was a similar size to him. A damning piece of evidence in favour of Leonard's innocence completely ignored.

'But, he had no memory of the crime.' Leonard had been shocked when police burst in, had asked the police what had happened before he asked anything else. He could have killed them all in blackout and still had the good sense to undress and dispose of the clothes. People did all kinds of things when they were under the influence. But hiding them so well that they were never found?

Nigel laughs. 'Well, no, but Diane said they'd been arguing Anita phoned her. Said he'd gone. But she was upset, scared.'

'That he might come back?'

He shrugs. 'I guess.'

'That's what Diane said?'

'I think so.'

'Think so?'

'God, I can't remember exact words. It's what she meant. Does it matter how she put it?'

Seb smiles, but it's tight. Of course it matters. 'Probably not. Sorry, go on.'

He shrugs. 'Sounded like Anita was downplaying it. Like she wanted to let her friend know she was all right, knew Diane would have heard them arguing.'

'They were good friends?'

'Diane and Anita?'

'Yes.'

'Sounded like it, and the kids were close. Diane's son was an only child, so I think she was glad he had some new mates and next door too. You would be, wouldn't you?'

'You questioned him?'

'Gabe?'

'Yes.'

'I imagine so. Like I said, I called it in but handed it over. Ben did some following up, things Mac told him didn't need to be done if you must know. But Mac got the confession, came in once we had Leonard there. I guess he'd have dotted the i's crossed the t's.' He hadn't though. No one had. Seb would look over the transcripts of the interviews with Diane, try to see if Nigel's memory was correct or not.

Nigel glances at his watch. Seb asks, 'Somewhere to be?'

'Yes, actually. My youngest son's due in, at the station. Heading home for the holidays, he's at university.'

'Right.'

'So without meaning to be rude…'

He's standing, so Seb and Lucy follow suit. Allow themselves to be led to the door. Seb stops and turns as they step out. 'One last thing.'

'Yes?'

'Do you think you did a good job?'

He looks at him wide-eyed. 'What, generally?'

'On that case?'

Nigel seems to deflate. 'I mean, maybe we didn't tie it all up.'

'But you got the right man?'

He straightens at that. 'Yes. Who else could it be?'

Lucy reads Hayley's statement to Seb in the car. They go over the times she'd given, the times witnesses at the party had seen her, and Lucy murmurs, 'A lot of her time was unaccounted for, wasn't it?'

'It was, yes.'

'Nigel said they believed her.'

'He did. Let's see if her story adds up now, eh?'

CHAPTER ELEVEN

I answer to a tall dark-haired man with an intense stare and a small blonde woman with a wide smile and an open face.

'DI Locke?'

'Yes, this is Detective Constable Lucy Quinn. May we come in?'

'Sorry, of course.' I have no idea what I'm apologising for. I step to one side, and they walk over the threshold, bringing a cool breeze in with them. I say, 'I've just put the kettle on.' Which is a lie, but I need a few seconds. 'No tea I'm afraid, but can I get you a coffee?' I picked up a packet of ground, sugar and milk at the shop in the airport along with a large cafetiere.

The woman smiles. 'Sure.'

I make a note of how they want theirs and step into the small kitchenette area. It isn't private exactly, but there is a long breakfast bar between me and the detectives, who are settled on the sofa, she with a small notepad in hand.

In New York, Sean and I have a coffee machine that does all the work so we don't have to. That's not exactly true though. I set it every night before we go to bed and by the time his alarm goes, coffee is ready to be poured. I take through two mugs for them, then come back for my own, pleased that I manage each movement with steady hands and feet.

The woman asks, 'How was your flight?'

'Fine, thank you,' I say, then add, 'I slept for most of it.' Pointlessly.

She nods.

I clear my throat, and it feels like I'm choking on gravel. 'So you spoke to my father?' My voice sounds even, and I mentally high-five myself.

'No recollection of taking Ethan anywhere.'

I say, 'He had blackouts.' My heart hammers as I think about my own lost hours. Coming to in the midst of a living nightmare. I squeeze my eyes shut, open them again to see both officers staring at me intently. I'm being weird probably. I force my face into a blank expression.

'He and your mother...?'

I take a sip of my drink. It has extra sugar in and full-fat milk. Sean would disapprove. We live amid a continuous, never-ending health kick. He is athletic and sporty so I am expected to be too. Also, it's important that we, he and I, look good. It's not something we've spoken about, but I know full well it is part of the deal. I am younger than Sean, as all of his superiors' wives are, as his mother was in comparison to his father. I was eighteen when I met him, and he was thirty-one, the age I am today. I look at eighteen-year-olds now and feel a faint swell of unease at the imbalance between adolescence, which can't know much, and adulthood with all of its relevant experiences. I am a trophy, and he is the security blanket that smothers me.

'Mrs Marriott.' A voice in the background. 'Hayley?' Pulling me from dense thoughts.

'Sorry. You want to know about my parents?'

He nods.

I put the cup down on a coaster. The woman does the same, pen in hand now, poised above her tiny pad.

'They married young. She was a university student, first year, met my dad playing at a student band night.' I shrug. 'She became pregnant.'

'With you and your brother?' His voice is soft, no malice there, and yet the words lash out at me in violent fury. My brother. My twin. Matt. I'd reached for him. I knew that. My hands were slick with his blood. It got into the grooves of my fingerprints, embedded beneath my fingernails. The next day there were still traces of it, and I thought, maybe I should leave it there, never wash my hands again so there would be something of him left.

'Yes. They were happy, I think, despite her parents being furious.'

'Because of the pregnancy?'

I nod.

'What happened between them that caused your mother to leave?'

'A year before... that night,' I swallow, 'my dad lost his job. He was okay for a bit then he started drinking too much. They argued about it a lot.' I pause again here, the words stuck in my throat. I think of their happy laughter, the unspoken bond my parents had always had. How quickly, it seemed to me, it had disintegrated.

He started getting drunk. There were bad signals only getting worse, building towards an awful climax. I remember him, blank-eyed, pushing Mum out of his way, carrying her once up the stairs slung over his shoulder. The sound of her crying, him walking back down, wobbly, inebriated, out the front door whilst we three watched in silent horror, wondering what the hell had happened to our dad.

'My grandfather died, left this house to my mum.' I shrug, not adding that I'd never met him, or my grandmother, who had passed when we were very small. 'She gave my dad an ultimatum. She was taking us there. He was to sort himself out or not bother coming to find her.'

'And then?'

'He hit her.' I turn to the detective now. The shock of the words still feels new and fresh.

He says, 'The first time?'

'I don't know.' I look away. It might have happened before. I'd seen bruises on her wrists, little round things the size of fingertips. Had I ignored the signs? I'll never know. All I'd wanted was for everything to be how it had been and how it never was to be again. I say, 'It was the time she had enough. She called the police. I believe they spoke to my dad after we'd left.' The memory twists my guts. Finding out after his arrest for quadruple murder that he'd been forced to attend a course for men who beat their wives. That he'd attempted to sober up, sort himself out, that it was too little too late.

'How long had it been going on, the arguing?'

'I don't know. Not long, when he first lost his job, he tried to stay upbeat. Applied for everything going. He sank though. I can't think how else to describe it. Mostly he was just sad. The anger wasn't all the time, and only ever when he was drunk.' Am I making excuses for him still? I am surprised at the defence in my words. 'He got in states, ridiculous messes. He'd go out to play a gig and one or other of the band would bring him back. Sometimes he'd be maudlin, or weepy. Sometimes he'd be mad, like raging. I'd never seen him like that. None of us had. My mum, she'd try and reason with him.' I shut my eyes. It is so difficult to speak about it, make sense of something that had no rhyme or reason. 'He changed,' I say, 'when he drank.'

'Had they had problems before?'

I shake my head. 'No. They were sickeningly happy if anything.' My mother's soft face when she looked at him. How he'd run a hand across her shoulder as he passed her.

'It must have been a very difficult time.'

I laugh. 'I thought that would be as bad as it could get.'

There is a silence then.

'You must have felt very confused by it all, a teenager, having to move away from everything familiar.'

'It wasn't great,' I admit.

'Were you angry, with your mum?'

'For moving us?' My heart seems to scuttle for a moment, jumping out of irregularity.

'Yes,' says the detective with the dark, intense eyes.

'Maybe a bit,' I say, unwilling to admit to my simmering, all-encompassing rage that I often felt towards her, towards my dad in his absence, towards Matt for dealing with it all so much better than I had. Eventually, I say, 'How was he, Leonard?'

'Sober, he says.'

I swallow and try to sound casual when I say, 'Oh yeah?'

'He took a degree in prison.'

'Sounds like he's been having a great time.' Bitterness pushes the words out.

'This whole thing must be extremely difficult.'

'When can I bury him? Ethan,' I snap, not wanting to have my feelings analysed. Not wanting to have to look at them at all.

'When we've finished this investigation.'

'What exactly are you investigating?'

71

'As I said on the phone, Ethan was found far away from your house and further still from where your dad was staying.'

I blink, icy tendrils slipping up inside me, little chilled slivers. I know what he's going to say, what he assumes I've worked out, but I haven't, not at all.

'I find myself not entirely convinced that Leonard would have had time to bury Ethan.' Each word a punch in the gut.

I stare at him blankly.

He says, 'Ethan was definitely home, when you left for the night?'

'I went in, checked on him.'

'What time?'

'Nine, maybe a bit after.'

'He was asleep?'

'Soundly.'

He and the woman exchange a look.

I snap, 'What?'

'We had considered that maybe he was killed and taken first,' the policeman says.

'Which you don't suspect?'

'We have no reason to, no, and you saying you saw him then makes it incredibly unlikely. Your mother called her friend, Diane, after your dad visited that evening. She said she'd just checked Ethan, worried he might have woken.'

'What... what time was that?' An image springs to my mind: me shouting at my mum and dad; my mum's voice strained and strangled; 'You'll wake your brother...', my feet hitting the ground. Running. A field. The sparkle of booze still in my blood. Later on, Danny walking me home.

'She called Diane just before midnight. She also said she was annoyed because you and Matt weren't home.'

'She sent him, to fetch me.' My voice is thin, distant. Flat-toned telling someone else's story. Hayley DaSilva. Hayley Taylor. Mrs Marriott.

Locke nods. 'I read that.'

'I told him to bugger off.'

'A normal teenage reaction.'

I look away. Out the bifold doors, onto the small patch of garden behind the house. It is an immaculate lawn now, but it was overgrown and wild when we were here. My mother had a ridiculous lawnmower that Matt had hacked at the too-long grass with, leaving uneven patches. We had a trampoline outside that summer, and Ethan and Matt had loved it, learning to flip themselves every which way. I envied them. Ached to join in, but instead sat sullen and prickly.

Another normal teenage reaction. I'd been full of hormones and hurt.

'You were at a party with...' The detective gets out his own little pad covered in hieroglyphs and says, 'Your neighbour Gabriel Smart and his friends, Cat Carter and Danny Morgan?'

'Yes.'

'Cat was in your year at school?'

I nod, think of Cat and I making notes into paper aeroplanes and firing them at each other during maths.

'You were friends?'

'We were.' My voice barely a whisper.

'Have you stayed in contact?'

'With who?'

'Any of them?'

'I'm friends with Gabe and Cat on Facebook.' I don't add that I've stalked Danny via their pages. That I've looked at photos of him on holiday, out with friends. Graduating with a degree in youth work. That I had printed out an article in the *Thamespark news* that detailed his community successes and that I kept it folded up at the bottom of my knickers drawer in New York. I add, 'They are married now. Cat and Gabe.'

'Oh yeah?'

I nod, manage a smile because childhood sweethearts, first loves, turning into a lifelong thing is good, right? Not for my mum and Leonard though. I say, 'They have a baby.'

The detective tells me, 'We will be speaking to them all.'

'What for?' A stupid question I realise as soon as the words are out.

He doesn't answer. Everything is heavy and oppressive in that silence. I know what for. He's said. There is a chance that my dad didn't bury Ethan. If he didn't bury Ethan, what are the honest chances that he killed him? If he didn't kill him, what are the chances he killed my mum and Matt?

I say, 'Maybe what you said is right. Maybe he killed Ethan first, came back for Mum and Matt.'

'It's possible.'

Possible. Not likely.

I pick up my coffee. Put it down without drinking any. Press the hard bottom of my palms against my eyes. I see my dad, hands held out, in the kitchen at Thamespark. Me shouting.

'Are you all right?'

I physically jump at her touch. The small officer with the fair hair and the soft, sweet face reaching across the nondescript table between us, touching my arm. I smile, a forced, small, sad movement. 'Tired. Jet lag and…' I wave a hand around.

She nods. The man, Locke, stands. 'We'll let you rest. Get settled.' And then, 'We'll be in touch.'

I see them out, his words lingering in his absence like a threat.

CHAPTER TWELVE

As they leave Hayley Marriott's small house and step out into the cold, Lucy says, 'Must be weird for her.'

Seb shakes his head. 'I can't even imagine.' His phone rings, shrill and intrusive. He looks at it with a frown, murmuring to Lucy, 'My daughter's school.'

She tries hard not to listen in to the conversation but can't really help it as they walk towards the car.

'Um. My kid's unwell, in the nurse's office, apparently.'

Lucy frowns. 'Oh no, sorry.'

Seb runs a hand over his face. 'My mother-in-law would normally get her, but this,' he glances at the time on his phone, 'yes, sadly this clashes with aquacise.'

'Aqua what?'

He grins. 'Don't ask. In real terms, it means out of the entire week this is the only bit of it where she's not available.'

Lucy stares at him blankly for a moment, then the implications for her sink in. They have a list of people they need to talk to. The Smarts and Danny Morgan today. Harry has found places of work and home addresses for all of them, and they've decided to show up without appointment: casual, unofficial, for now.

She says, 'You go. I can do the next interview.'

'Val will be around in an hour tops. I just need to get Tilly home and settled and let her know...'

'Seb, it's fine.' She smiles. 'I've questioned people on my own before.'

'I know, sorry, I didn't mean you couldn't, just...'

'I get it. It's a big case, and you feel bad leaving me on my own?'

He nods. 'Right.'

'Plus, you'll need the car.'

'Oh shit, I will, yeah. I could drop you in town though. Danny Morgan is at the Guildhall, right?'

Lucy says, 'Yep. Drop me then collect me after? I doubt it'll be a long chat. If you take a while, I'll grab a coffee, no hardship.'

'Okay, great, and thanks.'

She shrugs. 'It's fine. She can't help being sick.'

It's not until Seb has dropped her off and driven away that she realises he mentioned his mother-in-law but not his kid's mum, which makes her curious. She pushes it from her mind as she heads into the Guildhall.

CHAPTER THIRTEEN

Seb has been to the school only twice, once when they came to look round, and once for Year Seven parents' evening. Tilly is in Year Eight now. He can still barely believe she's at secondary school at all. Mere years from exams, sixth form and then… just thinking about it makes his pulse race. He tries really hard to be 'chill' about his daughter, as she now puts it, but he struggles. Even if he manages it outwardly, inside his love for her is so fierce that it terrifies him sometimes. If anything happened to her…

He spent the short drive running through various scenarios involving medical emergencies. He's pretty much jelly coated in skin by the time he's been buzzed in and made it to reception.

The school secretaries? Admin assistants? He's unsure but there are three of them behind a plastic partition and sitting at desks. One with a headset on, one typing and one smiling kindly and sliding a sign-in form towards him. 'Mr Locke?'

He nods. 'Is she…'

'She'll be fine, honestly.'

Relief. And then, if that's the case… 'But, she needs to go home?'

'I think it's best in this situation.'

He frowns at her. 'What situation?'

She flushes and looks around, but the other two remain absorbed by their own tasks. 'Maybe it'd be best if she has a chat with Mum when she gets in, yeah?'

'Her mum doesn't live with us.'

'Oh. Then you should speak to her, okay.' Her voice is gentle, but his heart is racing.

'Has something bad happened to her?'

'No. Not bad, just… a bit unsettling at school. Come round, Mr Locke.'

He nearly trips over his own feet in his rush to follow her to what ends up being one door along. They go into a small room with a long, thin bed and a hard plastic chair. The woman murmurs, 'Sick room.' And the pedant in him avoids sarcastically reminding her Tilly isn't sick, apparently.

But he takes one look at his daughter, whose face is pale and whose little body is hunched in on itself on the too-thin bed, and everything else is forgotten. 'Tills?' He's going over to her, reaching down to fold her in his arms. She doesn't look all right at all and worse still she's backing away from him, shuffling along and out of his reach, eyes wide. She's not, he realises, pleased to see him at all.

'Where's Nan?' Val had been widowed young after a terrible marriage. When Charlie went it made sense for her and Seb to live together. They raised Tilly as a team, but normally Tilly came to him with stuff first.

'Aquacise.' His arms drop. Adding: 'It's Wednesday.'

She looks from him to the school secretary, who averts her eyes.

'What's wrong? You're not sick, exactly, she said?'

To his absolute horror, she bursts into tears.

Whenever Seb is frightened, it distils itself into anger in milliseconds. He's a logical man and solution-based in his approach to everything, but where his child is concerned, rationality can run away on a pinhead. He spins on the secretary. 'What on earth is going on here?'

She goes over to Tilly, putting an arm around her shoulders. Seb notes that his daughter allows this and the anger slides away, replaced by a feeling of helplessness which, he thinks, is actually worse. She's murmuring something to Tilly. He can't make out what. Eventually, she looks up with a smile and says, 'Let's step outside and have a quick word, Mr Locke.'

He nods dumbly. Feeling useless and out of his depth.

Outside she says, 'She's given permission for me to tell you, but understandably I think she feels a little bit awkward talking to you herself.'

'She can talk to me about anything. We're very close.' The words sound defensive and desperate even to him. They *were* close, had always been tight. But recently... the door slamming, the loud music. He's had to tell her off more than once lately. A thing that probably pains him more than it does her, as he asks her to rinse out her cereal bowl, not trample mud through the house, hand over her mobile at nine p.m. on the dot. Most of his attempts at discipline these days are met with an eye-roll.

She puts a hand on his arm. 'I'm sure you are, Mr Locke.'

He frowns.

'She's said I'm okay to tell you, but, as I said, I get the impression she'd prefer not to discuss it with you directly.'

He nods, feeling annoyance simmer up again.

'Matilda started her period today.'

He stares at her. Blinks. 'She's only thirteen.'

The woman smiles. 'Some girls of her age have had them for years by now.'

Years. She's growing up. Part of that, it seems, is turning into the world's most selfish and inconsiderate housemate and treating him with what he can only describe as a faint disdain. This is another part of it.

After Charlie had gone, he consoled himself with the fact that there'd be nothing in the world that he couldn't handle. Nothing he couldn't do for Tilly. And he wasn't lying when he spoke to the school secretary. They *had* always been close. Only child, only parent. They had Val too, and he's always thought that had probably saved them from a sort of claustrophobia. Certainly, he wouldn't have his job without her there to help. In some ways, she's looked after them both, and he wishes more than ever that she was here now; she'd know exactly what to say.

The secretary's speaking. He says, 'Sorry?'

'If you don't have… provisions at home, you'll need to stop at a shop.' His brain fizzes. Val is in her sixties – provisions are highly unlikely.

They'll need to stop, accept that it will be awful for both of them. Actually, only for her – he isn't bothered by it. Maybe he can drop her home and go on his own, but he doesn't want to leave Lucy for too long, or the case. He needs to prove himself there. He wants to make sure he'll be considered for better investigations in the future, a promotion even. This investigation, pain in the arse though it is, feels important. If he can solve a fifteen-year-old puzzle… plus Tilly may want to choose herself. Val will be at least an hour, maybe even more if she stops for coffee and cake which she often does afterwards. He'd been planning to leave Tilly at home if she wasn't at death's door, maybe give her a paracetamol and tell her to wait till Val got back. But that isn't going to work.

They will have to brave the shop together. There is no way around it. He says to the school secretary, 'We'll be fine.' And winces at how unconvincing it sounds even to his own ears.

CHAPTER FOURTEEN

Danny Morgan reminds Lucy of a well-known singer, but she can't recall the guy's name. He is Britpop thin with hooded eyes and a penetrating gaze. She has found him tucked away in a musty-smelling office inside the local Guildhall. He doesn't look like he belongs in an office though; he looks like a rock star. Lucy figures this probably puts him in good standing with the kids he has to cajole, talk to and advocate for.

He stands now as Lucy introduces herself and shakes her hand.

She finds she is more nervous than she wants to be. She's questioned people alone plenty of times. In uniform she spent most of her days knocking on doors, but she was never this high up in an investigation. Granted, they are a team of three right now, but she desperately wants on to murder, and she knows that how she handles this is going to make all the difference. She asks him, 'Is it okay to talk here or would you prefer to go somewhere else?'

'That bad, huh?' He smiles, but there are questions there, of course. Lucy doesn't say anything, and Danny stands, picking up a beaten brown leather satchel, stuffed to bursting with papers. 'Annoyingly, I have to go to court, but you can walk with me?'

'That's fine,' she says, though it's less than ideal, which is confirmed as they stroll down the hall and out onto the busy street together. It turns out that, despite her mum's promises that cashmere is the warmest material in the world, it is no match for a bitter English December.

He asks, 'You here about one of our kids?'

'No.'

He frowns at that, looking down at her, and she wishes, not for the first time, that she was just a little bit taller.

'Oh?'

'I came to talk to you about Ethan DaSilva.'

Danny pauses, stops still and looks at her. 'You've found him?'

'We did, yes.'

'Dead?'

'I'm afraid so.'

He shakes his head. 'Sorry to hear it. I mean, I guess no one thought he'd survived, but still…'

They pass the technical college. A large group of teenagers sit on the wall, loud and raucous. One of them nods at Danny.

He says, 'Staying out of trouble, Aaron?'

He shrugs. 'Doing my best, sir.'

Danny grins and taps the lad's fist as they pass. Others in the group murmur hello and nod from under hoods. He says, 'they're good lads, you might know Aaron, one of the Chalmers kids?'

Lucy says, 'Went down for a burglary?'

Danny nods. 'He did, yeah. Gives it all the biggun, but it shook him up. He's training to be a plumber.'

'Good news.'

'I hope so.'

Danny cares about his work. She looked him up and was surprised she hadn't crossed paths with him at some point, but he's only recently moved from a local home for looked-after children to liaison work for kids with records. He is part of a rehabilitation team, and hats off to him. Not an easy job. Like he said, Aaron was shaken up, but the boy as Lucy recalls came from a home where criminality was rife and violence was the norm. If she remembers rightly, his uncle was the mastermind behind the bungled burglary and had dragged his nephew along to 'show him the ropes'. Whilst Danny seems hopeful about Aaron's course, Lucy wouldn't be at all surprised to see him in cuffs again.

'You knew the DaSilvas?'

'I knew Hayley mainly.'

'Via her neighbour?'

'Gabriel Smart, yep.'

'Married Cat Carter?'

'Cat Smart now.'

'Who you're still in touch with?'

He grins down at her, an easy, amiable smile. 'Yes. I'm their son Dylan's godfather, though none of us believe in god as such.' He waves a hand. 'You know what I mean.'

Lucy smiles. Godfather means close. 'Sure, and Hayley?'

'Are we in touch?' Wide eyes, surprise at the question. Lucy nods. 'No, though I tried, I mean, before she went to London, to an aunt's, I think?'

'You were close before that?'

'I thought so. I mean, we were a couple.' He shrugs, 'But, after what happened to her family she wanted nothing to do with any of us.' He shrugs.

Lucy says. 'That must have been tough.'

'We only knew each other that one summer, but god, that girl got under my skin and, yeah, it was pretty brutal. First love and all. I tried to approach her more than once in the weeks after. I figured maybe she just needed a bit of space. Then all of a sudden she was gone.' He shakes his head at the memory. 'I haven't seen her since. She's friends with Cat and Gabe on Facebook. I've never had the balls to send a request. Silly really, we were kids, but that rejection stung. I wasn't up for it a second time.'

'You were into her?'

'Yup. Head over heels, to be honest.'

'Still are?'

He laughs. 'Hayley left here what fifteen years ago now? Like I said, we were kids.'

Which hasn't really answered her question. 'Not married?'

'Not yet.'

'Single?'

A shrug. 'Nothing serious.' He's making light of it, but Lucy saw the look on his face as he joked about avoiding sending a friend request. He clears his throat, presses the button at the traffic lights. The courts are in sight now. He says, 'Gabe told me she'd got married, moved to America?'

'Yes. But she's here now.'

'In the UK?' Eyes off the road and onto her.

'In Thamespark.'

'I mean, it makes sense, of course. She and Ethan were close. Even if they weren't, it's her brother. Wow.' Eyes wide again and a pause that seems to hold more tension than the last one.

The lights turn green and start beeping. Danny is pulled from the memory. Across the road and in front of the courthouse, Danny shifts the sleeve of his leather jacket up, eyes on his watch. 'I have maybe seven minutes.'

'Walk me through what happened that night?'

86

'At the party?'

'Yes.'

'Okay. She turned up with Cat and Gabe. We were uh…' He looks sheepish.

She says, 'No judgement.'

'Drinking, smoking some dope.'

'So you were all a bit merry and high?'

'Right. I mean, not smashed, that's never been my scene, but I wasn't sober. I was a bit concerned about Hayley though.'

'How come?'

'She was drinking fast, and a mess. You know?'

'Was that usual for her?'

'I wouldn't say usual, but maybe she hit it a bit harder than the rest of us.'

'And she was smoking dope?'

'I think a joint went round to her a few times. Some of the older kids had bottles of spirits. She was swigging from them.'

'You were worried about her?'

'I mean, a bit. I went over to see if she was okay. She got up and could barely stand straight, that was when Matt showed up. I think Anita probably sent him to get Hayley home. They had a few words. He was concerned. It was understandable. Cat laughed, called him square. I told her to back off, I remember that, and she was a bit put out, Cat. But you could see Matt's point. Hayley was out of it. Like I said, we had all smoked dope, drank, but Hayley, she could get wild sometimes.'

'Who gave her the bottles of neat alcohol?'

'I don't know exactly, but she had her own mind. If she was going to do something she was going to do it, you know. But Matt kept pushing her about it, then he was asking if she'd taken something.'

'Had she?'

He frowns. 'I don't think so. She was battered but, I've seen people get that way on booze, you know. There were a few kids there who would have been holding, and Matt would have known that too.'

'Names?'

'Oh, come on.'

'We're not interested in getting anyone into trouble. But we need to follow up.'

He sighs. 'Douglas Beattie, a couple of his pals, he's not into that shit now though. He's a good guy.'

'We'll bear that in mind. So Matt thought she'd taken something?'

Danny nods. 'Said she wasn't herself, started asking for names. Glared at everyone there.' Danny shakes his head. 'He was a nice guy, Matt. I was glad Ryan had someone he could hang with. Ryan lived near me and Cat, was in Cat's year at school, and he liked to trail around with me and Gabe. Our mums were all mates. But I guess, looking back, we sort of left him out.'

'Year below, I suppose, matters a lot at that age.'

Danny nods. 'More so that year when we'd gone to college. When we were all at school together we'd hung out at break and lunch. Once we moved up, I think Ryan was a bit lonely. He was a nice kid, you know,' Danny's voice is soft, 'wouldn't hurt anyone. I got the impression Matt was made of the same stuff.' Two boys, on the verge of the rest of their lives. Good kids who wouldn't make adulthood. That night, when Matt had been trying to look out for his sister and Ryan had tagged along to support him, was their last. It wasn't fair. It wasn't right, and Lucy knows that Seb is starting to suspect the person who took their lives may still be out there. Unpunished.

'So, Matt was worried about her?'

Danny nods. 'Oh yeah.'

'They argued that night?'

He sighs. 'They did. I always felt sorry for her over that, in light of everything.'

'What time was that?'

'I don't know exactly, maybe half-ten, eleven, I reckon. Definitely before midnight.'

'Okay.'

'Then it calmed down. Hayley sat with me, Gabe and Cat for a bit and she was still messy but not falling over. Cat dragged her off to dance. Next thing, Matt's stressing, asking where she's gone. I said to dance with Cat, then all of a sudden, Cat's there and Matt's asking where his sister is. She said she was fucked if she knew. One minute they were dancing, the next she'd sodded off. Said probably with some bloke.' Danny's lips purse at that. 'I said unlikely.'

'You think it was?'

'I know it, man. That wasn't Hayley at all.'

Lucy thinks people do all kinds of mad things when they're drunk, especially teenagers, but she doesn't argue with Danny, whose eyes keep flicking around, evidently looking for the charge he was due to meet here. 'Was Matt upset?'

'He was worried. I know they had their differences, but they were close, I'd say, underneath it. She'd spent ages buying him this gift, a record he wanted, and she was making a card for him with tiny pictures of the bands he liked cut out on the front. For their birthday.'

That record was a gift she never got to give to him. Lucy can't imagine how her birthday was, staying with a foster family, devastated, unsure where she'd end up. The first birthday that wasn't hers and Matt's. Sweet sixteen soured. Lucy has had her fair share of fighting with various siblings, but she'd be lost without the buggers. 'So, did Matt go and look for her?'

Danny shakes his head. 'I said I would, and he looked relieved.'

'Why do you think he was relieved?'

'She was less likely to kick off at me, I suppose? Or so I hoped.' Sheepish grin. Lucy can imagine him then. A boy off to save his girl. Teenage brains were only ever half-tuned to reality. 'Anyway, I left and walked out to her house.'

Lucy's heart starts to speed up. This isn't in any of the case notes. She says, 'It looks on the map like it was quite nearby.'

'Yeah. The only thing in any kind of distance then, really. We always hung at that spot because it was isolated enough to be away from adults. I figured she'd probably headed for home so that's where I went. Didn't see her along the way then I heard shouting as I got near to the house.'

'Who was it?' She's desperately trying to keep her voice even, stay calm, but this is news. New news, that changes things. She wishes Seb was here.

'Hayley, a man and woman. Figured her parents.'

Hayley had been home. She had gone back to the house that was to become a crime scene? Drunk and... argued with her parents? How the hell was this information not found out fifteen years ago? 'Why didn't you say this, at the time?'

He frowns. 'I did.'

'Who to?'

'I don't know the guy who took my statement. One of you.' Ben Green was listed as having spoken to Cat and Gabe. It would make sense that he would have spoken to Danny too. The two officers who did most of the footwork were Nigel Baker and Ben Green. Mackenzie Arnold was 'in charge' but didn't seem to do much of anything beyond taking the credit. That had stuck out for Seb so much that he pointed it out to Lucy and it was spinning in her mind now. He told her that Mac had run a half-hearted investigation, that he had waited until Leonard was there and just showed up for the glory.

At that moment a teenage boy with a face like thunder and an exasperated-looking adult in a suit alongside him comes up to Danny. Danny shakes hands, says hellos and even manages to coax a smile from the boy.

He turns to Lucy with a kind of shrug. 'I'm so sorry.'

Her mind is racing. She'd expected this to be fairly straightforward, not to throw up this. She glances at her watch. Seb should be back soon. She says, 'How long will you be?'

Danny looks at the other adult, the solicitor. 'Dominic?'

'No more than an hour.'

He turns back to Lucy. 'Then I'll grab something to eat quickly, probably there,' pointing at a cafe across the road. 'I'll have forty minutes, I'd say.'

'My boss is coming back. I think he'll want to talk to you. Do you mind if we join you for lunch?'

Danny shrugs. 'Sure.'

Lucy gets out the phone and fires a message to Seb with shaky hands.

CHAPTER FIFTEEN

Tilly gets into the car in silence and stares out of the window. Seb can't find anything useful to say and eventually switches the radio on, sneaking glances at her as they drive.

She's dark like him, but her features are Charlie's and becoming more so each day. She is growing up and, for the first time ever, she needs things that he can't give her. Just the thought of that gives him a hollow ache in his chest. Raising her hasn't been easy, hasn't been the way he'd have chosen to do it, but he'd never once resented it and he's not ready for it to be done. Not yet.

He pulls up at the big Tesco. Tilly is still hunched over her side of the car. At first she doesn't move. He says, 'Tilly.' And she gets out with a huff, slamming the door. He flinches. He keeps up a steady stream of chatter as they go in. Her eyes stay on her feet. Inside, it's fairly empty at least. He's on to her school now, comparing it to his and moving on to possible GCSE choices for her. She says, 'Dad.' And he glances at her. 'Sorry.'

They head into the toiletries aisles. Her face is beet red. They are now standing in front of a dizzying array of products. Seb stares at the shelves and feels at an even greater loss. Tilly doesn't even look up. He grabs a box of the first thing he sees and is about to put it in the basket when a voice behind him says, 'Hello, Detective.'

He spins round. Faye Doyle. The prison psychologist. Just when he thought things couldn't get much worse. He stares at her blankly, blinks. She's smiling her easy smile. She's in another suit, grey with a pinstripe, and bright blue trainers today. A uniform of sorts, he supposes.

'What are you doing here?'

'Here Thamespark or here Tesco's?'

'Thamespark.'

She grins. 'I live here.' He swallows. She lives in the same town as him. Hardly a surprise. Half the people who work in South London commute from this suburb or one of its neighbours.

'You're not at work,' he says stupidly for want of anything else.

'I'm only at the prison two days a week. I lecture at the university here, and' – she leans forward conspiratorially – 'I've carved out Wednesday afternoons for report writing and marking. Which means I can also potter and do my shopping.'

'Right.' He realises he's holding a large box of Tampax.

She turns to Tilly. 'Hello.'

Tilly looks up. 'Hi.'

'My daughter,' Seb murmurs. 'It's our first... we uh...'

Tilly hisses, 'Dad.' And he feels heat rise in his face.

Faye takes the box from him and turns to Tilly. 'You don't want those, the size of them, honest to god.' She points to her own basket. 'Now, I'm a sucker for both pretty packaging and also a freebie. These come with a complimentary make-up bag this month.'

Tilly looks up. 'Oh yeah?'

'Yep. I mean, I have about five million already, but one more can't hurt, right?'

Tilly actually giggles. Seb looks from Faye to his daughter, now smiling at each other.

Faye says to him, 'Shouldn't *you* be at work?'

'I was. The school called. Val – Tilly's nan – isn't available.' Which is an odd statement, he realises, that must raise more questions than it provides answers.

She nods as though it all makes sense. 'Where do you live?' To Tilly.

'Alpha Road.'

'Not far from me.' She turns to Seb. 'If you're needed back at work, I'm sure Tilly and I can manage and I can drop her home? If that's okay with you, Tilly?'

'Yes, please.'

Seb says, 'Well.'

'Dad.' Tilly's voice is firm. He feels the decision slipping away from him and the relief he'll feel getting out of Tesco just within reach.

Faye says, 'I'm in no rush. Maybe we'll have a peruse of the make-up aisle too. Seems a shame not to get something to put in the bag.'

Seb says, 'Val will be home soon.' To Faye, who appears to have taken control of the situation.

'No worries.'

'You're sure?'

She waves a hand at him. 'A welcome distraction.'

Tilly says, 'Go, Dad.'

And he blinks at her. Faye reaches out and puts her non-basket-holding hand on his arm. 'Honestly, we'll be fine. I'll text you once she's home, okay?'

'You don't have my number.'

'I'm sure Tilly has?'

'I do. Go, Dad. I'll see you later.' And she actually smiles at him.

It's only as he gets into the car that he realises he hasn't given Tilly any money. He'll have to square up with Faye later. That sends a mix of frustration and... something else through him. Something unexpected as he realises that actually he's not too sorry that there will be more contact.

CHAPTER SIXTEEN

Seb sits across from Lucy, with Tilly and Faye at the back of his mind for now. His big hands circle a cup of coffee that still has steam coming off of it, and his face is set in a frown so severe, it's almost comical. Lucy imagines steam coming from his ears instead of the cup. She looks down at her mug of tea to avoid smiling inappropriately. 'I had no idea how important the interview would be.'

He shakes his head. 'Unbelievable.'

'I didn't take notes.' She adds, 'We were walking.' Flinching as she hears the defence in her own words.

He shrugs. 'You weren't to know. Like you said, we thought it'd be more straightforward. Besides, we'll record it now. You think he'll be okay with that?'

Lucy nods at the door. 'Ask him yourself.'

Lucy introduces Seb to Danny. Seb goes straight in, asking if he minds being recorded. 'No, but can I grab a sandwich?'

Seb says they'll get it, least they can do, and nods at Lucy who takes his order, goes and waits. Not just Seb's generosity, she's sure. He wants to hear what Danny has to say, doesn't want to waste time, and it's busy in the cafe now. Lunchtime next to the courts and literally just on the edge of the now-sprawling university campus.

She gets him a sandwich and a can of Coke, heading back to the table in time to hear Danny repeating the last of what he'd told her.

He takes the food gratefully and eats one half of the sandwich in three bites.

Seb is taking in what Danny has said and drinking his coffee. He tries to keep his voice even and modulated when he next speaks, though he can feel his jaw tense, the muscles in his neck making hard, twisted ropes. This wasn't something you left out. This mattered.

'So you heard arguing?'

Danny takes a sip from the can and nods. 'Not surprising – I mean, if your kid came back in that state...'

Seb makes an agreeable sound but all, that's running through his mind is that Hayley was off her face; she had fought with her parents. Hours later her mum and brother were dead, and she was sitting on the doorstep having trampled the crime scene covered in blood. 'So what did you do?'

'I figured me barging in wouldn't help, thought I'd sit, smoke a doobie, relax for a minute.' He adds, 'Sorry.' Sheepish, though Seb couldn't care less about a bit of dope then or now. He cares that this would have made Hayley a very strong suspect. He cares that Leonard might have thought the same thing.

He double-checks his notes, sprawled in shorthand in his small black pad. 'You heard arguing and a man and a woman's voice?'

Danny nods. 'Yeah, then Hayley came out like a storm was pushing her along, whoosh, right past me.'

'Then what?'

'I got up. I'd only just finished rolling my joint and I'd lit it, was just about to go after her when a man came out the house.'

'Did you know him?'

'Not then, but I recognised his mugshot later on.'

'Leonard DaSilva.' It's not even a question any more, and, along with a million things clamouring for attention, Seb feels a settled fury. 'Did you talk?'

'Yes.'

'What was said?'

'Who are you? I told him. He said, you sweet on my Hayley? Or something like that.' He shrugs. 'He, ah, pointed at my joint, I know that much, told me it'd turn my brain to mush and that she was smart and would probably expect better.'

'How did Leonard seem, when you spoke to him?'

Danny shrugs. 'I was seventeen, stoned. H was my girl-friend's dad. I was mainly grateful that our chat was brief.'

'You two were a couple?'

'Yes.'

'Taking that into account.'

He manages another bite of his sandwich, swigs from the can, flicks a glance at Lucy, back to Seb, 'Honestly, he seemed like a cool enough dude. Concerned about his kid, you know, giving me a heavy word but not too hard and it was fair enough.'

'Was he drunk?'

'He didn't seem it.'

'Then what?'

'I found her, Hayley, eventually. She was a mess.'

'A mess how?'

'Just drunk I guess, but too drunk, you know?'

Seb nods. He knows. 'Then?'

'We walked out into the woods, smoked a J together, uh, made out a bit I guess.' He flushes. 'Fell asleep for a bit, woke up cold.'

'What time?'

'Like early hours of the morning, sun coming up.'

'She was with you the whole time?'

'I mean, like I said, we slept for a bit but I think so yeah.'

'Did she have any marks or stains on her clothes?'

'Um, no, I mean maybe some grass and mud stains actually.'

Seb murmurs, 'Right.' No blood on her then. Which meant she probably hadn't been Leonard's accomplice. Jackie would be disappointed, he thinks, smothering a smile.

Leonard said he had been paralytic by the time he went back. Couldn't remember a thing, but since Leonard had never mentioned the meeting with Danny, he may not be a beacon of truth. Would this interaction with Danny have been after the initial argument? The one he and Anita had that they knew about? Yes, and before he went back to the Travelodge, Seb decides. Anita called Diane just before midnight. Danny said ten thirty, eleven, he went looking for Hayley. He instead bumped into Leonard but found Hayley a few hours later and walked her most of the way home, where she opened the door to the horrific murder scene. They know Leonard had stopped and bought vodka – or do they? Maybe he'd had it when he arrived – either way, the empty bottle had been by his bedside. He was a known drunk. No one had questioned his version of events. But what if he had been sober the whole time or what if he'd never gone back and knew full well that he hadn't? What if, as soon as he heard the news, his mind went straight to his daughter, who'd shown up drunk, angry and obnoxious? Seb needs to think this all through, and he stands, handing Danny his card, giving the man a tight smile and saying he'll be in touch.

Lucy shakes her head as they walk out of the cafe and murmurs, 'Bloody hell.'

Seb says, 'Ben Green must have taken that statement. Did you see it?'

She shakes her head. 'No.'

'What *was* in there?'

'That they spoke to Cat, and Gabriel, both of whom said that Hayley had been at the party.'

'And that was it, wasn't it?' He knows it was. Can see the reports in his mind's eye clear as day, can feel again his initial frustration when he'd looked at them – that they hadn't been full enough.

'That was it,' she agrees.

'Hayley didn't mention it either.'

'She didn't.'

'Shit.'

CHAPTER SEVENTEEN

I take the bus to the park. A small single-decker. It has been years since I've used public transport of any kind and I attempted to pay with coins only to have the driver smile softly and point to the card reader where I pressed and paid. The bus takes a convoluted route from the small house. It is like a surreal tour of yesteryear as he drives through the town, around the large sprawling housing estates here and on to the outskirts. Finally, we are at Thames Park. I am the last person to get off, and as I step from the heated bus out into the cold, I feel a tingle up my spine. We spent quite a lot of time here, that summer. Danny and I had walked through the woods hand in hand. We'd lain down underneath canopied green trees and kissed until our lips were sore. He had been such a wonderful surprise. The perfect gift for the girl who'd lost faith in true love after watching her parent's marriage disintegrate He was a sublime interruption to my anger and fear. Even now, just thinking about him, I feel the delicious flutter of butterfly wings in my stomach. I used to count down the days, hours and minutes until I'd see him again. I've never felt that way about Sean. Meeting him *had* given me focus though, and made me determined. I had wanted out, of England, of my limited options. I had wanted a fresh start.

The summer I spent with Danny I was so newly raw, so fragile after my family's split that I was unable to be anything other than myself around him. By the time I met Sean, I had no idea who my self was and, as I trample across the park now, wondering with each step on the jagged, crispy blades of grass if Ethan had trodden here too, I realise I'm still not entirely sure.

I am Mrs Marriott, Sean's wife. I'm the best one in my Pilates and yoga classes. I know lots of people by name and well enough to hold together some civil chit-chat. But I don't have real friends. Most of the conversations I have with my husband revolve around him, his work. I secretly suspect I would be better at his job than he is, but I don't have a job myself. I am thirty-one years old, and I am like a beautiful doll living in the pages of *Hello!* magazine.

I am not the girl who told Danny in a hushed voice about my dad, how much I hated him and how, even worse, I loved him still. I hadn't been able to tell Matt. The break-up of our family was the first thing in our lives that I hadn't spoken to him about. I had tried, and he'd told me I needed to pull myself together, help out Mum. I hadn't wanted to help. I hadn't wanted Mum. After that, I talked less to Matt; a distance grew between us that had never existed before. He tried to bridge it, tried to pull me back, and I wouldn't let him. I shut myself away in armour. It was the first time I felt he didn't understand.

Danny got me in a way no one else did then, and I got him too. I saw that he was kind and funny and smart. So super smart.

Everywhere I look as I cross from the playground and up the hill into the woods seems to hold an imprint of us.

I am warmer by the time I hit the outskirts of the woods. I pull my gloves off, scrunching them down into the pockets of my down-filled winter coat.

My breath streams out in front of me in cold puffs. Ahead of me is a two-storey building surrounded by scaffolding and signs. Behind it is a deep hole, where they had been about to build the car park to the luxury flats, it had been photographed in the paper. Surrounding that is police tape. Yellow with a white frosted coating. Cordoning off this place where someone had left Ethan.

It would look horribly ordinary, terribly mundane, if not for that yellow tape.

My heart thumps, as I stand, frozen, staring at the deep hole which shows layers of impacted earth. The cold creeps up on me again. Inching across the tips of my fingers. I let it. Glad to feel something other than shock.

Down there, that mud was the last thing that touched him, when he was still a boy. Still flesh and soft. I press my cold hands to my mouth. My whole body shaking. Tears streaming from my eyes, me only aware of them as they dry in quick icy trails.

Had he been scared, Ethan? Had he been in pain? Had he called out for me or Mum or Matt?

Hay Hay.

I sink down. My denim-clad knees press against the floor. Small, loose, sharp stones dig into them, a background kind of pain. I can acknowledge it, but I'm not really feeling it. Everything in me is mixed up and confused. Even if Leonard didn't do this, and I can't take that in right now, is it any less his fault? We had to leave him. He ruined our life. My family. He broke us apart. I don't know that I want his innocence, don't know that I want to have to even entertain the idea of forgiving him. He ruined *my* life.

I lost everything.

I stay so long the cold has got into every part of me, and by the time I stand on shaky legs, my body is shivering. I decide to walk back to the house, and as I go, warmth returns. The motion pushing out the cold and injecting pins-and-needles heat into my limbs, my skin. I think of everything, the inside of my head fierce and ferocious – a washing machine set on the fastest spin.

Danny, my dad, my mum, Matt and Ethan. Little Ethan. As I get back into the house, shutting the door and pressing my back to it, I make him a promise. 'I will find out, and then I will lay you to rest.'

It's all I can do. The only thing left.

CHAPTER EIGHTEEN

Lucy says, 'We'll need to speak to her?'

'Hayley?'

'Yes.'

Seb nods. 'We will, yes. It'll be tomorrow though. Let's speak to Cat and Gabriel, get as much information as we can before we go. Also, Harry found a name buried deep in the files, Dean Pike, a man Anita had been on a few dates with.'

Lucy frowns at him. 'I didn't see a transcript of the interview?'

'There wasn't one,' Seb says, the annoyance clear in his voice.

'A transcript?'

'An interview.'

'Bloody hell.'

'I know.' He shakes his head. 'Harry is going to look into it and contact him to arrange a meeting.'

'Okay.'

The Smarts live in a pretty bit of Thamespark on a nice road full of trees which are bare and jagged now but will blossom pale pink in the spring and lush green in the summer. A woman answers the door and frowns at Seb and Lucy. Seb flashes ID, and her face tightens. 'This'll be about Ethan DaSilva.'

'Can we come in?'

'Do I have a choice?'

Seb says, 'If you'd prefer us to come back another time...'

She sighs. 'No, may as well get it over with.' She walks away, leaving the door open, and says, 'Mind taking your shoes off though?'

Seb hates taking his shoes off. Finds questioning people clad in socked feet awkward, but it *is* her house. Lucy is even shorter without the half-inch heel of her work boots. Seb thinks Tilly is probably close to her in height and suppresses a smile. Lucy mouths *What?* And he shakes his head.

Cat Carter, now Smart, is in the kitchen, carrying on with what she had seemingly been doing when they arrived, which is some kind of cooking. There is a gurgling baby in a high chair who waves clammy, fat fists at Seb and Lucy. They both smile at him instinctively, and he grins back, delighted.

Cat says, 'Sit.' Pointing to the kitchen table. 'I'll be a second.'

She chops an onion quickly, scooping it up and throwing the diced bits into a hot pan. They sizzle and pop. The smell from it raw seeps into the air and Seb blinks, finding his eyes are tearing. Brilliant. Shoeless and tearful.

Lucy is dabbing hers with a tissue, and she slides him one from a plastic pack. The baby appears unbothered, and Cat seems oblivious. She adds garlic and herbs. Finally, everything is fried off, and she transfers it from the pan to a casserole pot, picking that up with oven-gloved hands and putting it in to cook. Lucy raises an eyebrow at Seb, who shrugs. She said she'd be a second.

It's closer to five minutes by the time she washes her hands, makes some cooing noises at the baby, who responds by waggling hands and feet. Then she sits down and says, 'If I don't cook now I won't get round to it. Gabe will come in hungry.' Adding, 'I work shifts.'

Lucy smiles. 'Oh yeah, where?'

'The Alms Wright Arms.'

Lucy nods. Seb scans the room: nice house, nice road, must have cost a pretty penny.

Cat tells him, 'Gabe was a contractor. Work has dried up a bit recently.' With a shrug that attempts to convey nonchalance and doesn't achieve it.

Seb murmurs, 'I'm sorry to hear that.'

'Happens, doesn't it? There was a change to taxation, then the lockdown, a lot of people were hit, not just him. Luckily, he's been able to pick up back at his dad's business.' Her mouth makes a tight line as she says that and Seb thinks that must be a blow regardless of how well you got on with a parent, to have gone out, made it alone only to have to go back.

'So you've gone back out to work?'

'I have, yes,' she snaps.

Seb smiles. 'What do you do with this little fella?'

'My mum's, or more often my mother-in-law's, and I'll need to pack him up and get going to her sooner rather than later I'm afraid.'

'We'll try and be quick.'

She turns her eyes onto him fully. They are nice eyes, wide set and hazel with an almost yellow undertone. They contrast sharply with her dark hair. He imagines that she and Hayley made quite the striking pair as teenagers. 'You read about Ethan, in the paper?'

'Yes.' Some of the hardness goes out of her then, she shakes her head. 'Awful.'

'You remember him?'

'Of course, Hayley adored that kid. We used to take him to the swings and whatnot.'

'You were close, you and Hayley?'

She shrugs. 'For that summer we were.'

'At school together?'

'Barely. She and Matt started about a month before we broke up for the holidays.'

'That would have been difficult for them.'

'I don't know. They had each other, I suppose. Matt and Ryan were chummy from the get-go. Hayley and I hit it off. We were at the end of Year Eleven, and, honestly, I can't speak for everyone else, but I was happy to have new people to hang out with.'

'You didn't have other close friends?'

'That's not what I said.'

Seb smiles. 'Did you?'

'I had mates, and Ryan was always around to hang out with if there was no one else,' she says, unaware perhaps how callous that sounded, especially in light of the boy's untimely death. 'I spent a lot of my free time with Gabe. She and Matt were living next door to him. The friendship just developed naturally, I guess.' She sniffs, and Seb wonders how happy Cat had been to have a beautiful girl move next door to her boyfriend.

'Were she and Gabe pally?'

Her eyes narrow slightly. 'I suppose.'

'She's here, you know.'

'What?'

Seb nods. Cat doesn't speak, but Seb sees a myriad of things flash across her face, which finally settles in a soft frown.

Lucy says, 'She'll probably get in touch.'

'Great.' Though the way she says it makes it sound not great at all.

'Can you tell us about that night?'

'We were at a party.'

'And you were all drinking?'

She nods. 'Hayley was a pain in the arse, drank way too much, too quickly. Swigging out of a bottle with some scabby bloke from the Lovelace who I'm sure served up all sorts.' She shudders at the mention of the estate on the other side of Thamespark to her house.

'You didn't take drugs?'

'No, nor did Danny or Gabe.' Sharp. Quick. He wonders if she doesn't count smoking weed or has chosen to forget it altogether.

'Why did Hayley get so drunk?'

She shrugs. 'I don't know. She was always angry about her mum, though Anita seemed nice enough.'

'Parental split-ups are difficult on kids.'

'I guess.'

'So you were all there, was she?'

'No, she disappeared.' An eye-roll now. 'Everyone went into a right panic. Danny made out it was my fault, for goodness' sake. I'd been dancing with her earlier, and Danny seemed to think that made me responsible for her whereabouts, but I wasn't her babysitter. It wasn't like Princess Hayley couldn't handle herself.'

Seb smiles in understanding. 'They were making a fuss, yeah?'

'Yeah. I mean she'd probably just gone to clear her head, or to throw up.' A smirk at that.

'Who was fussing?'

'Danny, Matt, Gabe, Ryan.' She shakes her head. 'Hayley could be a liability, to be honest. She always drank too much, and she and Matt argued a lot.'

'Was Matt in your group, would you say?'

She shrugs. 'Kind of. He and Ryan were, like, best buds and Ryan lived on the same road as me and Danny. All the kids there played out in the summer, but Danny and Gabe were tight and in the same year. After they went to college Ryan was maybe left behind a bit. We all got along fine though.'

'So who went looking for her?'

'Danny, to save Matt having another argument. Gabe wanted to go too, would have been quite happy to leave me there on my own, apparently.'

Lucy says, 'That must have been irritating.'

Cat shrugs. 'Hayley liked playing her damsel-in-distress card. Honestly, I think she used to get off on it.'

'Everyone worrying about her?'

She nods. 'I mean, why get that smashed when none of your mates are? Where's the sense in it?'

'So Danny went and got her?'

'Right.' A sigh. 'He was besotted with her.' Colour rises in her cheeks. The baby gurgles and she turns to him, the curtain of her dark hair covering her face. Did she have designs on Danny? Seb glances at Lucy who raises her eyebrows. Seemingly having caught the same thing.

'How long was she gone?'

'That I don't know. Like, Matt turned up at maybe eleven? She must have gone sometime after that. Danny came back later on, maybe about four, just after, he couldn't stop grinning.' Her voice is tight and stretched. Seb pictures Cat, young, flitting between Danny and Gabe, best friends. Boys she'd known forever. Danny lived on her road. 'And you don't know what time he got back exactly?'

'No. Sorry.'

'Why didn't you tell the police this?'

She frowns. 'They didn't ask.'

'What did they want to know?'

'If Hayley was at the party. Which she was.'

'And you didn't think to mention it?'

'No. It was all pretty scary and traumatic. Like, people we knew, whose house we'd hung out in, were dead. Danny was all fucked up over it. Gabe was a nervous wreck. We all tried to help her, Hayley, but she wasn't interested in us after everything that happened. She only came back to college for a few weeks then all of a sudden she was gone. No goodbye or anything.'

'Weird,' Lucy says.

Cat nods. 'I friend requested her on Facebook about five years ago, curious, you know.'

Lucy nods again.

'She lives in America, some rich husband, so I guess she landed on her feet as always.'

Seb smiles politely, though finds her obvious jealousy and utter lack of kindness towards a girl who was supposed to have been her friend interesting.

Cat says, 'I'm sorry, but I really do need to go.'

Seb nods, 'Your husband, what time will he be in?'

She shrugs. 'I don't know. We're like ships in the night on weekdays. He'll be at work now, and he's often late… hence mothers and in-laws helping with this little monkey.' Her face softens as she looks at her son, the hard edges fading, the frown melting. 'Try the office, Smart Builders. I'm sure you can google it.'

'Okay, thanks for your help.'

They walk to the door: Seb pulling on his shoes whilst trying to balance precariously, Lucy slipping into hers gracefully and making him feel like a lumbering oaf. It's only then that Cat asks them, 'Why did you come here anyway? I know you found Ethan, but no one thought he was alive, did they? Surely this is all done and dusted?'

Seb smiles. He'll be back to speak to her, not least to pick at what he has read as jealousy about Hayley DaSilva. 'Finding Ethan has raised a few unanswered questions.' She looks like she's about to say something else, but Seb gets in first. 'We'll be in touch soon.' And he hurries away, nodding at Lucy to do the same before Cat Smart has a chance to protest.

—

As they leave, Seb's phone rings. 'DI Locke.'

'Guv, it's Harry. I, uh, checked out Dean Pike.'

'And?'

'Assaulted a partner, got charged with it.'

'Tell me this was after the DaSilvas?'

'I wish I could.'

'Where is he now?'

Harry gives him a name, a home address and a work address. He hangs up and tells Lucy, who stares at him, open-mouthed. 'He wasn't even questioned.'

'I know.'

His phone beeps, and he checks it. A message from Faye Doyle, complete with a selfie of her and Tilly holding up matching make-up bags. *Home safe and sound.* A message from Val. *I was home by the time Tilly and Faye got back, invited her in for a cuppa. What a lovely woman. New friend?*

God. He says to Lucy, 'I just need to make a quick call.' She nods, and he clears his throat. 'In private.'

'Oh, of course, sorry.'

He feels doubly awkward now, but the last thing he needs is an audience. He tells her, 'I'll meet you in the car.'

Faye picks up on the first ring. 'Detective.'

'I didn't give you any money.'

'Don't worry about it. Val gave me a slice of cake.'

Faye Doyle has been in their house, sat at their kitchen table. She took Tilly shopping for sanitary products, she had cake with Val. The world seems off-kilter somehow.

'Still.'

She laughs. 'If you're that concerned, take me out for a drink at the weekend and we'll call it even.'

A drink? Does she mean a date? Or just a drink to say thanks? Would that even cover the cost? His mouth is dry and his tongue feels thick.

'Detective?'

'Yes.'

'Great. You're probably busier than me with the big case and all, so you text me a day and time.'

He meant, yes, he was there, but what can he say? 'Okay.'

'Cool. Have a good afternoon.'

And just like that, Seb has weekend plans that don't involve his daughter or mother-in-law for the first time in as long as he can remember.

He gets into the car and Lucy says, 'What are you grinning about?'

Is he? He frowns. 'Aren't I allowed to smile?'

She shrugs. 'I just wasn't aware that you did, is all.'

CHAPTER NINETEEN

Smart Builders has its own set of offices in a long, low building. It shares space with an accountant and a federation for tradesmen. Seb and Lucy are buzzed in and weave their way through the little warren of rooms, eventually arriving at the Smart Builders reception desk where a woman with many layers of false eyelashes asks how she can help. Seb flashes his badge and says they'd like to speak to Gabriel Smart.

Her eyes widen slightly, but she nods, dials an extension and a second later a tall man – 'I'm Gabriel Smart' – comes out and tells them to follow him. He leads them through a small outer office with three people, two on phone calls, one with a stack of filing, and into a private office at the back. There are two desks in here and, Seb notes, it is Nathan Smart's name on the door.

Gabriel unfolds chairs and tells them to sit. 'Drink?'

Both shake their heads.

'Cat said you'd been at ours?'

'We've come straight from there, Mr Smart.'

He nods. 'Hayley's here?'

'She is.'

Another nod. 'Where did you find Ethan?'

Seb tells him.

Gabriel doesn't speak but seems to mull it over. Finally, he says, 'That's quite a way from the DaSilvas' house.'

Seb gives him a tight smile but doesn't comment. Instead, he says, 'Tell us what happened, that night?'

He talks them through the same version of events that Danny and Cat gave.

Seb asks him, 'Cat said you were keen to go after Hayley?'

'I wanted to.'

'I got the impression, and please do correct me if I'm wrong, that there may be some jealousy on your wife's part.'

Gabriel sighs. 'Really? Still?'

Seb doesn't say anything. Gabe's eyes wander to the window. Outside there is a fine drizzle coming from the sky, which is slate grey. It's cold today, and Tilly has taken to endlessly wondering if it might snow soon. Seb hopes it does, not least to see a flash of his daughter in full-on child mode. Those moments seem to be fast becoming few and far between.

'So it was an issue? Back then?'

Gabe looks back at him. 'We were neighbours. Hayley – and Matt and Ethan, for that matter – had been through a terrible time.'

'She was your friend?'

He nods.

Seb asks, 'Would you have liked more?'

Gabe laughs. 'Wouldn't have mattered if I did. She was smitten with Danny. Though she dumped the poor bugger like a ton of bricks after it all happened.'

'She changed?' Seb says, making a note of the fact Gabe didn't really answer his last question.

Gabe nods. 'Yes. I mean, I wasn't at school with her. Only Cat was. Danny and I both went to the sixth form college, and she did attend for a few weeks after it all happened, but we were in the year above anyway'

'But you still saw her after it happened?'

'Only around and she never said more than hello. Cat told me it was the same in class, and Danny, god. He was devastated. He doesn't date much even now; I think the whole thing messed him up in that regard.'

'And you were a close group? Before that?'

'Yes. I mean Danny and I had been friends for forever. Danny, Ryan and Cat lived on the same road.'

Seb asks, 'Cat was friends with Danny first?'

Gabe nods, grinning, 'Oh yes. When she was a kid, she had a huge crush on him.'

'That didn't bother you?'

Gabe shrugs. 'They dated, you know?'

'Really?'

Gabe nods. 'Danny was never that into her.'

'How do you know?'

'We talked about it, at the time. It wasn't a long-term thing, a few trips to the cinema, Burger King. Nothing more.'

'Then you dated her?'

Gabe grins. 'I spoke to Danny first.'

'And he was cool?'

Gabe nods. 'He's a cool guy.'

Seb thinks about that. He'd assumed Cat's jealousy was about Gabe, but maybe it wasn't. Maybe it was about Danny.

Gabe says, 'That summer was one of the best we ever had. We'd all been friends since infant school. It was nice to have some new people to hang out with. Ryan was always a bit left out, and I was glad he and Matt gelled so well, and I was pleased for Danny. He was smitten.'

'And you?'

He looks away, a quick flicked glance to a frosted window which probably overlooked the reception desk but which you couldn't see through. 'I got together with Cat properly.'

'Still, the good-looking new girl next door...'

Gabe frowns. 'Look, Cat has her moments and an over-active imagination. She was also having a tough time. Her parents had some money troubles, arguments at home. I didn't know about it at the time, but it all made Cat a bit antsy, you know? Hayley and I lived near each other, so we'd meet at night at the back of our gardens for the occasional joint.' He grimaces. 'Sorry.'

Seb smiles. 'Don't be. It's minor.'

He nods. 'Well, you could see how Cat might have seen it as a threat.'

'But it wasn't?'

'No, like I said, Hayley only had eyes for Danny.'

Seb smiles, nods. Again Gabe has only pointed out that Hayley wasn't interested in him and suddenly Seb can imagine Cat, sixteen, a few problems at home, worrying whether she was going to lose her boyfriend. Also, he now wonders whether Gabe had been the booby prize all along. The man she'd ended up marrying, having a child with. The problem had been removed, of course, when Hayley left, he supposes. It will be interesting to see how things play out between them all over the next few days.

–

'Where to next?'

'Let's go and speak to Dean Pike.'

'Right.'

They decide in the end to just show up. He works shifts at a factory. Harry was able to source the rota and it looks like he'll be home today.

They get to a reasonably sized house on the edge of a large new-build housing estate. A thin woman with a nervous face and a baby clamped close to her chest answers the door. 'Hello?' she says like a question.

Seb smiles, flashes his badge and says, 'Is your husband home?'

'Dean?'

'Yes.' People often asked silly questions when there were police standing on the doorstep.

'Hang on.'

She shuts the door. They can hear the murmur of voices, a man's slightly raised, tinged with irritation. The door swings open again. He is medium-sized, thickset, with a scowl on his face, and says, 'Yeah?'

'Dean Pike?'

'Yes.'

'Can we come in?'

He glares for a second longer but finally moves aside with an audible sigh to let them know how inconvenient it is.

Inside, the place is spotless. There is another small child, a boy, who looks at Seb and Lucy with wide eyes. The woman, face down, shoulders hunched, comes in, the baby still pressed to her.

'Probably get them out of here, Eileen,' Dean snaps.

The woman jumps, murmurs, 'Yes, of course, sorry.' The boy stands silent and obedient. Seb thinks of trying to corral Tilly out at the same age. He would have been met with a litany of hold-ups.

They hear her, gathering things in the hallway. The baby makes a squawking sound, and she whispers something. The door opens, closes. 'Can't have a conversation with kids about,' Dean says, though in fact the children hadn't made much noise at all.

Nor, Seb notes, had Eileen even asked what was going on, which would have been a normal reaction. She's scared of him. He thinks: and so is the boy.

'What's this about then?' He's leaned back, legs spread wide apart, arm across the sofa.

'Anita DaSilva.'

The cocky man's face falls. 'Poor cow.'

Seb allows the vile choice of words to pass but senses Lucy stiffening next to him. He gives him a tight smile. 'You may have seen the news recently. We found her son's remains.'

'Oh yeah, the little one? Elton, was it?'

'Ethan.'

'Close.' He clicks his fingers, grinning. Then seems to remember the gravity of the situation. 'Terrible thing that was, and a lovely girl, Anita. Absolutely gorgeous. Such a shame.'

'You went out with her?'

'Yeah,' he says. 'Couple of dates but I wasn't quite ready for serious then.'

'She wanted more?'

He shrugs. 'They always do, don't they? And her with three kids. More than I wanted to take on.'

'Right,' Seb says. 'But you remained friends?'

'Yes, of a type, I guess.'

'Did the police contact you, at the time?'

'Nope, but why would they? Had their man, it's always the husband, eh?' he says with a grin. Seb can imagine that

120

he is exactly the type who makes that statement so awfully, endlessly true.

'You were charged, with assault.'

'Now, you wait a minute. That was years ago.'

'A year before you met Anita.'

'Whatever, some silly slag I was shacked up with.'

'Daisy Morris.'

'Yeah, we had a barney, she called you lot, I got sent on a flipping wife-beater course and community service.'

'Yes.'

'We weren't even married,' he says as if that's the point. 'Right uppity cow she was. I'll betI wasn't the first man to have lost my rag at her and probably not the last either.'

'You hit her, she said, several times.'

'She gave as good as she got.' He's huffing now, red creeping up his face from his neck. 'What are you here for? Spit it out.'

'Where were you?'

'When?'

'When the murders were committed?'

'You must be joking?'

Seb keeps his face set in serious lines to show he is very much not joking.

'For goodness' sake. I was with a Maureen Salter.'

'All night?'

'All night.'

'Know where we might find her?'

'Still in Thamespark according to Facebook. You can do your own legwork though, and also, if you don't mind, you can kindly piss off.'

Outside, Lucy looks at Seb. 'What a piece of work.'

'Yes.'

'Do you believe him?'

'I believe he'd be capable of murder and if I was his wife, I'd be worried.'

'Same,' Lucy says. 'The poor kids.'

'Yes, I know.'

'Could he have killed them?'

'Possibly, though he was very confident about his alibi.'

'Maybe, but Harry found that mention of him in the notes.'

'We don't know it was him,' Seb says. There was a note from one of Anita's colleagues that she had seen her in a 'heated discussion' with a man fitting Dean's description. Yet another thing that hadn't been followed up.

'Seems likely,' Lucy says with a scoff.

'It does, yes, and his confidence may be a bluff. I'd believe he killed Anita, but I'm not convinced he'd have killed Matt or Ryan or Ethan. Man's a coward but a classic wife beater. All misogyny and picking on people smaller than him.'

'He could have just panicked though; it's always looked like Matt and Ryan disturbed Anita's murder.'

'Yes.'

'We'll check it out anyway? His alibi?'

'Of course. We will check everything, Lucy, and follow every lead.'

'You don't think Leonard did it, do you?'

'Nope. The timeline doesn't work. I reckon the boy was killed after everyone else.'

'Why?'

'It's the only thing that makes sense, and I think he was buried after the others were killed, probably after Leonard had been arrested.'

CHAPTER TWENTY

The message comes through on Facebook Messenger and sends a stab of nausea into the pit of my stomach.

The word itself is so benign. *Drink?*

Saying yes means opening up so many other things. Saying no is insane though. I made my bed as soon as I stepped on the plane less than a week ago. I may as well lie in it.

I send back: *Sure!*

He writes: *Meet in an hour usual place?*

I half smile at that.

That summer I'd been here at almost sixteen, there was only one pub that served minors and, like generations before us and, I assume, the one after, we had flocked there in droves. So when I left, the 'usual place' had been that pub. The Coconut. It's dark by the time I get myself together. There's nothing in the house other than the coffee I picked up at the airport. I think about calling a cab and in the end decide to walk into town. Any hopes that it might clear my mind are dashed as I trudge along the familiar and yet somehow alien route.

I need to be here, in the UK. I can't leave my brother abandoned and alone a second time, but it is costing me. I am not that girl any more. I have recreated myself. Made the very core of me malleable and different. As soon as I got away from Thamespark I felt like it might be possible.

I'd have the nightmares forever; it would always be with me, but it was buried so deep inside that sometimes I could forget. Over the years I've heard lies slip from my tongue like honey, 'Hayley Taylor. Nice to meet you...' and, sometimes, I've believed them too. I trained my brain to look away fast from dangerous places. When things sprang up, uninvited and excruciating, like a fever threatening death, I could force my mind on to something else. The only time it ever seeped out was at night when my consciousness was at rest. Then my memories would sneak in like a furtive, awful night stalker and assault me fast before my body could react, yanking me from the dredges of rest.

As a result, I didn't sleep well. There were many nights when my husband would be lying in bed, snoring softly, peaceful and untroubled, and I'd be up, brutally wide awake. It was a secret world at three a.m., four, even five. Just me and my past. I'd never told him. I'd not looked at it as deception.

How well can we ever know another person? How well do we want to? I let Sean whisk Hayley Taylor away. I worked out fast what he wanted and gave it to him. I let him into my body and allowed my life to be hoovered up by his. But my mind wasn't a place that welcomed visitors any more, perhaps, than my heart was.

I wonder if he ever senses it, the bits of me out of reach and unseen, if that is why he has strayed. I wonder still when it will hurt. His betrayal. I keep waiting.

My husband is having an affair. With his secretary, of all things. I suspect it isn't his first, but now I have concrete proof, because once, whilst I was awake and he wasn't, I unlocked his phone and looked around. The first thing I did wasn't to confront him or phone a girlfriend (I don't have any of those, after all). I looked through the clauses in my prenup and started researching for the best divorce lawyer.

Being here, the scene of a crime, the place where I lost everything, is almost a relief when I compare it to waking up next to my husband, his searching hands warm on my skin, my perfect smile frozen on my made-up face. Fun wife. No hassle, never nags. Works out, works hard on whatever's thrown at her. Help me with this business plan, Hayley, write this, phone my client, come to dinner. Help me cinch the deal. Be the decoration on my arm. Wear this, laugh, smile, sigh when I touch you. I'm probably being unfair. Sean has always been what he is. Other than the affair and a lot of money spent in strip clubs, there was little I hadn't already known about him. If I want to be honest, I'd probably known that he was the kind of man who might have a roving eye. I had always planned to be the kind of wife who could look the other way. If it meant having the lifestyle that my mother never could. If it meant not being stuck in a never-ending cycle of mourning. The irony of being back here now when I am questioning my careful choices isn't wasted on me.

It's cold out, and everything is the same but different. There are new shops, plenty between the housing estate and the town centre, and buses running between them now, judging by the amount of quaint little stops I pass on the way. Chocolate-box-pretty things made of wood with lantern street lights illuminating a thin bench within. Enough to keep you dry while you wait, a nice way to get from A to B. It hadn't been the case when I'd lived here and had been an annoyance for Matt and me, as well as a worry for my mother, who would wait up, on hand to come and collect us at all hours of the night and day.

As I get into the town itself, I see lots more nail and hair salons, but there are still a lot of the old pubs, the playground where I had my first kiss. Sitting on a swing on a bright day that summer, where I grew into myself for such brief moments before who I might have been was snatched away. I pass the record shop where I bought Matt's sixteenth birthday present. A gift I never got to give to him, still somewhere in the loft of my mum's house. My house. My heart contracts beneath my ribs. I picture it red and bruised. Aching.

The Coconut is now a student bar, according to Tripadvisor. Back in my time, the university had been a crappy polytechnic that nobody wanted to attend. Now it ranks highly, and a large portion of the town is made up of students. There is more money here, more than there used to be. The cars are better; the houses all seem to have at least two on their drives. There seems to be a lot more people. After the hustle and bustle of New York, of course, it doesn't feel crowded. But it does feel close. There are too many memories here crowding around me, screaming for attention.

This wasn't where I grew up. It was where we *ended* up, a place I resented coming to. The place my mother brought us when we were broken, shattered, needing to regather and lick our wounds. She'd grown up here, but because her parents so adamantly disapproved of my dad, we'd never visited.

I am walking by the Thames now, a cut-through I'm surprised to find I remember no problem. The water throws a chill up into the air which whips across my face. Swans glide haughty and stiff; the tall bridge ahead is grey. Everything looks subdued. Like a black-and-white photo from yesteryear.

I walk into the pub.

Bars in America don't smell like this.

English pubs have a distinct odour and a special feel. I loved being a kid and watching my dad on stage in them. I loved the sticky bar seats, the patterned beer mats. The people laughing, having a good time, the heavy cloud of cigarette smoke that made my eyes water. He was fun, though even then in the good old days, he always had a few too many. He had my mum to rein him in, smiling softly, taking his arm, leading him home.

I see Gabe before he sees me. He has changed, of course, in fifteen years. We are friends on Facebook but scrolling through only the best pictures of someone doesn't give you the reality, does it? He uses it more than I do, but nowhere near as much as Cat. I'm a lurker, lately a private detective in my husband's life. I thought about sending Sophie, Sean's secretary, a friend request, for what purpose I wasn't sure. But her profile was public, and so instead I browsed her photos. Saw that she was young and pretty and carefree. Something I put on for Sean, a man who liked light and breezy. But maybe I didn't pull it off well enough? This role I'd created for myself. Perfect wife; woman who kept up with yoga, Pilates and running. Whose highlights never grew out, whose nails were always polished and coloured. Whose face was marked with permanent make-up so that even first thing in the morning I looked my best.

A far cry from the angry teenager I'd been. When I see photos of myself back then I am hardly recognisable, and as Gabriel looks up, it takes a few seconds for him to realise.

'Hayley? Hayley DaSilva?' A smile spreads. He is handsome. That hasn't changed. I find I'm smiling back, the first real smile for... how long? I don't know, but I'm glad to see him. For the first time since my plane landed, I am really, momentarily happy to be here.

'Hey, Gabe.'

He signals to the barmaid, orders us both drinks. I sit opposite him on a tall bar stool. I don't drink often and certainly not in the early hours of the evening, but I take a sip of my Jack and Coke to steady my nerves, I suppose, because it's what fifteen-year-old me drank and it feels like a nod to the girl who is haunting my every step right now.

He shakes his head. 'I barely recognised you.'

I laugh. 'Have I aged that badly?'

He snorts. 'Hardly.' His face rearranges itself, slipping into serious lines. 'They came to talk to me, about Ethan.'

I nod. Embarrassed to find tears spring into my eyes. I sniff, blink, and find as I attempt to force myself to smile that it doesn't work. Pretending is so much harder here, where everything is jarringly, horribly familiar.

'Yes. DI Locke. He called me, in New York. Ethan, his bones... what was left of him was far away, from our place.'

'Out by the park, he said?'

I nod.

Gabe shakes his head. 'Damn.'

'Right.'

'Will there be a service of some kind?'

I swallow thickly. 'I'm not sure. I think the police...' Then: 'I'll do something eventually.' Mumbled, because will I? Who will come? Will it be just me and my baby brother's slender bones? Would I bury them here with Mum and Matt, or would I take him back to America? A

128

secret package, hidden from Sean, that I would commit to ground somewhere there. I'm glad I don't need to do anything right now. My thoughts are cluttered and confused. In the past twenty-four hours I haven't managed anything more than walking out of one life and back into another.

My words tailed off, but Gabe is still nodding. Understanding in his eyes. He knows what I am not saying: that he is evidence, my little brother.

'How are *you* doing, Gabe?' I ask, suddenly needing the conversation to not be about this, me, my family.

He shrugs. 'All right.' A pause. 'I mean, I was doing all right.' He grimaces.

'Oh?'

'I, uh, had a bit of trouble finding work.'

'I'm sorry.'

He nods. 'I'm back working for my dad.' He sighs. 'I'm shit, to be honest.' A pause that I don't try and fill. 'Where are you staying?' he asks.

'At the old house.'

'Fuck, really?' And in those two fast words, I actually feel seen and understood.

I grin, a real smile. 'I know, but it made sense. I've been renting it out and there are no tenants in it at the moment.' I shrug. 'I took it as a sign.'

'Wow.'

I laugh then. 'I know. Honestly, it's weird being there. Here.'

We talk about the baby I've seen on Facebook, *So we don't forget where we are.* I say, 'Cat seems to have taken well to motherhood.'

His face falls. 'She has, yes. She's keen for another but' – that shrug again – 'money, you know?'

The root of all evil. Can't live without it. I say, 'I'm sure you'll get back on your feet.'

He nods. 'I will.'

He asks for my number, before he forgets, and drop-calls me so I can save his. People start coming in. We chat about nothing and everything. I tell him about New York, and he listens to the very sanitised version of my fantastic life in the Big Apple. I tell him about Manhattan and the restaurants and clothes, our apartment with views to die for, complete with the pictures saved on my phone.

He shakes his head. 'Wow, Hayley. I'm so pleased for you.' And I manage to smile right back.

I say, 'Look at us all grown-up and married, huh!'

He nods, eyes down on his drink, cheeks reddening. 'Me and Cat, guess it was always going to play out that way.'

'Guess so.'

'Do you remember how we used to get stoned at the back of our gardens?'

I laugh, thinking of us, sitting out there, obnoxious and carefree, late on those hot summer nights. I shake my head. 'And yet you somehow managed to ace your A levels and go to university?'

'My mum would hardly have had it any other way.' The words are spiky, and I think this must be tough for Diane and Nathan too. His job loss. She'd been so desperate for him to go on and 'do well', and now he is working for his dad again.

His phone beeps and he reads it, swearing softly.

'Everything okay?'

'Fine, I have to check one of my dad's sites. Apparently, someone forgot to lock up.'

'No problem.'

He says, 'I can come back, if you want to wait? I can drive you home?'

'That's sweet, but I should go. I have to make a few calls.' Which is true. Sean will be waiting for me to check in. I don't say that I am also glad to get out of there before I have mustered up the courage to ask him the question I really want the answer to. *How is Danny…*

I avoid thinking back as much as possible but find that it is not as easy here where I feel so much like Hayley DaSilva and less and less like Mrs Marriott. I trudge back through the town, my breath pushing out in a long stream in front of me. I am assaulted by memories. Walking sulkily around behind my mum as she went about her days with false, forced cheer. I remember her taking us all for ice cream shortly after we'd arrived. Matt and Ethan ordering more food than they could manage, laughing amongst themselves. Me, sullen, hard and scowling. Refusing to eat. To join in. Feeling so very separate from them, my mood making the bridging of that gap all but impossible.

I'd looked down on my mum. That's the horrible truth.

From my point of view, she was failing at life. She hadn't seemed to do much of anything that I could see other than look after us and, at the end, argue with my dad.

One of the things I was saddest about when she died was that she'd been in contact with a local college, had gone so far as to apply for an access course. It looked like she was finally going back to finish the degree that ended with the arrival of Matt and me. She never found out. Only I was ever to know. The acceptance letter arrived cruelly just days after she was bludgeoned in her own living room. Mingled in with circulars and bills that ended up with me in the terrible foster home before Nancy, my mother's second cousin, came back from her travels smelling of sand and sun and whisked me away to London.

Hayley Taylor. Nancy's niece, shop assistant, bar girl. Orphan.

I can only hope I'd have expressed some pride and admiration for my mother's efforts. I can't be certain that I wouldn't have just rolled my eyes.

I suppose that's the stage most fifteen-year-olds are at with their parents. Even ones who'd had more success than mine. Unfortunately for me, I would never get to grow into an adult who made her peace with her mum and dad.

I'd been a hard fifteen. An angry fifteen. I'd tell her all the time that I'd be gone as soon as I could. I'd spit out words like vomit. That I had plans. I was going to do something with my life.

Not. Like. Her.

I'm out of town now and annoyed to find I have tears streaming down my cheeks. They settle in cold, chilled lines as the wind whips at them. I turn out, step back towards the river. Embarrassed, though there's no one to see.

For goodness' sake.

I walk and get to a section where there are no lights. The sun is long gone, and it is dark. I fumble with my phone, turning on the torch so I don't trip on a tree root and plunge into the Thames.

It's quiet out here, and I focus on that, shining my torch out onto the water. I always find it soothing, even now in its inky blackness.

I'm pulled from it by a sound behind me, a snapping twig. I spin, my phone held out ahead like a pathetic weapon.

I yell, 'Hello?'

Nothing.

I wonder if I'm going mad. If my brother's stark white bones protruding from tumbled earth like spring crocuses will be the final thing that tips me over the edge.

I'm imagining things, I'm sure. But I speed up anyway, almost running the last few minutes, and feel a swell of relief when I finally get back to the house, locking the door behind me.

I put on all the lamps, turn the TV to E4, the channel of my youth along with MTV and The Box. I think about vying with Matt for the controls, being scolded by my mum for calling the overpriced number to request a song on The Box that I had to wait all day to hear. I think about my dad and his potted lecture on each and every song. I'd hung off of every word. Wanting to soak in his passion for music, make it my own. When I grow up, I used to think, I want to be just like him. I blink away tears. Fifteen years he's been there, in prison. An innocuous sitcom blares back at me from the telly now. I take off my coat, wash my face.

My phone beeps. Gabe.

Good to see you.

Good to see you too, I send back, wondering if he has told Danny that we've met. If he might pass my number on even.

I look up 'Leonard DaSilva' on my phone and a whole stream of awful articles comes up. I close the window, put my phone on the table and try and focus on the TV.

CHAPTER TWENTY-ONE

Seb wakes up thinking about Charlie. Coming to with a start and for a brief second, he has no idea where he is. He rarely remembers his dreams but wonders now if maybe he was dreaming about her. He looks at the empty side of the bed next to him. Tries to imagine what it would be like to wake up and see someone there. Not anyone though. He's imagining Faye Doyle. But is he ready for that? Wouldn't it just complicate his relatively simple personal life? How can you know?

Downstairs, his hair still damp from the shower, Tilly is at the kitchen table, laughing with Val. He steps into the room, almost holding his breath. She'd been in bed by the time he got home after staying late at the station rereading every statement to see if he had somehow missed something. If Dean Pike had in fact been questioned and eliminated, but no. The more he read the more annoyed he got about it. A previous charge, for Christ's sake. He found Maureen Salter no problem, a home address and phone number too, which did make him think that perhaps Dean had been telling the truth. Because why would his life, or this case, be that easy?

Tilly says, 'Nan made pancakes.' Seb grins at his daughter, happy to see her smiling, eating, talking with her mouth full. He offers to drop her at school, and she looks at him in horror. 'I'm meeting my friends.'

'Okay.'

She's gone before he is and Val asks him, 'All right?'

'Think so. She seems fine?'

Val grins. 'She'll be grand. I think she had a nice time with that lovely Faye woman.'

'Yes.' Heat creeps up his neck.

'You'll be seeing her again, yes?'

He looks at his plate, focused on cutting his pancake up into tiny mouthfuls. Val sits waiting for an answer.

'I didn't give her any money for… you know. Said I owed her one. She suggested a drink.'

Val beams. 'Marvellous.'

He frowns. 'To settle the money.'

Val looks at him seriously. 'She suggested the drink, did she?'

He nods. 'Do you think…?'

'She helped out your daughter when she needn't have. Brought her home, sat and chatted to me with a million questions about you.'

'Like what?'

'Just chit-chat.' Val shrugs. Then, 'Where Tilly's mum was.'

'And you said?'

'Long gone and left it at that. She didn't pry.'

He let out a sigh of relief. 'Good.'

'She was just checking you were single anyway.'

'She was probably being polite.'

'She was not.' She looks at him and he stares studiously at his plate. 'You're allowed to be happy, you know.'

'I *am* happy.'

'You know full well what I mean.' And then gently, 'They won't all be like Charlie.'

He chews slowly.

Val says, 'Seb?'

'I have Tilly to consider.'

'Tilly seemed to like her well enough and, besides, Tillywon't be here forever.'

He shrugs, shoving the last bit of pancake in and standing, having no desire to discuss his somewhat pathetic love life with his mother-in-law. He mumbles, 'Got to get going.'

She nods but has her thin-lipped, disapproving face on.

CHAPTER TWENTY-TWO

I suppose he suspects me. The tall, dark policeman. Certainly, he stared at me intently, watching me as I sat, assaulted by the words he had delivered yesterday. Not his fault. The quivered memory of my baby brother has always been there but hidden within, like a bruise yet to be drawn out onto the skin. Now the pain of him has risen and is spreading in purples and sickly yellows, making me tender to touch. Making me fragile.

Ethan.

Matthew.

My mum.

The detective has dark, dark eyes, deep pools that deny what he presents as an easy-going demeanour. I'm not stupid. He was studying me from the start. He wanted to know if perhaps I had been privy to Leonard's movements that night; perhaps I was involved. The thought of it makes panic rise even now I am here, home, alone, wondering how bad it is that I was relieved when my husband sent a message saying he was too busy to talk. The policeman was, of course, casually taking every reaction in. It's well-practised that, I think, and I imagine he has a knack for putting people at ease. I'm a tough audience though. I live on a knife-edge.

Even before that night, I had become adept at being tuned into the frequencies around me. Children who live through domestic disturbance often are, apparently. I learnt to await disaster. Trying to pre-empt all that could go wrong and act quickly. Sometimes that would be Matt and me, a team of two, ushering Ethan upstairs; sometimes it would be one of us pleading with my dad, or standing in front of my mum. Towards the end it would be all three of us getting out.

They were young when they had me and Matt. Ethan had been an unexpected arrival, but they'd welcomed him, loved him as they had us.

We were happy. I hadn't imagined that.

I brush my teeth, trying to scrub away last night's remnants of Jack and Coke. The alcohol sits in my mouth, and it makes me frightened. I know its power. All the things it can steal. The way it can get into a person and make them something they are not. Something other. I am angry again now: a new, fresh, stinging rage. I've made the best of things, if not entirely made peace with them. No one could expect me to make peace with them. But mostly I only think about it a few times a day, and briefly. I've trained myself to blot it out as best I can. I've married a man who knows nothing of my past. I've managed to pretend so beautifully, so convincingly that I'm okay that he has never even asked. Never poked or prodded my, still sad, story about losing two parents to cancer, extra sad for me – an only child. I've pretended so well and for so long that even I could half believe it. And now here I am, forced to think of reality all over again.

As though the universe is laughing at my feeble attempts.

Someone strangled Ethan.

Someone drove him forty minutes away from our house. They dug a grave that hot summer, breaking through layers of what must have been hard–baked earth, and put him in.

And that someone may not be Leonard DaSilva, who is sitting in a cell in Brixton.

CHAPTER TWENTY-THREE

Messenger pings on my phone. Before I have a chance to check it though, it starts ringing. Sean.

'Hey, babe.' It's lunchtime here. He must be on his way to the office or already there. 'How's it going?'

'Okay.' And then, 'The damp in the property is fairly extensive.'

'Oh no.'

'Right.'

'Can you sell it as is?'

I close my eyes and tell him, 'I'll get less money if I do.' Appealing to his innate greed. It'll be my money, and the terms of our agreement are quite clear that we are, financially at least, fairly separate. I have what I have based on our marriage and his goodwill. The second it disintegrates, I will have exactly what I came in with, which is this house and a very short career in tending bars. He won't benefit from the sale, but he'll still find it an affront not to maximise.

He says, 'Get builders out and some quotes, I'll move money to your account. Ten k should cover it?'

My heart thrums its *badaboom badaboom*. Ten thousand dollars. Enough to keep me going here for a while? Enough to see me through a divorce? I still haven't had a chance to open my laptop, peruse documents. I need to find out where I stand. I still haven't decided whether I'm ready to walk out of my American dream. Nothing I do is based on reality, so what is one more lie in the big scheme of things? What does it matter if I turn the other cheek and let him carry on with his affairs whilst I continue to take the pill and he wonders where our planned and longed-for child is? That's the problem. The real snag. Because I am accustomed to my own misery, comfortable in it even, but to put an innocent child in its midst is something else altogether.

'Babe?'

The doorbell rings and I jump.

'Sorry, Sean, yes, that's brilliant, you're brilliant, thank you.'

'No problem, gotta go, speak later, yeah?'

—

I answer the door to the two officers. Detective Locke has a scowl on his face; even Quinn is frowning, and it is she who says, 'Can we come in?'

I shrug, stepping aside. They follow me into the living room. Eyes searching for what, I don't know. The room is bare, show-home perfect, other than my yet-to-be-opened laptop and a now cold cup of coffee. The TV is on low, and I switch it off.

The man starts talking. 'You left the party, went home and ran out again.' My brain fizzes with images. Me shouting. My dad running after me. Coming to later on chilled grass. Danny helping me up.

By the time the detective is finished speaking, I have tears streaming down my face, and I look at him wide-eyed. 'I didn't go back again, to the house, not until I... found them?'

He frowns, exchanges a look with the woman. She leans forwards. 'Hayley, is the reason you never said anything about this because you thought you were involved in their deaths?'

Now the tears have started, it is like a dam has been let loose and I cannot stop them.

Locke stands up, walks over to the kitchenette area, comes back with a roll of kitchen towel and holds it out to me.

'Thank you.' I tear a piece off. Swipe it across my cheeks. Dab beneath my eyes. It is rough against my skin.

'Did you think you'd killed them?'

I shake my head and shrug at the same time. 'No. Yes. I don't know.'

That is the truth. I had wondered, of course I had. 'I… I can't remember it properly.'

They exchange a look. The man says, 'Talk us through what you do remember.'

So I do. Starting with the daytime when my mum told Matt and me that our dad was here, that he had a job interview locally on Monday and was hoping to visit us that evening. 'I was so confused by it all. On the one hand, I missed him so much.'

Quinn nods. 'I can imagine.'

'On the other, how dare he saunter back in, and I could see my mum bending towards him. You know?'

The man says, 'You were angry?'

'I was.'

'Do you know if your mum was seeing anyone else?'

I frown at him, vague memories of a large man with pale skin and red hair. 'There was this one guy, um… Dane?'

'Dean?'

'Yes,' I say, 'that's it. He got chatting to Mum in the supermarket. Took her out to dinner. Actually, she spoke to me about it, said it was a nice evening but that she wasn't ready.' I felt relief at that and also my usual default setting of anger, that she'd even dared to go out with another man. 'I think he was a bit upset about it.'

'Oh?'

'Yeah,' I say, 'he kept ringing.'

The two police exchange looks.

My heart beats. I did not bury Ethan. I keep coming back to that thought. I lost a matter of hours that night but surely not enough hours to have done that? Sean sees a therapist fairly regularly. Everyone in America has one, and as that's the life I've been living, I had the same. 'You're not very open to the process,' she'd said with narrowed eyes. I stopped going. There was no way I was going to be divulging anything to her. There were things left blank that I wanted to remain that way. My own husband didn't know the terrible things that kept me awake at night, why should she? Besides, there was no fix for my ills. No resolution to be had. Nothing could bring them back after all.

'What?' I ask, looking from one to the other. Locke smiles, 'We just need to talk to him is all.' I open my mouth to respond.

'So you were with your friends?' The policeman's voice comes in before I have a chance to add any questions. I don't suppose he'd share it with me anyway.

I nod. 'I went over to Cat's. Gabriel and Danny's friends from college were setting up the rig out in the woods, and we started drinking.' I sniff. Wipe a finger under my nose, realise how foul that is and reach again for the kitchen roll. 'I remember being in the woods. This guy we barely knew had bottles of vodka. I drank some, quite a lot, then there are missing bits.'

'What was the guy's name? Who gave you the drink?'

I shrug. 'I didn't ask. Didn't care. Danny and Gabe had a few beers with them, and Cat had a couple. They were smoking dope. Cat came and got me, I think. I remember leaning on her.' I look down at my hands knotted now in my lap, the sodden sheet of tissue twisted between them. 'After that, it's a mess. Everything is disjointed and out of sequence.'

'What do you remember?'

'Arguing with Matt.' My voice is barely a whisper. My brother's face in my mind's eye. *Why are you doing this to yourself…?* Me laughing at him, unable to say I couldn't take it. Couldn't handle the horrible hope that came with my father, which he had shattered before with his unkept promises. 'I won't drink again, I'm sorry,' I had shouted. 'Sorry I scared you, sorry sorry sorry.'

'He was with Ryan?'

I nod. 'I think so, yes. Yes, actually, definitely. I remember Ryan trying to calm the situation down. Between me and Matt. God.'

'You're doing really well.' Quinn. I'm not though. I'm doing terribly. I'm saying things fifteen years too late. I'm Hayley DaSilva, scarred and raging. All that rage hiding so much fear because whilst I don't think I'm a killer, don't think I'm awfully, irredeemably broken enough to do that to anyone let alone people I love, maybe I *am* more like my dad than I'd like. There was a time I'd have told you with one hundred per cent confidence that he wasn't the kind of man who'd hit his wife, and yet… I'm here in this house, smashing into a million tiny pieces. Mrs Marriott is somewhere in the depths, she just hung up the phone to

Sean, and now she's looking for a builder to talk to about fictional damp.

'You and your dad were close?' Locke.

I nod. 'We were, yes.' That look between him and the woman again. I say, 'What?'

'The information Danny gave us about when he saw you and where means that you really couldn't have done it. You'd have had to be in two places at once and covered in blood when he saw you last, which you weren't. But you said yourself that you wondered about your own guilt, and if *you* wondered...'

'Maybe Leonard did too?' I say as it clicks into place.

CHAPTER TWENTY-FOUR

Lucy watches her boss carefully as he settles into the car. His jaw is tight, shoulders hunched. He is fuming, but it is a quiet, simmering thing. He makes a call on his phone, leaves another voice message for Ben Green.

As he hangs up, she says, 'We'll need to speak to Baker again.'

He nods, rings through to Harry at the station.

'Hey.'

'Harry, contact Nigel Baker and tell him we need him to come in.'

'Okay.'

'He won't want to, but it's vital that he does. Let's see if he's more or less talkative off home ground.'

'Sure thing, when?'

'Tomorrow preferably, and can you chase Ben Green again? We've still got no answer.'

'I'll chase it, no problem.'

As he hangs up, Lucy says, 'You still want to go and see the Dudleys?' Ryan Dudley's parents.

'I do, yes, then we'll be headed to the prison. I arranged to go in for ten thirty, so we'll see the Dudleys first. After that, I think we're going to have to just follow the trail under the assumption absolutely nothing was done right.'

She shakes her head, eyes on the road.

Seb says, 'And I'll have to speak to Jackie.'

Lucy flinches, glad it won't be her, at least. She says, 'You believe Hayley?'

'I do, yes.'

'She should have said something.'

He nods agreement. 'And I reckon she would have at the time, if she'd been pushed. They knew. They had a statement from Danny that no one bothered to record.'

'I guess from their point of view they had their guy.' The argument is weak even as she says it and Seb makes a huffing sound.

'That may be so, but they left things out. Things that would have meant a longer wait before the case was tried and closed. They wanted it ticked off and filed away.'

'Mac was due to retire.'

Seb says, 'And nothing was going to stand in the way of it.' His voice is a hard snarl.

'No one could have foreseen finding Ethan now.'

'No one other than the killer.' And it's then that Lucy fully gets the impact of all of this. Seb doesn't think Leonard is guilty of any of it. He thinks Leonard lied to protect Hayley and that means that a killer responsible for four deaths has walked free for all these years.

CHAPTER TWENTY-FIVE

The officers leave, and I feel as though the inside of me is on fire. An internal combustion whose finale will be an explosion in my brain. My heart beats too fast and my head is pounding, my vision jarring and blurred. Migraine, a physical manifestation of the full-throttle thrum in my mind. I'd get them after every 'therapy' session. As if the weight of holding in the truth was backing up in my brain and threatening to spill out of my ears.

Did I think that I'd killed my mum and my brother? It had been there protruding, a whisper on the boundaries of consciousness. A stark green bud poking proudly from ploughed ground. I'd never let it blossom. Always kept it clipped and contained, unable to flower. It was a sprinkling of disjointed things. The sound of our front door slamming, me shouting. My dad's stricken face in our kitchen on the only day he'd ever been at that house. It was a cool summer's night filled with the sound of my feet thumping against the floor and then... nothing.

It was the absence of anything, the black unaccounted-for bits which could have been seconds but were more likely hours that have haunted me. That missing time that pulled me from sleep in the small dark hours. Clammy with sweat, my body acutely alive and vibrating with the terror of possibility. That's as far as it went, as far as I let it go. Before I settled into being Hayley Taylor, young barmaid in search of an eligible husband, it had played on a continuous loop that I picked at all the time. I'd tried to approach it from every angle. I'd tried hard to imagine picking up a knife, using it to cut and open flesh. Filleting my beloved twin – my other half before birth, throughout my childhood – like a fish gutted for dinner. I hadn't been able to summon it though. It hadn't *seemed* feasible. But my anger was a hot, fizzy thing, and I'd seen how that could look untempered and left to run wild. My dad had never, ever seemed anything but a kind and loving family man. I had years and years of proof of his good heart, his good intentions. I knew they were true. But I'd also seen him, with my own eyes, hit my mum. I had felt the brutal disconnect between who I thought he was and who he had become. Just as she must have. I still remembered so very clearly, standing horrified as the flat of his hand connected with her tear-sodden cheek. A wet, resounding, terrible sound breaking into the chaotic noise of an argument. A moment where I had stood mouth agape, suspended in a bubble. It couldn't be happening, and yet it was. It had. He'd stood looking at the offending limb, swayed by alcohol. Unsteady on his feet.

He was not a wife beater. Was not an abuser. Until he was. Until things within him, the right – or more correctly, the terribly wrong – combination of deadly ingredients turned him into something he was never supposed to be.

And there was I. His daughter, a girl raging at the unasked-for injustices heaped upon her, who took after him, who looked like him, sung like him, with his awful tainted blood running through her own veins. What might she become if left unchecked?

I had played it out and played it out until I was exhausted. Until all I could do was pack my bag, leave this town, this country, and never look back. To go and keep running.

Until now, when not only am I being forced to stare the town and the crime straight in the face, but it is also looking right back at me with questions in its eyes.

Ethan.

Poor little Ethan. Someone took him, buried him. Left him all alone. A sob escapes me. My body shakes, the store-bought, hardly used sofa cushion adjusts a little under the weight of me and my heavy, heavy grief.

I think I knew then, with that phone call from DI Locke. That I couldn't have done it. And I doubted very much that my dad could either.

A beep. My phone, Messenger, a second time.

Danny. His face in a tiny circle smiling at me from the corner of an app. *I saw the police. They said you are here?* Sent before they left my house. Now: *Can we talk?*

My hands typing out words, responding. Relief hitting me in the background behind my throbbing head and aching eyes, even though I have no idea if that is misplaced. I squint at the blurring letters as I type a message back to the boy whose lips swept over mine.

The last sweet thing before everything rotted.

He suggests dinner later on, and we arrange a time to meet. It's still hours away, and I contemplate what to do with the time. In the end, as my headache becomes more and more fierce, it is decided for me. I rummage in my handbag for Migraleve, taking two pink tablets and swallowing them with tepid, cloudy water from the kitchen tap. Then I force myself upstairs on shaky legs, pulling deep breaths in. I set the alarm on my phone, crawl into this new bed in this old room where I had lain so many afternoons before, headphones on, attitude up, my barrier between me and my family, me and the world. But never between Danny and me, and it's him I'm thinking of as I drift off.

CHAPTER TWENTY-SIX

Seb can't imagine what it's like to lose a child. Just contemplating anything happening to Tilly fills his heart with wretched dread. He can feel her starting to grow up more each day. Pulling away from him little by little. This week proving it isn't something that could or would be delayed. Even that has its own small pain, even though it's right. It's the way things are supposed to go.

They are standing at the door of a pretty Victorian cottage. It's answered by a well-presented woman with a friendly face and neat clothes. She looks at them quizzically, her head tilted to one side. 'Can I help?'

'Mrs Dudley?'

'Yes.'

'I'm DI Locke. This is DC Lucy Quinn.' They flash their badges.

She laughs – a nervous tinkle. 'Oh my.'

'Can we come in?'

'Sorry. Yes, yes, of course.'

They follow her through to the living room where she gestures to a sofa. Seb sits, Lucy takes the space alongside him.

Mrs Dudley is still standing, and says, 'Drink, can I get you a drink?' as though it's just the ticket.

Seb shakes his head. 'No need. We shouldn't be long.'

She nods. Slips into the armchair opposite. 'It'll be about Ryan, won't it?' The words come out fast, her eyes flicking to the mantle over the fireplace. Family photos. One of her, a man Seb presumes is Mr Dudley. Two boys. One of whom must be the son stolen by violence.

'It is, yes.'

She nods. 'Right.'

He realises then that she genuinely has no idea why they are here, and he asks, 'Do you keep up with the news?'

She shakes her head. 'No. I avoid it. So does my husband.' She laughs. 'Silly probably, but after everything, it became a kind of obsession. Not every day you're the lead story. One of you. Him.'

She looks down at her hands.

Lucy says, 'I'm so sorry, Mrs Dudley, what happened to Ryan was terrible.'

She looks up, her eyes damp, and gives Lucy a quick, tight smile. 'It was a tragedy, yes.' And then, 'But what does the news now have to do with...' She gasps. 'Ethan?'

Seb says, 'His remains have been found.'

'Oh.' It's an awful sound. Sore and twisted. She slinks back into the armchair. 'That poor boy. I mean, we all thought he was... but you hope, don't you?'

'I suppose you do, yes.' Though what hope there could be for a child missing that long, he doesn't know. Nine-year-olds came home. They showed up. When they didn't, it never indicated anything good.

'Was he... how long?'

'We think he was killed when the others were.'

'Leonard DaSilva finally get his memory back?'

'No.'

'Oh?'

'That's the thing. We have reason to believe there may be another person involved...'

'Who?'

Seb knows instinctively that Mrs Dudley doesn't know anything about it. He never suspected she did, but in light of the slapdash way the case was originally approached, he's determined to leave no stone unturned. He tells her, 'We're not sure, but there is some question over timings. I'm afraid I can't go into any more detail, but we'll update you when we can.'

Mrs Dudley nods but is visibly pale, and Lucy says, 'Are you all right?'

She looks at her. 'It's not something that ever goes, do you understand what I mean? We've made the most of it. My husband and I were determined to make things as normal as possible for Rupert.'

'Your other son?'

'Yes, I also refuse to regret befriending Anita. I liked her, thought she was brave. What she did, I mean. Moving her family, starting afresh, well.'

'You were friends with the DaSilvas?'

She nods. 'Oh yes. Well, I was friends with Anita. She was a lovely woman. A lot of the mums around here turned their nose up at her, and at Diane for that matter; her husband had a bit of a reputation.'

'Did he?'

'Yes, drinking, chatting up women in bars.' She shakes her head. 'Drugs.' Said in a whisper that's almost comical. Seb nods sympathetically. 'I overheard Ryan on the phone to Matt one evening. I shouldn't have been listening in, of course, but the teenage years, they pull away, and the more they do, the more you want some information, any information. Anyway, from what I could gather, Matt was concerned about his sister smoking weed and also thought he knew who was responsible. Not long after Anita told me herself, she also said it was a bit awkward because I think he suggested to Anita that Nathan might be into it, which meant possibly Gabe?'

Seb nods. They know Nathan was arrested and let go for a minor offence. A bit of weed would fit that, and teenagers nicking it off their parents wasn't beyond the boundaries of possibility. He can also see that Mrs Dudley is fairly shocked at the thought of it. He supposes it is more frightening to consider it being your own child.

She says, 'Anita didn't know what to do about it. I mentioned her concerns in passing to Ryan. Said I wasn't sure if I wanted them all hanging out, told him to be careful.' She smiles. 'He laughed, said I could trust him, and I believed I could. But, overall, I was happy when he had Matt to hang out with. There's a lot of difference between that last year of secondary school and college. I didn't make a fuss over it, we all knew each other, and it would have caused problems, maybe over nothing. Diane's son was friendly with Danny Morgan, and I've known his mother forever.'

'Is that how the boys became close? Through Gabe?'

She nods. 'Initially, I guess. To be honest, I always felt that Ryan was a little left out with Gabe and Danny. They were that bit older, taller, better-looking probably. He told me Cat mostly ignored him at school, said to him over and over, your time will come...' Her voice trails off, she shakes her head, 'I'm sorry.'

Seb says, 'Don't be. It's understandable. Are you still friends with Diane?'

'No. After everything, we had a period where we were just about surviving. We had to carry on for Rupert.

Thank goodness for him, to be honest, or I might have given into it all. The grief. When we came out of the worst of it, I found it hard to see Gabe and Danny. Not their fault, of course, nor their mothers, and I didn't wish the horror on to anyone else. It's just, I'd see the boys go past, with Cat usually, and I could almost picture Ryan trailing along behind them. We moved here because the road became too awful to stay on. My husband wanted to leave town, but Rupert had been through enough without having to move schools.'

'And you've stayed ever since?'

'Rupert's not far, has two children of his own. My grandchildren.' Her face breaks into a smile and Seb finds himself responding in kind, glad she has found some happiness, that her family is intact in part at least.

'Did you know the man Anita was seeing?'

She frowns. 'Seeing? That oaf she went to dinner with?'

'Oaf?'

'Well.' She pulls herself up. 'That sounds unkind, but, yes, I remember him. Big man. They went out once. Anita said afterwards that she wasn't ready for a relationship. He said let's be friends. She bought him over here one afternoon for a barbecue.'

'You didn't like him?'

She sighs. 'I didn't like his intentions, and I said so to Anita.'

'Intentions?'

She waves a hand. 'He was sweet on her; anyone could see that.'

'Could she?'

'No, and he seemed the persistent type.'

Seb glances at Lucy, who raises her eyebrows.

'What?' Mrs Dudley asks.

'Did you mention him? At the time, to the police?'

'Yes. I distinctly remember doing so. They assured me it was Leonard. He confessed after all.' She shrugs.

Then he asks, 'You think it was Leonard DaSilva?'

She looks up, meets his eyes. 'I do, yes. She told me they were having problems.'

'Oh?'

'Yes, it sounded awful. He was drinking too much and turned on her one night. She grabbed the kids, packed her bags and headed down here. It took enormous courage I imagine, not least because, as far as I could ascertain, they'd had a good marriage for the most part.' She sighs. 'A terrible tragedy but, judging by the news, not an unusual occurrence, a man harming his wife.'

'No, not unusual,' Seb agrees.

CHAPTER TWENTY-SEVEN

Lucy and Seb get to the prison, cut through the red tape as fast as they can and are taken to the visitor room to see Leonard. It is a large space, like a common room, and smells of old coffee, chipped cigarettes and desperation. Lucy always feels sad that this is where families, already dealt the blow of having an incarcerated relative, are forced to meet. What should be precious moments are snatched in this awful place. Children come in here, wives, mothers, fathers and siblings. Leonard, though, hasn't had any visitors other than his solicitor and Seb in fifteen years. He stands now, shakes Seb's hand, and Seb introduces Lucy.

They have barely sat down when Seb says, 'You didn't kill them.' The words hang in the air, almost accusatory and expectant, in desperate need of clarity and explanation, which doesn't come.

Leonard leans forward, hands clasped together, curled under his chin, and he asks, 'My daughter?'

'We don't think she killed them either, nor had anything to do with it.'

'Don't think?'

'It's highly unlikely, and she is not a suspect.'

He seems to deflate. A tall man, straight-backed and with proud features, very like his living child's, collapses in on himself.

Seb says, 'She's here, in England.' And Leonard looks up at that, dark eyes sharp, homing in on the words.

'How is she?'

Seb says, 'Jet-lagged, confused. Her memories of that night aren't exactly reliable.'

Leonard murmurs, 'She'd been drinking, was in a mess. Learnt it from me.' The words themselves could be construed as self-defeating, but they are said in a stoic way with no hint of self-pity. He asks the detective, 'You know who did it?'

Seb shakes his head. 'And you won't be leaving here today.'

'God.' Leonard runs a hand over his face, through his hair.

'You confessed because you thought Hayley did it?'

'I'd do anything for my children.' He smiles a small, sad smile. 'When I'm sober, that is.'

'I'm sorry,' Seb says.

Leonard sighs. 'I've made it worse, haven't I? Whoever did do this is still out there, still free?'

'You did what you thought was right,' Seb murmurs. Leonard's thinking was crooked, short-sighted and lean on this matter. 'I get it. It was your instinct to protect your child.'

'Yes.' Leonard agrees, and Lucy thinks but doesn't say his confession suited a police force keen to get him to sign on the dotted line and close the case.

Leonard asks him, 'What have you found out?'

Seb tells him about Danny, what he'd told them, the timeline they'd worked out around the information and the fact that Danny had been with Hayley after the murders took place and had no blood on her. Leonard says, 'She blamed herself anyway? All these years?'

'I think it nagged away at her, but she moved abroad, started a whole new life. She changed her name when she left Thamespark.'

'Oh yeah?'

'To Taylor.' He nods, though Lucy imagines it must sting to hear it. The only two DaSilvas left, and she'd opted out.

'She knows now, that she had nothing to do with their deaths?'

Seb tells him, 'She knows as much as we do so far, yes.'

'And you'll keep her in the loop?'

Seb shakes his head. 'Can't guarantee that, but I'll do my job. Lucy here will do hers too.'

Lucy nods.

'What do you need from me?'

'We need you to sit tight.'

Leonard grins. 'You don't want me phoning a lawyer, the papers or causing a stink, right?'

'In our defence, you did confess,' Seb says, adding, 'You'd be within your rights to if that's what you want to do.'

'But it wouldn't help.'

'It wouldn't help, no.'

There is silence then. Lucy tries to imagine how Leonard feels. Fifteen years he's been here. Locked away on the most heinous of charges. She says, 'You didn't black out?' He smiles but doesn't answer. 'Were you even drunk that night?'

He meets her gaze, dark eyes studying hers, then Seb's, who doesn't look away even in the midst of this: a ballsed-up investigation. The wrong man sitting here. Their colleagues who'd done it.

'I had an interview, for a job that Monday. Before I went to Anita's, I'd gotten it in my head that if she refused to take me back, I was well within my rights to get drunk, so stinking was my thinking.' He grins.

'And?' Seb now.

'She cried. My wife cried. When I took a step towards her, she jumped, cut herself with that knife.' He shakes his head. 'I was sober for the first time in a long time, and that cut me inside as much as it did her skin. Then Hayley.' He pauses. His eyes dampen. 'My clever, driven daughter, out of control. Raging. I saw a flash of how it must have been for them, her.' Lucy doesn't know which her he means, doesn't suppose it matters. 'I'd done that. Broken them. My family. I went back to the hotel, poured the vodka down the sink and decided I'd go to that interview regardless because what mattered wasn't what I got out of it, but what I did. If she wouldn't have me back, I'd pay maintenance anyway, and move to Thamespark so I could help with the kids.'

The words sit there, and the three people around the table take them in. Seb feels the sadness of it, a man who'd been ready, willing to do better, had shown up, and the chance was snatched away from him.

Lucy says, 'Did you think it was Hayley?'

'Yes. Maybe. I don't know. I didn't think she'd be capable when she was in her right mind. But she was in a state that night. I got like that, and when I did, I did all kinds of things I wouldn't normally… and she's my daughter. So yeah, she was there, she found them, she was covered in blood and told the police she had no memory of what happened. That's what the officers told me anyway. They strongly implied she was the next logical suspect.'

Seb feels fury at that. The confession had been manip-
ulated from him. They'd used his remaining child as a
kind of awful pawn. He manages to keep his face straight,
composed and calm.

Leonard says, 'It was months after I was arrested,
after I'd confessed, I started thinking maybe she hadn't
committed the crime, but I thought maybe she was
involved in something bad, maybe it was connected to
her somehow. I liked the kid I met that night, Danny,
but Anita had said she'd been drinking too much, smoking
weed. That boy was stoned. Maybe she was in with a bad
crowd, maybe it wasn't her who'd lifted the knife, but
maybe it was people she was involved with? I wasn't as
freaked out as Anita about the weed, I'm a musician after
all, but she was young still and drugs don't always attract
the best people.'

'You wanted to spare her from any legal involvement?'

He shrugs. 'Legal, emotional. If she thought it was me
and if she was in blackout, which I suspected and which
officers at the time confirmed, hopefully, she wouldn't
wonder if she had any part. The least I could do was keep
her free, physically and emotionally.'

Seb sits back, doesn't point out that after something like
that, Hayley could hardly be free, that knowing the truth
would have been the best thing, for everyone. He needs
Leonard on side, so he doesn't say these things to him.
The man thought he was doing right by his kid, and, in
some ways, Seb guesses he sees the punishment as fitting.
Seb would do anything for Tilly. He knows that. He'd lay
down his own life for his daughter. He'd sit in prison and
not say a word. He can understand losing the power of
rational thought when it comes to your children.

He thinks it's possible Leonard is right, and Hayley and her life had something to do with the whole sorry mess. He keeps coming back to her, at the house, the party. Drugs always brought trouble, not because they were any worse than alcohol, but because they were illegal, illicit. He needs to know who Hayley and her little gang had bought weed from, who the boy had been handing her, a minor, neat vodka. He needs to find out where those trails lead. So many things he doesn't know, but he can feel motive starting to peek in, nudging at his brain. People got killed all the time. That was a sad fact, borne out by the existence of his job. They usually died for passion, revenge or money. Drugs were the criminal's capitalist empire. Drugs were cold, hard cash when you drew it right back, and people would do all kinds of things to protect that.

He says to Leonard, 'So, what are you going to do?' almost holding his breath. Jackie wouldn't be impressed that he'd come and spoken to the man, which is why Seb has put off seeing her until afterwards.

'I'm going to sit tight and wait for you to figure it all out, Detective.'

—

Jackie Ferris glares from Seb to Lucy and back to Seb again. Lucy feels as though she might wither and die under that gaze and instinctively curls in on herself, shifting like a naughty child on the hard-backed chair in Jackie's office. Seb doesn't move, looks completely unruffled and also doesn't apologise. Whilst Lucy understands he hasn't done anything wrong, *they* haven't done anything wrong, she feels the urge to say sorry a hundred times herself. Such is Jackie's incandescent ire.

'You're saying that we, this team, locked up the wrong man?' She spits the words out like rotten food and Lucy winces.

'Yes. He couldn't have done it, plus he's now told us he gave a false confession.'

'Well, that one is on him.'

'Yes,' Seb agrees. 'Well, partly.'

'Partly?'

'He indicated that Mac suggested Hayley would be the next logical suspect.'

'Shit.'

'None of us were on the team then.' Seb: even, calm.

'I know that.' Jackie's voice drips with sarcasm. 'Do you think the papers will take that into account in their headlines?'

'No.'

'You've written a press release?' To Lucy, who nods.

'Well, I'm writing one.' She is embarrassed to find her voice cracks slightly, and she winces.

Seb says, 'It'll be a holding piece really, but I'll make contact with Mike as soon as is feasible, let him know I'll give him an exclusive if he holds things back now.' Mike Townend is an old family friend of Seb's. He works on the crime pages of one of the broadsheets. They've used him before, and he is as tame as a reporter can be.

'You'll give him an exclusive what? When you solve this fifteen-year-old case?'

'Exactly.'

'You're very confident.'

Lucy glances at her boss, sees Seb's jaw clench. 'I'm determined.'

'You'd better get on with it then.'

CHAPTER TWENTY-EIGHT

My eyes open a few seconds before the alarm on my phone starts blaring. My head still aches, but it is a dull background thing. Nothing like the full sledgehammer effect of earlier. I also find that I feel surprisingly calm. As if I have put myself through so much anxiety that my body cannot take any more of it and now it is shutting down. Whatever the reason, it feels like breathing space, a life raft to hold on to after flailing in deep water, terrified you might drown, and I'll take it. No questions asked.

I have six messages from Sean and two missed calls. The last message says he's concerned and now he is out at a business thing (unspecified) and won't be able to call again. Am I all right?

I am relieved. That I don't have to stumble my way through a conversation with him. Here in Thamespark, in England, I just don't have the energy to be Mrs Marriott. She feels as much someone else as Hayley DaSilva does when I am there. I slip out of bed and my head judders slightly.

In the bathroom, I drink straight from the tap until the water moves down my gullet, then I shower, brush my teeth and wonder what to wear.

Last time I'd been here, before I moved to London, I mainly wore old DMs tattered at the tops, fraying where the laces rubbed the leather into softness, and band T-shirts. My favourites had been ones that had belonged to my dad. Big-named bands he'd picked up at concerts, soft from years of wear and with the faint scent of his aftershave hard-baked into the fabric. I threw them out before I left for Nancy's. The awful day I had to come into this house, accompanied by a social worker with horribly sympathetic eyes, to pack the remnants of a life that was over.

These days I wear clothes that cost a small fortune and come recommended by a personal shopper who keeps a running list of 'pieces' I already have, upcoming events, trips and ideas for what will be needed. I have no idea how much she costs, but I'd say a small fortune. I have been a dream for her, a blank canvas even to myself when I arrived in New York knowing only that what I wanted to be was Sean's wife. When I was Hayley Taylor, I had a kind of uniform: black jeans, black top. I was nothing, waiting to work out what something I wanted to become.

Somehow, she found things that worked, and all of my clothes are tailored, go together and suit me well. I didn't pack a bag full of cocktail dresses and heels though, I'm not here to party after all, and I find I'm nervous. In the end I go for black jeans, ankle boots, a soft green cashmere jumper, leather jacket, silver jewellery, minimal make-up.

I call a cab, too nervous to dither with buses and walking and still slightly freaked about the, probably paranoid, feeling of someone being behind me when I'd walked home after meeting Gabe.

I get to the restaurant Danny has suggested – a place I've never been before, that wasn't here when I last was – early because I'd prefer to be seated, waiting when he arrives.

I see him before he sees me and feel my breath catch in my throat. His eyes scan the tables, finally settling on me. His face breaks into a smile.

I stand, and as he leans in to kiss me on the cheek, I almost headbutt him. I'm a fierce shade of red by the time I sit back down, but he is grinning easily. He says, 'You look great.'

And I smile. 'Sorry for nearly nutting you.'

He laughs. 'I can take it.' I laugh back, relaxing.

We order wine, olives, bread, and start talking.

About his work, which he clearly loves, about New York, which he wants to know all about. I find myself telling him all the things I do actually love about that city. The record stores, thrift shops. Weird one-off performances at small theatres hidden down backstreets, and cinemas playing strange sci-fi and foreign films. The side of the city that I consider mine alone. The things I do whilst Sean is at work. I tell Danny in fifteen minutes things I have never told my husband. Sean doesn't really do the theatre unless it's a musical with clients. He wouldn't see the point in watching a film with subtitles and all of his music is stored in the cloud, and it is all kinds of dull that I wouldn't listen to anyway.

As I speak and Danny nods, makes jokes, pulls things out of me, I realise how little I have in common with the man I married. How little I have in common with the woman I created to be his wife.

There is a lull, easy, not awkward, and the waiter comes and takes our order. It's a non-stuffy place. Pizza, which I don't normally eat, and as I relay what I want, I'm adding the calories and can almost picture Sean murmuring about carbs being the devil's work. When the food arrives, we eat in companionable silence. I sneak glances at him and every time I do I feel a flutter in my belly. This is how my mum was about Leonard. Not how I am about Sean. I'm reminded why when the conversation turns to the reason I'm here, and I feel tears spring into my eyes. Feelings are hard to control. They make you vulnerable. Loving can cost you so much.

Danny says, 'I'm so sorry, about Ethan. Poor little guy out there for all this time.'

I nod. Unable to speak. He takes one of my hands in his. My left and the oversized rock from my engagement ring presses between our fingers, hard, sharp and intrusive. I pull my hand away, reach for the napkin and dab at my eyes. 'Sorry.'

'You have no reason to apologise. This must suck.'

'It really does.' I manage a smile.

'So what are the police saying? I met the one in charge... Locke?'

I nod. 'Yeah, he seems okay. They are saying it looks like Leonard, my dad,' I say, stumbling over the unused word which feels sharp on my tongue, 'is innocent.'

Danny stares at me. Those intense eyes. 'Jesus Christ.'

I smile. 'Right?'

I stop at one glass of wine. and Danny asks, 'Not a drinker any more?'

I shake my head. 'Figured it had cost my family enough.'

'And your husband?'

'Sean's a total health freak. We don't even eat pizza as a rule. Or any bread.'

Danny frowns. 'You're kidding?'

I shake my head. 'Nope. Honestly, Danny. I spend a lot of my days running, doing yoga, waiting to support him in his business, drinking enough water and eating sensibly.'

I meant the words to come out jokily, like I was poking light-hearted fun at myself. But they fall flat, not helped by the fact that my voice catches on the word 'sensibly'.

'I'm ordering cheesecake.'

'What?'

'Screw your joyless diet. I'm ordering cheesecake, with ice cream, for both of us.' He's grinning. I smile back.

He puts me in a cab to take me home, kissing me softly on the cheek, and I spend the journey smiling, looking out of the window at thin rain. I float into bed, stuffed with sugar, my headache gone, and sleep soundly.

CHAPTER TWENTY-NINE

Whilst Seb is in no way happy that the force he works for locked up an innocent man, he can't help feeling a buzz as he and Lucy set up the incident room. His team has just been expanded from the two of them making some enquiries, with Harry to help if need be, to a fully functioning squad under his command. This case is going to be huge, and it needs to be done right, not least because of the implications for the historical investigation and everything that will mean in terms of coverage. He will be the senior investigating officer, a first for him, and though he doesn't have the same powers as Jackie nor the rank that would normally accompany this role, he has her blessing, so any searches that need carrying out will be signed off by her. He'd asked if Lucy could remain his right-hand woman and oversee the team of DCs and that was okayed. He's not stupid and knows if this goes well, he might just make that promotion sooner rather than later.

He stands now as his new team starts to file in. Lucy takes a seat at the front. She is also aware that this is a trial of sorts, that this could mean a step up for her. The last person to arrive is Jackie, who scowls at Seb from the back of the room. He grins back, and she rolls her eyes. The chatter dies down to almost silence, and he clears his throat.

'Thank you all for coming. For those of you who don't know me that well, I'm DI Sebastian Locke. I prefer Seb. This is Detective Constable Lucy Quinn who has been assisting me over the past few days on what we initially thought was a closed case with a minor question mark hanging over it and is now looking like an unsolved quadruple murder from fifteen years ago.'

Harry lets out a low whistle, and there are a few murmurs in response.

Seb holds up his hand for silence. 'I don't need to stress to you all how delicate this is going to be. We have a man in prison who I'm now certain is innocent. We have ascertained that logistically there is really no feasible way he could have killed and buried Ethan DaSilva in the time between Anita's last contact with another person, which was a phone call to her neighbour and friend Diane Smart just before midnight, and the time Leonard DaSilva was picked up at his hotel room and placed under arrest at five a.m. He also had no dirt on him, no spade was found and no weapon. Whilst the initial reports all suggested that he had changed his clothes en route to his hotel – an explanation of why there were no bloodstains – I now believe this to be incorrect. I think that the reason his clothes were clean, bar a few specks of Anita's blood, was because he was long gone before a crime was committed.'

There is quiet now. Everyone in the room has worked at least one murder, and Seb is sure they are going over in their minds the usual chain of events.

He takes a sip of water. 'Leonard DaSilva has now admitted this to us. He was in fact sober when he left and remained so until his arrest. He seems keen to co-operate, so far at least, and he isn't giving us any hassle. He has agreed to remain where he is until we have this thing solved, so we not only have a duty to the victims here, but a likely innocent man's freedom also hangs in the balance.'

He lets silence reign for a beat, two, as the enormity of those words settles on the people in the room. He sees Jackie flinch, and he can't blame her. Leonard DaSilva has been in prison for fifteen years.

'The case involved the DaSilva family. It is thought that the crime took place in the early hours of July the eleventh, two thousand and eight. Anita and Matt DaSilva were stabbed to death in their own living room.' He takes out copies of the photos, handing them to Lucy who passes them around the room. 'Matt had a friend with him, Ryan Dudley, who was also killed. It looked for all intents and purposes like a rage killing. Spur of the moment, though I'd hazard a guess that Ethan may have been killed elsewhere. Why I don't know, but we need to find out. Anita DaSilva had recently inherited her family home after her father passed away. This coincided with her and her husband, Leonard DaSilva, having marital problems. The main problem being that after being made redundant and possibly suffering some kind of breakdown, Leonard DaSilva became an unpredictable drunk. He was verbally abusive culminating in at least one act of physical violence against his wife though, as far as we can tell, never the children. Either way, Anita had had enough and moved her and her three children – twins Matt and Hayley, youngest Ethan – out here.'

Seb pauses and checks on the room. There is at least one detective who worked under Mac in here, and they may not like what is coming next. He runs through his words carefully in his mind before opening his mouth. Lucy hands him back the images which have made their way around. He pins them to one of three large boards where visual evidence will be collated.

'We have a suspect: Dean Pike, who Anita had been on a date with and decided very quickly it wasn't for her. They decided to remain friends, but Ryan Dudley's mother said he was after more and Anita was too kind. He had previously been charged with a violent assault of a partner.'

The room breaks out in frantic murmurs.

Seb lets them talk amongst themselves and then says, 'He was not questioned though it looks like the original team was aware of him. Nor was his background checked, or the assault charge would have come to light. He claims he was with a Maureen Salter. Unfortunately for us, she is currently abroad and won't be back for a few days. We found that out via her place of work, and I must assume she's using a different SIM while she's away, as her number is going straight to voicemail. The original investigation was headed by Mackenzie Arnold. I know some of you worked with him and I completely understand the need to be loyal to our colleagues. Unfortunately, and I cannot state this more clearly, this case was mishandled, and that is why we find ourselves here.'

There are a few more whispered ripples.

Seb adds, 'If any of you feel you'd prefer not to work on this investigation because it causes a conflict of interest, please do speak up to either me or Jackie. I'm going to take a fifteen-minute break now. Please come and see one of us during that time if you would like to be removed and replaced. Sorry not to give you more time, but fifteen years is already too long to wait for justice.'

—

The room clears aside from him and Jackie. His boss comes over and rests herself on the table with a sigh.

He asks her, 'All right?' – feeling suddenly concerned that maybe he dealt with a difficult situation badly.

'We have no choice but to reopen.' It isn't what he asked, but it is an answer of sorts.

'You think anyone will come in?'

'No, but that doesn't mean that Ken might not feel a little bit pissy about it.'

Seb agrees but adds, 'It'd be useful if he stayed. He was here during all of this after all.'

'Not on this case.'

'No, but he might remember things.'

'He's a good guy.'

Seb doesn't answer that. He knows Jackie is right, and Ken *is* a good officer, but he probably wouldn't have chosen to have him on his team because he doesn't want anyone here whose loyalty to Mac might get in the way. Out of everyone on murder though, Ken is one of the few who's never given him any overt hassle.

The fifteen minutes lapse. Jackie goes back to her office for most of it, poking her head around the door when the time is finished and giving Seb a thumbs up.

The team is intact. Excellent.

Seb asks Ken to be the office manager, a vital job. Seb has picked him because he is pedantic and finicky, but also as a way to hopefully keep him on side. It was a decision between him and Harry. Ken nods. Seb adds that Harry will be assisting him. Harry looks pleased with that, and he thinks they will make a good pair.

'Lucy Quinn will head up the DCs, so although she'll be out with me most of the time, she'll be overseeing where you put your time and effort. Lucy.'

She stands, nods at him and says, 'The first thing I'd like you to do is go and question teachers and school friends of Hayley and Matthew DaSilva, Ryan Dudley, Gabriel Smart, Danny Morgan and Cat Carter. Spread the net as wide as you can, it'll be tedious, but I want whatever you can find, with particular interest in the weeks leading up to, and the day of, July the eleventh, two thousand and eight. We'd really, really like to know who was selling them weed and who gave her neat vodka as, alongside Dean Pike, any dodgy drug dealers are also being considered as suspects. Hayley has told us the guy who served them was a tall, thin guy with shaved short hair who lived on the Lovelace estate. Danny has suggested Douglas Beattie; we need his details ASAP.'

She looks to Seb, who stands and reels off the names of the DCs who will be under Lucy's command.

Then, 'Dr Mathewson' – Martina stands and waves – 'will be our liaison with the scientific team though there probably won't be a lot in the way of DNA evidence this far after the fact. I have Nigel Baker due in this morning, and I'm waiting for Ben Green to get back to me. We've finally found out that he lives in Spain, so we were initially calling an old phone number. We've left messages, but so far, no joy. Perhaps we can try and find out if he has a next of kin here and if so contact them ASAP.'

Harry is standing, red-faced and kind of waving. It can be intimidating going from a small team of three to this.

Seb suppresses a grin and says, 'Yes, Harry.'

'He's at his daughters, in Sussex. Ben Green.'

Seb grins. 'Great work. How did you find out?'

Harry goes even redder. 'I called their neighbour, in Spain. She was listed. She said Mrs Green needed an op and they'd gone private in Sussex, hence staying with the daughter.'

'Very good. Anything else?'

'Actually, two things.'

'Go on then.'

'Right. I got Douglas Beattie's address. He's still at his mum's on the Lovelace. And Nigel Baker's wife is his second. I don't know if it's relevant, but I looked at the interview notes and he didn't seem to mention it.'

'He didn't, no. Did you get her name?'

'And contact details.'

'Nice one, Harry. Pint on me when we're done and dusted.'

Harry sits down looking like a small child who's been patted on the head. Seb is pleased to see Ken give him a thumbs up.

He says, 'There are long and tedious discussions about this case on a godforsaken site called Reddit.' Lucy sniggers. Seb frowns and tells the room, 'My thirteen-year-old daughter is probably more tech-savvy than me, which is why, I assume, Lucy is amused.' She shrugs. There are smiles around the room, and Seb starts to relax. He's headed small teams before but never one this big, nor for a murder or a case this complicated. 'The threads are full of true-crime junkies, I'd say a select few, but this will be making the papers, no way to avoid that and more and more people will start nosing about.' He pauses, takes a sip of water. 'Nigel Baker and Ben Green were both officers who worked the original case, and we've spoken to Nigel once already. Today, in light of what we know now and thanks to Harry's gem, I'll be going in on him harder, especially around the fact that no one questioned Dean thoroughly. Everything we do, no matter how minor, gets fed back to Ken. If Ken isn't available, it goes via Harry. We cannot afford mistakes or to leave any stone unturned. This is going to be a hard slog, and we're going to be looking closely at our own which I know is tough. But if we can get a solve, this is a career-making case, not just for me and the senior team but for everyone involved.' He nods. 'Let's get to it.'

He glances at his phone, a message from Val. She says she hopes his briefing is going well and that all is well at home. This case is going to consume most of his waking hours at least for the next few days, and he is grateful for the reminder that he is not alone. If Val *wasn't* around, there is no way he'd be able to be a detective at this level. Seb's parents had stopped speaking to him the day he packed in the cushy journalism job his dad had got him after he'd flunked his A levels and announced his girlfriend was pregnant.

Retrospectively, he can understand how that situation might have been worrying, disappointing even, to them. He'd been just five years older than Tilly was now, which seems impossibly young.

They'd told him to make Charlie get rid, and if she wouldn't do that, at least consider walking away, to think about his future. Which, they reminded him, they had invested so much in.

But he had been adopted, and there was no way in the world that he was going to allow patterns to repeat by walking away from his own child. More than that, he and Charlie were madly in love. They got married. A small ceremony with witnesses they didn't know, and he was full of hope because, all you needed was love, right?

He pushes the thoughts from his mind. No point dwelling on yesterday. He has Tilly, Val and his job. He is good at it, and he reminds himself of this as he nods at Lucy to follow him into the interrogation room where Nigel Baker is waiting, looking less than amused.

CHAPTER THIRTY

Have you had breakfast? Cat.

The bluntness of the message, written as though it was fifteen years ago and we were discussing ditching science, makes me smile. Where we'd lived in London, I had had two really good girlfriends who I'd known since infant school. Initially, we'd stayed in contact, but eventually, the phone calls dried up, and I couldn't be bothered to keep writing. Three is always a crowd, isn't it? Maybe we'd have grown apart anyway, but my absence made the decision of who would get cut out fairly easy. I toyed with the idea of looking them up when I was at Nancy's, but I was on the other side of the river and, besides, what would I say?

I missed them badly when I first moved to Thames-park though, and when Gabriel introduced me to his girlfriend, I was pleased to start up with her and we gelled fine. At first, it was as though we'd always hung out. Gabe was at the sixth form college, but she was in my year at school, and most of our classes overlapped, we wore the same size clothes and shoes and liked the same bands. I was grateful to have someone to show me around and sit with at lunch, and, despite being on good terms with everyone, Cat didn't have any close friends at school other than Ryan, who 'got on her nerves'. She'd hung out with him, Danny – who lived on her road – and Gabe for years and still tended to do stuff with them at weekends. I think, to start with anyway, she was glad of some female company. By the end of the summer though, I knew she had the hump about my getting stoned with Gabe at night, and I'd seen her look at Danny with a longing he was oblivious to.

I text back, *Not yet, are you offering?*

I'm still a shit cook, I'll pick you up and we'll go out yeah?

I send a thumbs up.

Her car is a large people carrier. The car that, in New York, would be the preserve of the soccer mom. I guess she is Surrey's equivalent. I let out a low whistle as I step into it. She shakes her head. 'Yeah, looks lovely, but we can't really afford it any more.'

I say, 'Gabe said he couldn't find a contract.'

She nods. 'You met for a drink?'

'Yes.' I add, 'He invited me.' Surprised at how quickly I can slip back into this role. Although our friendship had started off well, he fast became a sticky issue between us. I recalled her being quite jealous about Gabe and possessive. Though she had no need to be where I was concerned.

'Yeah, he said.' She puts the radio on and we listen to that while she drives. I sneak glances at her. In America, I've known my 'friends' a lot longer than I knew Cat. But she knows more about me. Basics like who I actually am for a start. She doesn't look so very different. She's well dressed, her hair is darker. Her face is still pretty, but it's also made up of hard lines, and she has a small frown in place even as she drives.

Eventually, we pull up at a cafe. Cat parks and we go in. Evidently, they know her here, and the waiter asks after her husband, then says, 'Where's the little man?' She smiles, makes small talk, and we are finally seated with coffees and menus.

I say, 'What's it like, having a "little man"?'

She grins. 'Dylan is adorable, though ridiculously spoiled. Between my parents and Gabe's...' The smile drops as she remembers my lack of parents. I keep grinning stupidly. This is the shit I haven't missed. Sean does it sometimes; even just 'orphan' status in your twenties and thirties engenders sympathy.

I say, 'It's great that he's got a lovely big family. I love your pictures of him. He's very cute.'

She nods, takes off the sunglasses she was wearing – despite the cold it is a bright sort of grey out there today. She looks at me closely, and I feel almost as if I'm standing before her naked. 'What's it like being home?'

I keep my forced smile in place. 'It wasn't my home for very long.'

'I suppose not.'

The waiter comes, and though I've barely had time to glance at the menu when Cat orders overnight oats and fruit, I go for the same. Adding a pastry, enjoying the amount of sugar I'm managing to cram into my trip. A break from my marriage and my dull-as-dishwater diet.

Cat says, 'Still don't have to worry about what you eat, eh?'

I shake my head. 'No, my husband is a total health freak actually, so I spend my entire life on a bloody diet.'

Her eyes narrow. 'Really?'

'Either that or in yoga, or running.'

'Jesus.'

I laugh. 'Everyone we know in New York is super health conscious.'

She says, 'What's he like?'

'Sean?'

She nods. I swallow, and I'm saved from answering straight away by the arrival of our food.

I use the time to get a few of the best pictures up on my phone and show them to her. She says, 'He looks like a film star.'

She's right. He does.

'What does he think about all of this?'

I shrug. 'We haven't discussed it in much detail yet.'

'And he's not here?'

She knows this. Gabe and Danny both know it, and I've no doubt at all they'd have told her. I say, 'He's working.'

'Still, what about a bit of moral support?'

I shrug. This was how it became between us after that first initial rush of friendship. She always made me feel this way, picked at and poked. She used to make underhand remarks about Matt, my mum, me coming from a broken home. Nothing overt. Nothing I could ever pinpoint, and back then, I was so glad of her friendship. So keen for her to like me, to let me into their little group, that I'd let a lot of stuff go. Now I feel annoyed.

I say, 'Are you working?'

And she sighs. 'No choice since Gabe lost his last contract.'

'I'm sorry.'

'To be honest, we'd hoped for two kids by now.'

'Not pregnant again yet?'

She shakes her head. 'Gabe doesn't want to keep working for Nathan, so he wants to wait until he has a job again, like a contract or permanent role in an office.'

'That must be tough.'

She shrugs. 'Gabe's back working for his dad now, sure, but he stubbornly refused to ask him for his old job for about six months which meant we've depleted our savings or I'd be able to get on with it quicker. Now I guess we'll have to wait. What about you? No kids?'

'Not yet.' I smile a too-bright smile.

She says, 'You'll likely get pregnant as soon as you try, and your husband looks unlikely to run out of cash.' Spite is woven between her words — so she's had a good nose at my Facebook page too then. I shrug. Focus on my pastry. I don't tell her that the thought of children in general terrifies me. The thought of being tied to Sean forever fills me with dread. And that being here, even under the most abhorrent of circumstances, is making me homesick, and I'm not even sure what for.

My phone rings. I excuse myself, stepping outside.

It's a woman called Jackie Ferris. Apparently, she is Locke's boss and had been updated on 'recent events'.

I say, 'Okay.' Wary that the queen police bee is deigning to call me.

'How are you, Hayley?'

'I don't know. All right, I guess.'

'Good, that's good.'

It's a lie but a polite one and better than telling her I'm exhausted, freaked out and have no idea whether I'm coming or going. It's the middle of the night back at home so no confrontation to be faced there yet. But Sean will no doubt ring as soon as he's awake, and I'm dreading it. Knowing that we need to have a conversation urgently that will likely take the crack between us, that he is blissfully unaware of, and widen it even further. Two cliffs with no bridge to link them. When I am there, I can almost convince myself that who I am pretending to be is who I actually am. Here, I don't have that luxury, and I'm now one hundred per cent sure I'm not in love with my husband and that I never was. I'd settled for that, been okay with it, because being in love was what had got my mum killed, after all.

Except it wasn't.

The woman on the phone is apologising. She is making some sort of speech, but I am having trouble focusing, and I drift in and out of her words. Hearing 'miscarriage of justice'. And 'compensation'.

Tears spring to my eyes as I think of myself then.

Fifteen. Angry, my heart smashed into a million pieces, because they were dead, yes, but also because now I had no choice but to hate my father, throwing myself fully into that feeling because I hadn't wanted to unpick the other possibility. The missing hours, blood on my hands, wet, slick, drying hard and cracked like scabs. That terrible tightrope I had walked whenever I thought of him, Leonard, between love and its darker counterpart no longer existed.

He'd killed Matt.

He'd killed Mum.

He'd taken my baby brother, who I'd rocked to sleep, sung to, kept wrapped in my arms in bed on cold nights.

Instead, he was innocent and knew it. Protecting me like he always had. That's what this woman is saying whilst also carefully trying to feel out how much trouble I'm going to cause for her, which, right now, is absolutely none.

Maybe that day, when he'd shown up with smooth words and tempting promises for my mother, he'd meant them all. Maybe we had been on the verge of a new happiness, one that surely we'd all appreciate more, treasure because we'd come so close to losing it.

'We've reopened the investigation. Officially.' I'm yanked back to here. Now. The woman at the other end of the phone.

'My dad is definitely innocent then?' And we will never know if we might have regrouped. Blended back together. The DaSilvas.

'We're heading down that path.' She says, then adds, 'But it's the most likely scenario. Which is as good as an admission.'

'God.'

'This must be a huge shock.'

I don't bother answering. It's cold outside the café, and my coat is inside on the back of my chair. I shiver a little. 'Can I see him?' The words are out there before I even knew I was going to say them.

Jackie Ferris says, 'That's fine by me, if it's something you think you can handle. I'm sure DI Locke could drive you. You could bring a friend or arrange for your husband to come over; we could wait?'

'I'll bring a friend.'

'Great. How about if we contact the prison for you and arrange it?'

'Thank you.'

'Any specific time that is good for you?'

'My diary is wide open.'

She chuckles half-heartedly at my shit joke. I suppose she is relieved that I am not going mental, which I'm probably within my rights to do. But I'm tired, exhausted actually, and I think I should see him though I'm not sure if I exactly want to. We say goodbye.

I get back into the cafe and Cat asks who that was. 'The police, they are reopening the investigation. My dad is innocent.'

CHAPTER THIRTY-ONE

Nigel is frowning as Seb and Lucy take their seats. Seb moves slowly, taking the time to line up his pad, pen and settle down. It's a cheap trick but one that works, even on Nigel who has perhaps used the same pop psychology himself in the past. Lucy sits to his left. She has her pen and pad in hand as she'll actually be taking notes. Seb's are just for show. The last thing he does is put the file on the table. Opens it up to the most gruesome pictures from fifteen years ago. Lays them so that they are facing Nigel. He adds a new one, the bones they recovered, all of them, laid out on a mortuary slab with a long tape measure next to them for scale. Then the material, nylon pyjamas with superheroes on them. Tattered but not disintegrated. And the grand finale. The little boy himself with flesh on his cheeks and a gap-toothed grin. Ridiculously cute. Undeniably adorable at that age between babyhood and adolescence.

A time when he should have had years of possibility spreading before him. Instead, that picture was taken at the end of his life. An unfair cruelty that Seb wants to drive home to Nigel, whose eyes follow each image as they are laid down. His Adam's apple bobs as he swallows. A thin perspiration makes his brow glisten.

Seb says, 'Hayley DaSilva was at her house that night.'

Nigel looks at him with a confused frown. Seb doesn't say anything more. Instead, he lets the words stretch out between them, filled as they are with accusation. Of what, he doesn't know exactly.

Nigel says, 'She came home in the morning. From the party. She was the one who found them.'

'She was, but she'd also been back that night.'

'She told you this?'

Seb shakes his head. 'Danny Morgan did. He also said he told Ben Green at the time.'

Nigel's eyes widen. 'My god.'

'You're claiming you didn't know?'

Nigel frowns. 'Claiming?'

Seb remains stony-faced. Lucy pauses from scribbling notes to look levelly at Nigel. He attempts to smile at her and it falls flat.

He runs a hand over his face, leaning forwards onto it, fingers digging into his scalp. Massaging slowly as if wishing to rub away this information. But facts are facts. Seb believes Danny. He has no reason to lie. He also has no idea, and very much needs to find out, if Ben himself was hiding information. There were processes in place even then. Seb is struggling to believe that someone as junior as Ben had been would have let that information go uncatalogued, but you never knew. Until he could actually speak to the man himself, that question would likely remain unanswered.

'Talk to me about Mac and that case, Nigel, and do it now before I have to hear it from Ben.'

Nigel says, 'We had our man.'

'It wasn't Leonard DaSilva.'

He looks up then, sharp eyes meeting Seb's, hands dropped to the table clasping at each other. Belying nerves and anxiety. 'For any of the killings?'

Seb snorts. 'What are the chances of two murderers targeting one family on one night?'

'What are the chances of it not being the abusive husband?' Nigel asks, his voice full of wary defence and also, in fairness to him, making a valid point. He goes on. 'Leonard was the obvious suspect.' But there is doubt there now. Edging into his words, making them cautious.

'And you were going to get him at all costs?'

Nigel's face closes down. 'I don't like the tone you're taking.'

'I don't like having to pick up the pieces of a botched investigation. I don't like that we have a man in prison, who's spent the best part of his adult life there when he needn't have.'

Nigel stands. 'With no malice intended, I'm going to take some legal advice.'

'Really?'

'Yes, really. You can't keep me here, and I need room to think.'

'I was hoping your conscience would have opened your mouth.'

Nigel leans forwards. 'I have a wife, children. I was a junior officer, doing what I was told, so was Ben.'

'Your second wife.'

His face turns a deep shade of red. 'Excuse me?'

'Your second wife. First wife, Angela Baker, who we'll be speaking to shortly.' He smiles. Nigel looks like a deer caught in headlights. 'We'll also speak to Ben. If I were you, I'd be desperate to help. This is your chance to put things right.'

'And I will. I do want to help. But it was years ago. He confessed. I want some advice first. I think I want a lawyer.'

They can't hold him, can't force him to stay. Seb needs to know what Nigel knows. Needs to find out what exactly had gone wrong. He can understand him wanting to cover his own arse, of course, but he has no respect for it.

—

An hour later Seb's phone starts ringing. He's about to pick up when Harry comes over to him. 'All right, sir?'

'You can call me Seb.'

'Seb then. I found an address for Angela Baker and a number, thought I'd give her a ring, make sure that's where she lived.'

'Is it?'

'Yes, and she's in all day if you want to speak to her. If not, I said I'd call to rearrange.'

But Seb is already standing, getting his coat on and calling out to Lucy. As they head out, he checks his phone and says, 'Val called. I'll meet you in the car.'

Lucy goes out, assuming she'll be driving then, and has just settled herself in when Seb taps on the window. He looks like he might explode. She asks, 'Everything all right?'

'Um, kind of, but I have to nip home.'

'Your daughter?'

He nods. 'Can you manage this one?'

'Of course.'

He gets in his Golf, drives home, his heart racing and his hands damp around the steering wheel. Despite the fact that it is close to freezing, by the time he gets out of the car, he is covered in a thin film of sweat. It's barely even the afternoon, yet it's so dark that their Christmas sensor lights have come on and twinkle at him as if mocking his panic with their wretched cheeriness.

Seb has never really struggled with being a parent, even when he found out he'd be doing it alone. Tilly gave him life; she gave him reasons. A reason to go to work and do well – keep a roof over her head, make her proud. A reason to look after himself – so that he is always there for her. A reason to connect to the outside world once in a while because she lives so fully in it. Without her, he doesn't know where he'd be. Maybe he'd be just fine. Maybe there is an alternate Seb thriving in journalism somewhere and still in frosty contact with his adopted parents. But he can't picture it.

She changed everything. In ways he hadn't been expecting and for which he would be eternally grateful. He had been a frightened child, had hidden it well behind calm eyes, but inside, the fact his real parents hadn't kept him, for whatever reason, and that he could genuinely feel the disappointment he caused his adopted parents, made him wary of love. Suspicious of anything good. Charlie taught him the same lesson in a newly painful way. But Tilly – she was the one pure, uncomplicated thing he had.

But now…

God. He takes a deep breath in, turns his key in the door. Val is there before he hears the click. He takes one look at her thin-lipped face and feels even worse. 'Where is she?'

'Kitchen.'

They go through into the warm hub of their little cottage. He is gearing up to give her a bollocking, to tell her this – fighting at school, for goodness' sake – is completely unacceptable.

But as he sees her, sitting at the kitchen table, streaks of mascara, which she's not supposed to wear to school, down her cheeks and large eyes damp, the anger slips away.

He sits opposite her. Val takes a chair beside her granddaughter and gives Seb a kind of sad shrug.

'Tilly?'

A sniffle.

Suspended. For two days. His straight-9's bright, clever, kind daughter.

It's then that he sees her bruised knuckles. Red now, by the morning, they'll be swollen and multi-coloured. He lifts her hand; she snatches it back. Wriggling it up into the sleeve of her royal-blue school jumper.

He doesn't know what to say, how to approach this.

Eventually, she says, 'Am I grounded?'

'What happened?'

A shrug, her eyes stray to the window. The cat comes in through the cat flap, noisy and oblivious to them and their silly human issues. She lands in the kitchen with a squeak of a meow and heads to Tilly, who picks her up, rubbing her face on her fur.

'Tilly?'

The cat wriggles and jumps back down, staring pointedly at her bowl.

'Carla Simon said my mother is a junkie bitch.'

Seb feels the blood drain from his head right down to his toes. One look at Val's shocked face suggests she feels the same.

Simon? Simon… Oh god. He remembers her mother now. Older than Charlie and him but had lived on the Lovelace when they did. He didn't know her well, not at all really, couldn't even remember her name. But right now, he'd gladly brain her.

The first year of Tilly's life had been okay. Happy even, maybe up until she hit eighteen months. Then Charlie got depressed, got bored, got restless. She started drinking in the daytime. Then she was smoking dope, hanging out with old friends. People Seb didn't want his baby daughter to be around.

She felt trapped.

She felt swamped.

She just wanted to be young.

She couldn't cope.

She left when Tilly was two and Seb had come home to their tiny flat to find his daughter in the playpen bawling her eyes out and Charlie in their bed with some lowlife who'd sold her coke.

Val, Charlie's mother, came down from her small house in the north of England to see if Seb was okay, realised fast that he was far from it, and stayed. She sold her house. Seb joined the force, studied at night for a degree in criminology and sociology. Crime had always fascinated him, and it was the one aspect of journalism he'd actually been interested in. Seb and Val bought the place they now called home.

By the time Tilly was five, Charlie had proven she couldn't be relied upon to show up or offer her young daughter anything meaningful.

Seb told her to leave them alone and she did just that.

There had been a lot of loss in his life. His birth mother. His adopted mum and dad who'd never been quite happy that he wasn't their son and, worse still, that he didn't share their traits and ambitions.

Charlie.

The silence is too long, stretching out around them and blanketing the little family unit of three with unsaid words. Seb swallows thickly, presses a hand to his forehead. Tilly knows her mother is mentally unstable and isn't able to look after her. That is really all Seb has given her, and he's been relieved, if he is honest, that she hasn't pushed for more. He's told himself that she hasn't asked because she has everything she needs. In him, in Val. That is probably bullshit though, and he of all people ought to know that. He is in his thirties and still wakes up wondering who his real mother was. If she loved him.

'Is she?' Tilly's voice is strangled. A desperate tinge to it. He cannot protect her from this any more than he can stop her from growing up and all the natural, necessary pain that entails. He looks at Val, whose eyes are damp, hands clenched on the table in front of her. Her daughter, her only child, a continuous source of both guilt and shame.

'Yes.' Seb's voice is barely a whisper.

'What?'

'I said yes.' He looks straight into his daughter's eyes. 'Your mother is a heroin addict.'

She bursts into tears. Val puts an arm around her shoulder, crying now as well.

Seb sits, watching the scene unfold, his insides numb as though he is watching someone else's life.

CHAPTER THIRTY-TWO

Angela Baker lives on a nice road full of skeletal-looking trees and grass verges frozen white. In the springtime, Lucy imagines, those trees blossom and look picture-card pretty. But winter gives everything its own kind of beauty, though she could do with a bit more daylight and less excruciating cold.

The house is detached with a large drive and must have cost an absolute fortune.

A woman with fading red hair and dark eyes answers.

Her kitchen is blissfully warm, and Lucy gladly takes a cup of tea from her, wrapping her hands around the cup and lifting it so the steam hits her face. What she wouldn't give for a bit of winter sun, maybe she'll book a last-minute thing after this case. If she gets on to murder, yes, that's what she'll do – a little well done to herself.

Angela Baker settles across a long kitchen table on a thin bench. Lucy is in a white plastic bucket chair which is more comfortable than it looks.

'You're not the one who phoned?'

Lucy shakes her head. 'No, that was DC Fitzgerald.' She shakes her head. 'So sad.'

They both leave a respectful beat. 'It must have been a difficult time for you, when your husband was working the case?'

She laughs. 'What, because he was so wracked with pain over it all?'

'Are you saying he wasn't?'

She shrugs. 'I honestly wouldn't know. I was busy with the kids, he was at work a lot of the time, and if he wasn't, he was rarely home.'

'You didn't have a good relationship?'

She smiles, and it looks sort of playful. 'Well, we got divorced around that time.'

'Can I ask why?'

'You can ask, but I can't be overly specific, and it's probably not an unusual story. We got along well enough, and all of my friends were getting married. When he asked, it seemed the right thing to say yes. Gosh, that makes me sound awful, but I don't mean it like that. I wanted a family you see, and I'm a couple of years older than Nigel, which probably didn't help. Anyway, I could see thirty heading towards me, and I wanted children, so did he. So we had two of them, and then I realised he really wasn't up to it.'

'Being a father?'

She nods. 'Right. I also found out he was still hanging round that Diane Smart far more than he should.' Lucy makes a scrawled note of that and underlines it.

'They'd dated, he said, nothing serious?'

She nods. 'I don't think it was for Diane, but I think he was fairly hung up on her. Anyway, I wasn't overly bothered which is a sure-fire sign you're not madly in love, I suppose.' She chuckles. 'Sorry. Anyway, we got divorced. But there genuinely weren't a lot of hard feelings. He still gets on well with the children, and he has always provided very well.'

Lucy's ears prick up at that. Married money, he said. He'd left the force only eighteen months after the DaSilva case. Maybe he'd been seeing wife number two during the end of his marriage? 'How well?'

'Well enough to pay half the mortgage on this place and put the kids through school. Private for both. Always paid the fees in advance.'

'His second wife is very wealthy?'

'I don't know.' She frowns.

'When did he remarry?'

'Gosh, maybe ten, eleven years ago.'

Lucy takes that in. 'And before that, after he'd left the force, he was paying half the mortgage then, and school fees?'

She nods. 'And decent maintenance too.'

'How did he come across that sort of money?'

'Said he was consulting and that his parents had helped him out. They weren't loaded but weren't exactly destitute either. Like I said, once we were over, aside from the kids, we went our own way.'

Lucy smiles, finishes her tea. 'Thank you for your time, Mrs... ah...'

'Still Mrs Baker. Never got around to changing it. It's the kids' name too, after all. Why are you asking about Nigel now?'

'We're sifting over everything from the original case.' Which doesn't really answer her question but seems to satisfy her well enough.

'Well, hope it goes okay. I saw on the news it was being looked into but didn't really want to believe you had the wrong man! That poor bugger, in prison all this time.'

Poor bugger indeed.

Lucy gets into the car and all she can think is – *rich cop, leaving the force?*

She calls Seb, who sounds harassed but also says he's on his way back. She fills him in, breaking off to beep at a lunatic taking a corner at great speed.

Lucy says. 'Not looking good, is it?'

'Not for him, no.' Says Seb.

'Think it's linked to the murders?'

'If I had to guess, I'd say it's more likely linked to Nathan Smart's drug charges.'

'Which were dropped.' Lucy reminds him.

'Yes, and we're going to need to find out exactly why. It may have nothing to do with the DaSilva killings directly, but police who need to cover up corruption don't want the spotlight, do they?'

'They probably do not, no.' She agrees.

'The thing about Diane Smart is interesting, isn't it?'

'Yes, very. He made out like it was a fleeting schoolboy crush.'

'He did, yeah.'

'Not how Mrs Baker made it sound at all.'

'No.'

'Will I meet you at the station? I'm almost back?' She asks him.

'Yes. We'll go and see Ben Green's daughters. Let's see if we can get a clearer view on all of this.'

CHAPTER THIRTY-THREE

It's first thing in the morning in New York and getting on for lunchtime here. WhatsApp buzzes to life with an incoming video call. I take a deep breath, trying to imagine my insides being made from molten steel instead of wobbly jelly. My husband's beautiful face jumps to life on the small screen clutched in my damp palm.

I feel that jarring sensation as if observing myself from somewhere far away.

'Hey, babe.'

'Hey yourself.'

'How is it?'

I shrug. 'You know.' My heart thumps hard. *Badada-boom badadaboom.* 'What's happening there?' Quick words fired at him before he can ask any more.

'Okay, closed the deal with Murray, paperwork all done and dusted.'

'Oh brilliant.'

He grins. 'Yup, and you helped cinch it.'

'I wish I was there to celebrate with you.' As I say it, I realise it's not true. Though I'm not entirely sure I want to be here either, I find I want to be there, with him, even less.

'Me too, babes. I'll go out with the guys here tonight though.'

'And Sophie?' The words slip from me before I know I'm going to say them. He pauses, his face so still that for a moment I wonder if we've lost the Wi–Fi connection. That invisible line that draws us all together all of the time. No matter where we are, we are within reach. Even if we don't want to be.

'Yes, probably.' His voice is smooth like silk. Everything about him is that way. Soft, luxurious, expensive. He is a tactile man, a man who likes the feel of things. Material, fine wine, women. Status. 'She did do a lot of the legwork, you know.'

My smile holds; underneath it are slippery thoughts rushing round my mind like fast eels in a bucket of clear water.

The words from their email liaisons flash through my mind. *Want you. Need you. Fuck me.* Things he's said to me often enough, worded in exactly the same way. I wonder if he ever got confused between chats. Now isn't the time for this argument. I'm not even sure if it will get to that. But I probably need to speak, to say things I haven't yet. 'Sean, there's...'

A beep in the background, the familiar sound of an email arriving on his laptop. 'Hang on, babe.' He props the phone up and I see him swivel away from me. He's back, picking up his mobile, I see the downside of his chin, and now his face, screwed up in concentration. 'I need to get on before I meet with Len.' His boss, to discuss Sean's latest success, I guess.

'Okay, but I really need to talk to you.'

His face softens. 'God, sorry, babe. This different–times thing is a pain in the ass, right?'

My brain whirrs through his day, which will be manic leading up to celebrations tonight. Then what? Will

Sophie spend the night at ours? Would he stoop so low that he'd bring another woman home, press her body into our bed, on our sheets as he has done mine, or would they get a hotel? Would that rule out a conversation tomorrow morning? And how would I start that conversation? So my dad is actually alive, but I stopped speaking to him after he killed my mum and brothers, except – plot twist – turns out he's innocent, and no one knows who killed them after all.

I force Mrs Marriott's smile again and it comes out like a grimace. 'No problem, let's try and catch up tomorrow when you finish work. I'll wait up.'

'Plan.' His mind is already pulling away from me on to the next part of his day. 'Love you, babe.'

'You too.'

He kisses at the phone. I kiss back and feel relief as his face disappears and my home screen takes its place.

Ping – a message from Lucy Quinn. *You can go in at two today. Please let me know if that suits? Also I am happy to accompany you.*

I pick up the phone and dial Danny.

CHAPTER THIRTY-FOUR

Seb meets Lucy back at the station. He has a face like thunder and her attempts at small talk when they get in the car amount to nothing. When he finally murmurs, 'Sorry for being quiet,' she feels a swell of relief, then reprimands herself – not everything is about her, as her mother often reminds her. She says, 'No problem.'

Ben Green's daughter answers the door with a perturbed scowl. 'Yes?' Seb flashes ID, and she presses a hand to her chest. 'Goodness.'

'Nothing to worry about.' Lucy's words are as quick as her smile. 'It's your dad we're after, about a case he worked on.'

The hand drops, the smile is returned along with a tinkly laugh. 'Oh well. Not every day the police knock on the door. Dad's been off the force so long I almost forgot he was there at all. Come in. 'Scuse the mess.'

The house is cluttered, and two children in the midst of a game involving brightly coloured guns and foam bullets whoosh past, stopping only momentarily to look at the visitors. Ben's daughter says, 'Call me Miriam.' Then she tells the children, 'Here for Granddad.' They go off on their way.

Seb says, 'Nerf guns?'

She half grimaces. 'You have children?'

Seb nods, smiling at the memory of Tilly hiding, badly, behind the living room door, one bright blue end of a Nerf gun hanging out, waiting to shoot him, Val or the cat, whoever came first. She didn't do much of that any more. Playing. He hopes that the news about Charlie won't make it even worse. He should have talked to her, of course he should. He'd put it off and put it off for so long, and now look. He sees her in Val's arms, tears running down her face and, worse, looking right at him. 'Why didn't you tell me?' The trust he was so sure of, so certain they had, eroded by his omission. Val had said a few months back that the conversation would have to be had and he'd agreed, yet still… he'd put it off, figured he had plenty of time yet. But time runs past when you're not looking, and it turns out time will force you to do the things you should if you don't manage it yourself. He pushes the thought away; he'll talk to her later.

They are in a conservatory now where a man sits and looks at them, 'This is my dad. Dad… Oh, I forgot your names already.'

'DI Locke, this is DC Quinn. Ben Green?'

He stands, a solid man with cauliflower ears and a flat nose that has obviously been broken and reset badly. He takes Seb's offered hand, shakes it, then Lucy's, gesturing for them to sit. Miriam says, 'Tea, coffee?'

Both decline.

Ben says, 'Awful weather here.' Pointing to the grey slate outside.

'Nice in Spain?' Seb asks.

'It is, yes. Gets cold, but it's usually bright. Part of the appeal for us. No more grey drizzly winters.'

'Yet here you are.'

'Wife needs an op.'

'Nothing serious, I hope?'

'Nothing serious, no.' He smiles then. 'You're not here about my wife's health though, are you?'

'No.'

Ben nods. 'That little scrote Baker just messaged me.'

Seb makes a mental note of 'scrote'. 'Not friends?'

Ben sort of snort–laughs. 'No, we're bloody not. Not now, not then. He must have found my email address somewhere though. Said you wanted to talk to me, then your man at the station called.'

'How come you didn't get on with Baker?'

Ben smiles. 'You can't like everyone, Detective.'

'No, but your dislike seems quite intense.'

He looks out again across a generous garden which probably is beautiful in the summer but now is just a large expanse of wet dullness. If you stepped out onto the lawn, you'd be plastered in mud in no time at all. Seb thinks Ben has a good point about winters.

'You're here about the DaSilva boy?'

'You read about him?'

Ben nods. 'And Baker was blathering on about it in his email. All affronted like.'

'Oh yeah?'

Ben smiles and meets his eye. 'I'm going to assume that you know full well you've pissed him off.'

Seb gives a slow nod of agreement and Lucy suppresses a smile.

'Have you contacted the sister? Hayley.'

'We have, yes. She'd moved to New York, married an American.'

'Yeah?'

'Yes. She's back now.'

'What's the husband like?'

'Haven't met him.'

Ben nods. 'Difficult to find happiness after something like that.' Eyes back out to the thin rain but not really looking. A pause while he thinks back, remembers things he'd probably rather forget. Then, 'It was a terrible scene.'

Lucy says, 'We've seen the photos.'

'Can't give you any indication of the horror of it. Mother and son, looked like the boy was taken down trying to protect her. Ryan, nothing to do with anything, I suppose, other than wrong place, wrong time.'

Seb says, 'Often the way.' He is thinking of a case he worked recently, a bar fight that had spread out, a woman, nothing to do with anything, hit full force with a flying bottle. Punctured an artery. By the time anyone looked away from the main event and realised she'd been hurt, she was dead.

'Awful.' Ben shakes his head.

'And Hayley walking in on it.' Lucy's voice soft, the words not.

Ben sighs. 'Unimaginable, isn't it? I think she kept a steady nerve at first, certainly she went in, saw her mum, her twin brother, Ryan. Then she went upstairs, no Ethan. Managed to phone us from the landline before she completely freaked out.'

'Didn't use her mobile?' Lucy asks, it was in the notes that she'd dropped it in a pool of blood in the living room.

Ben shakes his head. 'No battery.'

'She must have messed up the crime scene?'

'She did, yeah, touched Matt and her mum, found her bloody fingerprints on the phone, and she was covered in the stuff, looked like bloody Carrie on prom night. She threw up all over the doorstep.'

'Jesus.'

Ben smiles, but it's sad. 'She'd been out, was all strung out and sweaty, stank like a brewery but was sobering up fast.'

'You spoke to her?'

'Me and Nigel. Nigel was first on the scene. First murder for him. He was rattled, and I took over as much as I could. He called it in to Mac though.'

'And Mac said?'

'Go pick up Leonard,' Ben shrugs, 'the logical thing to do.' But there is a hesitance in his voice.

Seb says, 'What would you have done?'

He looks at Seb from clear blue eyes. 'I'd have searched high and low for the little one.'

Seb nods. 'Me too. Why didn't you?'

'Mac told us to get Leonard first then get a search team out, which we did, but not for long. It should have been until the kid was found.' He shrugs. 'For all we knew, the kid was alive, and we could have got to him. Mac wasn't having it though. He'd turn up, he said.' His voice is hard, bitter bits embedded in his words.

Seb says, 'You think it was the wrong call?'

'Judging by the fact you're here now I think we can all agree on that.'

'Mac's not here to defend his decisions.'

'He's not, no.'

'You didn't write up the statement from Danny Morgan.'

Ben frowns at him then. 'I not only wrote it up, I harangued Mac about it. It'll be in the file.'

'It's not.'

Ben stares at him open-mouthed. 'You're kidding?'

'Why were you haranguing Mac?'

His eyes narrow. 'I wanted to do your job, you know.'

'Murder squad?'

Ben nods. 'I was all bright-eyed and bushy-tailed, but that case...'

'You found it too much?'

Ben shakes his head. 'No, not that. I was prepared for that. I'd served in the army, seen plenty of gore there. I didn't like how it was handled.'

'Which was?'

'Quickly.'

'Mac had his man.'

Ben snorts. 'Mac wanted to retire.'

'And Nigel?'

'In love with one of the bloody women involved.'

Seb and Lucy exchange a look. Angela had suggested as much. Seb leans forward. 'He said he dated Diane Smart a few times when they were kids.'

Ben snorts. 'Dated? A lovesick puppy he was. Adored her. Her idiot husband was a known dealer; did you know that?'

'I saw he'd been cautioned a couple of times.'

'Always got off because Diane turned puppy dog eyes on Nigel.' Ben shakes his head.

'Nigel was married?'

'Yes, but he divorced her. That started while I was still on the force.'

Seb ponders what Ben has said. 'What do you think should have been done?'

'Should have followed up about the man Anita had dated, that was mentioned and dismissed.'

'Dean Pike?'

'Yes.'

'He'd been done for assault.'

'You're bloody kidding?'

'No,' says Seb, who feels fresh anger at it all over again.

'We didn't even question him,' Ben says.

'No, I know.'

'I wanted to.'

'I believe you.'

Ben nods.

Seb asks, 'What else would you have done, if it had been up to you?'

'We should have pressured the kids.'

'Hayley?'

Ben nods. 'Yes, and Gabe, Cat and Danny.'

'You think they were involved?'

Ben shrugs. 'Matt was concerned about his sister. Hayley, the lot of them were smoking weed fairly regularly which wouldn't have been cheap. I would have liked to have known where they were getting it from.'

'Hayley said she'd been drinking with a skinny bloke from the Lovelace estate. Danny suggested there was a then-known dealer there, Douglas Beattie?'

'There you go, stuff like that ought to have been looked at. Were they buying weed off him, or was Gabe swiping from his dad's supply? If so, what else was there?'

Seb nods. The same line his thinking had gone along. He tells Ben, 'They're married now, Cat Carter and Gabe.'

'Oh yeah?'

Seb nods.

Ben asks, 'How did he do? Gabriel?'

'Well for a bit, I'd say. He was contracting. The bottom fell out of it, I understand, and he's back working for his dad.'

Ben grimaces. 'Bet he hates that.'

'What do you mean?'

Ben screws up his face. 'There was… tension.'

'Between the boy and his dad?'

Ben nods. 'His parents, really. Mum doted on him. I figured that was it. Classic spoiled only child, dad maybe a bit pushed out.'

'Nathan was jealous?'

Ben shakes his head. 'No. I mean, I don't know, but I didn't think so. I wasn't sure if Nathan actually picked up on it; not the brightest bulb, to be honest. But Gabe was scathing about his dad's business, and Diane was adamant she wanted "better things" for her son.'

'And yet his company has been quite successful, Nathan's.'

'Yes, but Gabe was to go off, get a degree. Mum felt he could do better than building, which isn't a crime, of course.' Ben waves a hand. 'It wasn't anything tangible that I can give you an exact example of.'

Seb sits back, mulls that over. Cat had seemed fairly scathing of her husband's misfortune. History repeating itself? If so, what, if anything, did it mean for this case? 'What did you make of Hayley?'

Ben's face falls then. 'Poor kid.'

'Other than that?'

'Not much. I didn't get to question her. I wanted to, but Mac spoke to her about Danny's statement.'

'He didn't.'

'You what?' He looks from Seb to Lucy aghast.

Lucy nods.

'That useless fucker.'

No one disagrees.

'In the brief time you spoke to her then.'

'She was a kid, you know? I mean, at fifteen, you think you're all grown-up, and certainly she'd been acting out, wasn't managing her parents' separation. That would have been hard on her.'

'Of course.'

'But that morning, god. Like I said, she'd obviously been on the lash the night before, but she looked like what she was, a scared little girl.'

'You were there when Leonard was picked up?'

He shakes his head. 'No, but I sat in on the interview.'

'Where he confessed?'

'He easily agreed with everything Mac said.'

'And what did he say himself?'

'Absolutely bugger all, which was my main issue with the whole thing.'

Seb frowns. 'You raised this?'

Ben sits back, contemplating the question. 'I was a young man then. I came up on a shitty estate the other side of London, started boxing in a local gym and joined the army. It was a good life, the right one for me. The police force seemed a logical progression once I was home. I had my wife, who'd waited it out for me raising two kids while I did various tours, and the force meant being home at least. I was eager, keen.'

'Yet you left.'

Ben nods. 'Yet I left. That case.' He shakes his head. Seb senses he's trying to formulate his thoughts, put them into words. 'The boy, Matt.' He shook his head. 'You've seen the photos, yes, but when I first walked in, I thought Matthew DaSilva looked like his hand was reaching. Sounds stupid, but that's what I saw, a boy reaching for his mother. And the little 'un missing.' Again, that head shake, not so much a no as a clearing of thoughts. 'All I could think of was that little boy, alone, alive? I didn't know. And worse, no one seemed to care much.'

Lucy asks, 'You said there was a search?'

Ben laughs, a hard bark from this gruff but empathetic man. He would have made a good detective. Seb suspects he was a good coach. The force's loss which, he thinks, it needn't have been.

'We looked within a five-mile radius. Back then that was mostly woodland. They had one nearby neighbour.'

'The Smarts.'

Ben nods. 'Right.'

Seb says, 'And you're saying Nigel Baker had the hots for Diane?'

Ben nods. 'You couldn't blame him, she was drop-dead gorgeous, but I'd have looked at her husband and his associates a lot more closely.'

'You think you didn't because of Nigel?'

Ben shakes his head. 'No, actually. I think we didn't because of Mac.'

'Nigel said he was a good boss, a good man.'

Ben sighs. 'He was a lazy boss and a pig of a man.'

'Oh yeah?'

'Yeah. He was due to retire, like within weeks of the DaSilva case coming in. He didn't want it dragging out, so if you're asking why corners were cut, that's your reason.'

Seb says, 'To be fair, he stayed on an extra month, saw the case through.'

'Yeah, showed up to every press conference, went out in an undeserved blaze of glory, if you ask me. If we'd held out, put more time into finding the boy, chased up the kids at the party, the local dealers, Nathan, Dean, I mean, what a mess that was – well, it would have taken a lot longer, wouldn't it?'

'It would.'

Ben shakes his head, 'Dealt with terribly.'

Seb tells Ben, 'There's no way Leonard DaSilva buried Ethan.'

'Thought that when I read the story, all it said about location was that it was near a building site for new developments. It'll be the ones heading out past the lakes?'

'Yes.'

'He wouldn't have had time, would he, Leonard, to bury the boy there?'

'No.' Seb says.

'Why did he agree it was him?'

'He thought Hayley might be involved.'

'And you?'

Seb shakes his head.

Ben says, 'You believe Danny Morgan?'

'I do, yes.'

He nods. 'So did I.'

'One last thing.'

'Shoot.'

'Did Nigel know about you haranguing Mac about Danny Morgan's statement?'

'Oh yeah, we argued about it. He told me to stop rocking the boat, causing unnecessary aggro.' He shakes his head again.

Seb stands, and Lucy follows. Ben pushes himself to his feet with the sprightly balance of a man thirty years his junior.

He walks them to the door, and as they turn to say their goodbyes, he clasps Seb's hand and meets the taller man's eyes. 'You're determined to get to the bottom of this?'

'I am, yes.'

Ben nods. 'I'm not sorry with the route my path took, the gyms were where I was supposed to be all along, but I am sorry justice was never found for them. The girl, the dad if, as you say, he's innocent, and that babe who was left alone all these years.'

Seb says, 'I am too.'

'Then I guess you're the right man for the job.'

CHAPTER THIRTY-FIVE

I am standing outside, the cold biting at my cheeks, my breath pushing out in front of me in a wispy plume, when Danny pulls up. I find my stomach flip-flops at his arrival, and I marvel at the ability to feel almost... giddy. I remember those feelings from way back when. When he was Gabe's best friend. The last member of the group I met. When I longed to have him kiss me, hold me. When I was absolutely certain that if I was his girl, all would be right in the world. Before I knew how cruel and messed up life could be. How pain could score itself on you like a branded scarlet letter burnt crisply onto pale, singed skin.

I get into his car. It's warm inside, an instant contrast to the chill I bring. He reaches over, squeezes my hand, looks at me – really looks, and I let him.

'All right?'

'I don't know.'

'Understandable.' And it is, isn't it? Because these are terrible, big things I'm having to do. See the man I'd tried to remove from my mind and heart. Look my past in the face and say... what? I have no idea.

We don't speak much as we drive out of Thamespark and into London. The city I spent my suburban summer longing for looks less appealing now to my adult eyes. It doesn't have the gritty glamour of New York. Or maybe it does, and I'm just not seeing it. I've been surprised over the past few days at how pleasant Thamespark is. Things I didn't notice at fifteen. A pretty town with a marketplace crowded with Tudor buildings – black beamed, white painted – and the Thames cutting through its centre.

The South London prison is awful by contrast. Grey, tall, foreboding. My heart stammers as we draw up to it.

Fifteen years.

He's been here for so long. For me, to protect me from questioning, to stop my life being picked apart. I never questioned it either, his guilt. But, I think, he had made himself into someone who I could believe did this. That's real and not imagined.

When we get inside, there are various hoops to jump through, doors that clatter and clank, open and shut. Locks on everything. I cannot imagine what it must be like walking in here knowing it will be years before you can leave. A lifetime of confinement stretching ahead. We get to a point where Danny cannot come any further, and I smile and nod to him that I'm okay when I'm not at all. I take off my jewellery and place it in plastic bags, then my belt. Everything smells of stale cigarette smoke, and the space where I am to visit my father is like a tatty, decrepit common room. Thin, worn linoleum under my feet. Walls, once painted white, now faded to yellow. Vending machines stuffed with sugary goods packaged in too bright colours which look out of place. And there, sitting at a wide plastic-topped table, hands clasped in front of him, is my dad.

I stand frozen to the spot. The guard behind me. I register his presence in the background but don't think I could turn my head to look at him if I tried.

My father, Leonard, stands. His hair is long. Longer than it was. Tied back off his face and white at the temples.

Not old, but not young any more either. I go to him on shaky legs. Voices seem to hum, but they are just my thoughts. Whispered words from yesteryear. Loud enough though that I stop for a moment, close my eyes. When his voice breaks in. 'Okay, Hay Hay?' I am back, whoosh. Here. Now. Hay Hay.

I am opposite him. So close I can see the pores on his skin. He is tall. As tall as I remember. I don't think I've grown since the last time we saw each other.

Shouting in the kitchen. Mum wide-eyed. Me, turning and running on Bambi legs, drink making my progress odd and disjointed. My father shouting. The rage. Propelling me away from him. Them. The last time I saw my mum. The last time I ever would.

I find my legs give now. My knees crumbling in on themselves and my body lowering into a plastic chair. It feels flimsy and insubstantial, but it takes my weight.

He sits down, eyes searching me. His hands reach across the table and lift my fingers, familiarity races through my nerves up my arm. I feel his calloused hands, rough against my soft-skinned, manicured ones. I am a child again. For the first time in as long as I can remember, suddenly, I am only one person, one thing. I am not separate identities held in fragile compartments. I am Hayley DaSilva and he is my dad.

'Hay Hay.'

I pull back my hand. It is too much, and I yank my eyes away, focusing on the table where my fingers tremble, grabbing at each other.

Finally, I look at him, meet his eyes. Neither of us speaks, but when he reaches for my hand again, squeezes it, I don't pull away.

I feel everything all at once, anger, the absence of family. The terrible aloneness that I hardly understand and can never fully explain. What it is like to be only you out there in a world that makes no sense. For a few unexpected seconds, I allow myself to imagine everything is all right, my hand grasped in his. But that hand hit my mum. That hand started all of this. But it is not the hand that stole them. Not that at least.

Then a voice. 'Come on, Leonard.'

The guard who followed me in, an unwanted shadow. Who has taken up silent residence across the other side of this vast, vile place.

Leonard, Dad, nods. 'Sorry, Carl.' Then to me, 'We're not supposed to touch visitors.'

He settles back into his seat. The momentary illusion of safety is shattered. He is still here, and so am I. He'll be getting out. The detective has promised that he will find the real culprit and that when he does, Leonard will be free – and then what? I can't even think that far ahead, can't contemplate any possibilities.

'Have you had many?'

He frowns.

I add, 'Visitors?'

His face crinkles into a smile. 'More recently than ever before.'

'They found Ethan.' My voice struggles as I say his name. I think of small white bones laid out on cold steel, of my brother trailing along behind me. Hay Hay.

Leonard nods. 'I know.'

'Someone…' I pause, swallow thickly, feeling phlegm clogging up my throat. I inhale sharply as though gasping for air. I clutch the side of the table, release my breath. 'Someone strangled him.'

He shakes his head. All of the sorrow, all of the sadness. My grief mirrored in him. Ethan, small, happy-go-lucky little thing. Someone squeezed the life out of him. We don't speak for seconds. A minute. My brain stilled with that horror. His too, perhaps.

I ask him, 'You were sober?'

'When I came to see you guys?'

'When you were arrested?'

He nods.

I say, 'Did you think I…'

'I don't know,' he says, the honesty painful. 'I thought it was possible. You always had the best of me. I guess I entertained the idea that maybe you had the worst of me too. If not, that you… did it, then I thought maybe you'd got into trouble, maybe something you were involved in. That night you looked…' His voice trails off. A father talking to his daughter about a difficult subject. A normal subject? Most parents probably have the 'drink and drugs' chat with their kids. We didn't get that conversation. My mum had tried, carefully because every interaction with me was like walking over barbed wire for her. 'It crossed my mind, Hay Hay, as a possibility, and once it had, I figured I could take the blow instead.'

I say, 'I thought it was you.' My voice is small compared to the massive betrayal in those tiny, hurt words.

He nods. 'Everyone did.'

I want to say I'm sorry, but I don't know if I am. If he hadn't lashed out, hadn't given in to the bottle, had chosen us over it, I'd never have even considered it.

He shakes his head, goes to take my hand again before his eyes flick to Carl and they settle in the Formica space between us. He sighs. 'You saw me lose it, Hayley, and I did lose it. You didn't imagine that, and it must have shocked you. That last year, those months, I wasn't myself. Not at all.'

I can't disagree with that, but I do find the anger releases, just a little. Like a pressure valve being turned and steam coming out. I imagine I can feel it in my body. A deflation of the hot, acidic ball of bile that festers in my gut, shatters in my head, giving me unspeakable, unbearable headaches. My body rebelling against all the tricks I use to try and forget. Never letting me. For a moment the lessening of that rage is like blind panic. It has been part of me for so long. The internal refrain. *I hate my dad. He ruined my life.*

I think of Sean on one of our first dates. 'Tell me about your parents…' he said.

'They are both dead,' I replied, hoping if I said it enough, it would be as good as true.

Leonard. Here alone. Unforgiven for crimes he'd never committed. His love for me still so strong that he never contradicted it.

I tell him, 'They've reopened the case.'

And he nods, thoughtful, considered. 'He's good.'

'The detective?'

'Yes, I think so.'

'He said you're going to wait quietly, not cause a fuss.'

'I think that's best.'

'Aren't you angry?'

He shrugs.

I say, 'I am. All the time. My whole life, everything is based on lies.' Tears come then, hot and uncontrolled. I swipe at them, annoyed, my face screwed up and hard.

He watches me, staring as if he's trying to memorise every bit of me. I remember that, way back when. He was like it with all of us. Desperate to get to know us, find out what made us tick and respond to it.

He asks, 'You're married?'

I nod.

He says, 'Mrs Marriott.' And I flinch before I have a chance not to. 'You're not happy, Hayley?'

My damp cheeks, my sore heart. 'I never thought happy was within reach.'

'You should never settle for anything less.'

'Really? When your whole family is taken out, when your dad's in prison.' I add, 'My husband thinks you're dead.' My words are hot, red and hard. The anger is back, filling my voice, whispering wicked, hurtful things in my mind. Things intended to wound that slide from my mouth unchecked. I've lived like this for so long that I don't know any other way.

'Do you love him?'

'No.' No pause. No moment of contemplation. 'I never have.'

'I loved your mum.'

'And that went well for her.'

He smiles a sad smile and I look away. 'We'd have sorted things out, I think. Or I would have at least. It wasn't on her. She'd done nothing wrong.'

'You'll never be able to now.' Bitter words that leave a bitter taste.

He says, 'No. But I'm still here, and so are you.'

I look at his smiling, warm face. No malice there. No resentment. 'You still don't drink?'

'No. Haven't done since before I came here. Never did me any good.'

'You've been here for fifteen years for something you didn't do.'

He nods. 'I did enough harm though.'

'But you didn't kill them.'

'No. I didn't do that.'

'I miss them.'

'Me too.'

'Matt and I argued. That night.'

'Siblings will do that.'

'I was awful to Mum.'

He smiles. 'She said you had your moments and I saw you that night.' He shakes his head. 'You were hurting, Hayley; I could see that, so could your mum. We'd hurt you.'

'Matt and Ethan didn't act like that.'

He shrugs. 'You were different people.'

I find my breathing is easier, my shoulders rise and fall softly. The jagged, suppressed sobs gone. 'What's going to happen?'

'Right now?'

I nod.

'We let that policeman get on with it.'

'Should I go home?'

'To America?'

I nod.

'Do you want to?'

'No.'

'Then don't.' That simple.

I say, 'I'll have to tell him. My husband, Sean.'

'Yes.'

'He's having an affair.'

Leonard raises an eyebrow at that. 'What a dick.'

I laugh then, before I can help myself. Giggles tip out and I feel them, really feel them. They are pretty bubbles floating high on a summer's day. Leonard is smiling too. I want to say *I missed you*, but I can't. The words get stuck in my throat. Held there by memories of my mother's scared face, of having to pack a bag and run from London.

I manage, 'Then I guess I'll be here, when you get out.'

He nods. 'I'd like that a lot.'

–

Prison, it turns out, is a place of little inconveniences, and leaving proves just as discombobulating as my arrival did. I put my belt and jewellery back on under Carl's watchful gaze. I sign something to say I'm going and return the plastic visitors card I had to use to get in. Outside, Danny is waiting, and he steps from the car waving as I walk towards him. Just like he was back then, he is a sweet moment in an otherwise sour situation. Before I can register it, something flashes in my face. I turn, startled to find a man and a woman, the man waving a large camera with a flash which I assume is the thing that almost blinded me. I murmur, 'What the fuck?' before I hear, 'How does it feel to visit your father, the murderer?' I stare in stunned silence and feel like my knees might buckle. Then Danny is by my side, hand on my elbow, leading me to his little car, with a firm, 'No comment.'

CHAPTER THIRTY-SIX

Seb has just finished going over Leonard's confession again, with Ben's words in mind. Leonard had indeed been fed a lot by Mac which gives him the strength to deliver all of the bad news to Jackie now. Her face is so red it's almost puce, and Seb flinches every time she speaks. Her words have broken down into nonsensical muttered curses now. He risks a glance at Lucy whose wide eyes indicate she is equally horrified as him, if not more so.

The front page of today's paper, this one a national tabloid rather than the local rag no one ever picks up, has Hayley DaSilva's stunned face staring back out at them. Alongside it is the prison that currently houses Leonard DaSilva, and finally a photo of Danny Morgan, arm wrapped around Hayley's shoulders ushering her into his car. A few opening paragraphs lay out that she has visited her father for what is suspected to be the first time in fifteen years. Continued on page four...

And page four is where the real problems begin. The exposé of a 'secretly' reopened investigation with all the leaps you can't help but make from there. Police incompetence, a bungled original investigation. Secrecy, an innocent man in jail, and the real icing on the shitty cake: a murderer walking free.

Jackie has stopped her venomous spouting, and Seb opens his mouth to say something. Closing it again quickly when he realises he has no words for this.

Unfortunately, Lucy pipes up. 'They'd have found out sooner or later, I guess.' Her face goes bright red before she even finishes the sentence. Jackie's hard eyes make her look down studiously at her feet.

Jackie: 'Who knew about the visit?'

Lucy looks to Seb, who says, 'Us, Lucy and I, the wider team and the prison.'

Jackie's eyes are fierce. 'The leak had better have come from the prison.'

'Okay.' Seb's voice is even, reasonable though he is pretty certain it has come from one of them. He hopes from a junior officer too chatty in the pub rather than a malicious leak, but how would the prison know details of the case? It does little to calm Jackie down because she probably knows it too.

'Are we any closer to solving it?'

Seb pauses.

Jackie's scowl deepens. 'Well?'

'Nigel Baker has clammed up, but his current wife is wife number two, and it's looking likely that she is not where his money came from. Wife number one said he has paid generous child support over the years. Wife number two is considerably younger, and I'd say the chances that she and Nigel got together soon after it all are as slim as her being minted – which we can find no proof of at all. Also, Baker was way too involved, at least emotionally, with Diane Smart, whose husband was a small-time drug dealer from what we can work out. This has been mentioned both by his ex-wife and Ben Green, the other officer from the original investigation. Incidentally, Green left the force because the case was handled so badly. Then there was Dean Pike who Anita went on a date with and who had a previous conviction of assault.'

'Your view of him?'

'He's a wrong'un, classic abuser, should have been a prime suspect at the time and is our most likely one though my gut feeling is it wasn't him and, actually, his alibi has been confirmed. I got hold of Maureen Salter who said she was indeed with him all night and added that he was a prick which I would agree with.'

She groans, 'Great.'

'Sorry.'

'Any other leads?'

Seb and Lucy exchange a look.

'Any other leads?' she says again, louder now. Lucy jumps slightly.

Seb says, 'Nathan Smart was a known drug dealer, though never charged. We think he may have got away with it because of Diane's relationship with Nigel Baker.'

'Relationship?' Her voice is shrill now.

'As I said, at least in Baker's mind. They were childhood friends. Ben, and Nigel's first wife, Angela, suggested Nigel was still soft on her.'

'And Diane and Anita were friends?'

'Yes, and with Ryan Dudley's mum. Anita had concerns about Nathan.'

'Then follow that up.'

'We are. We also have officers out speaking to teachers and school friends of both Matt and Hayley.'

Jackie says, 'Whatever you're doing, make it quick and get a press release out ASAP. I'll hold a conference later which, I have to say, is not my bloody best.'

'Lucy's doing a new release next. We'll send it to you first.'

'Yes, make sure you do.'

Lucy is pale-faced as they step out of Jackie's stuffy office and start walking back to the incident room. Seb asks, 'You all right?'

She shakes her head. 'She's hopping mad.'

Seb laughs. 'Jackie's default setting is pissed off. Don't worry.'

'Really?'

He shrugs. 'Sure, all we need to do is solve this fifteen-year-old case and we'll be right back in her good books.'

Lucy swallows thickly.

CHAPTER THIRTY-SEVEN

What I remember most about back then, before it all ended so awfully, is Danny. I spent many nights sneaking into his house after we'd been out. We'd lie in his single bed, candles lit in old Baileys bottles, his room covered in posters and a red lamp with a skull-and-crossbones shade that made scarlet patterns on our skin. We'd kiss, of course, and explore, but we'd talk for hours until the sun started to peek in and then he'd walk me home. I loved those nights, those talks about music, films we liked and the things we wanted to do. Then the following morning I'd float all the way back to our house, his hand holding mine, and find myself smiling dumbly, stricken throughout the day by the memory of him. His touch, his words. His intense eyes drinking me in. In the midst of all the turmoil, the wrench from my dad, the hostility between my mum and me, my siblings and me. He was an oasis. A calm port in the middle of a fierce storm.

Last night reminded me of then. It was the kind of night I haven't had since… well, since I had it with him. He is warmth and heat, and I am ice that is slowly melting. We didn't have sex. We have never done that. I'd decided that on my sixteenth birthday, he'd be the one and I remember it being such a big deal: the anticipation, every touch of his hands, fingers, lips, ran a buzz through me. He wasn't the one though.

It was Sean in the end, and by the time it happened, sex felt like something that hardly mattered at all. Who cares what your body is doing when you are just a ghost within it, after all?

We didn't even kiss last night, Danny and I, but my heart beat hard and fast, and my stomach fluttered in ways I'd forgotten it could. By the time the sun came up this morning, a pale white orb in a grey featureless sky, he had to go to work to start his day. I said goodbye to him at the door like a silly schoolgirl, and after he left, I stood with my back pressed against it, happy nerves coursing through me. I went to bed. Because we hadn't slept, and suddenly I was exhausted. Now my eyes are groggily opening as my phone buzzes.

I grab it, noting the time, one o'clock, and the fact I have five missed calls.

Sean. I come to, rubbing my face and am pulled back to reality with startling ferocity.

Something has happened. He's called five times. I'd messaged him to say I was going to get some sleep.

I call him back, my hand shaking as I hit on his details.

'Hayley.'

'Sean. Is everything okay?'

'No, it's bloody not.'

I scrunch my eyes shut. I'd gone to sleep with the curtains open. It's overcast outside and not overly bright. Still, it is more than I'm ready for. As is his cross tone.

'What's happened?' I ask, watery and thin. My whole self, jolted between saying goodbye to Danny at the door this morning and the churning anxiety of Sean's voice pummelling me from miles away now. I say, 'Babe.' Flinching at the word I've always hated. One that belongs to Mrs Marriott.

'Len bought me a copy of the paper. From over there.' Len gets an international news round-up every morning. Sean spits out the last two words and they hit me like bullets.

Over there.

Where, in the midst of impossible circumstances, I feel calmer than I have for years. If you'd have asked me six months ago, I'd have told you I was happy in New York. With my shiny Manhattan life and my shiny, loud husband. Even after Sophie, I'd have said I loved it there. Had a life, a home. A marriage I wasn't ready to give up on.

Now. Here. In this town I'd once hated, once blamed for all the wrongs, I feel like I am waking up from an odd dream. Back to myself. Back to a reality I'd denied for so long.

I say, 'I've been asleep.'

'Look at your WhatsApp.' It bleeps as I pull the phone away from my ear, transferring Sean to speaker, my sleep-crusted eyes focusing on the image as it downloads.

Two pictures. Me leaving the prison, stricken-faced. Me under Danny's arm getting into the car. Danny with hard eyes turned on the photographer.

The headline: *DaSilva survivor visits murderous father for the first time in fifteen years.*

The phone slips from my hand. Falling soft on the plain white covered duvet on the blank pine bed in this little house where I lost everything. My breath catches.

'Hayley. Hayley, for fuck's sake, speak.'

His voice, hard, brittle, angry. He has a right to it. Of course he does. His wife is a liar. She is not who she said she was. But is that true? If I hadn't known her, how could

229

I reasonably have expected to present the correct, proper, real version to him?

I close my eyes. Hayley Taylor. Hard heart, wide smile, tending bar in London. Not touching a drop while she worked but storing bottles to take home. Drinking quietly, secretly, in Nancy's flat, left alone as she went off again on her travels. Those were dark times, where I sometimes wondered if death would be preferable to the... nothingness.

Then there was Sean, big, bold. Gorgeous. Sweeping her up, me up. Hayley Taylor rearranging herself to fit him. Being the perfect girlfriend, then fiancée, then wife. The relief as we stepped onto that plane. The idea that I could pretend it never happened. And I had almost managed it.

'Hayley.'

'I'm sorry.' For what, specifically, I don't know.

'Your dad's a killer. For god's sake.'

'He's not,' I say. My mind full of Leonard surrounded by the smell of stale nicotine, under Carl's watchful eye. My dad. Tall, strong. My heart swells. Innocent.

'He's in prison. Says in the paper he killed your whole family?'

'They thought that. I thought that too.' Did I? Or did I think it was me? Full of my father's faulty genes. A girl who moved back to London and drank to sweet blackout every night. Who knew what I could have done? What I was capable of?

'So, what – he's innocent now? All of a sudden.' Hard words. Mean voice.

'Sean, please.'

'No. You've had years to accept this, this... shit. This isn't the kind of thing you fucking hide.'

I flinch.

'If you were damaged, I should have known before we got married. This changes everything.'

Damaged. Should have known.

'How do you think this makes me look?'

I hang up the phone. He rings again, and I send him to voicemail. Pulling myself out of bed, into the shower.

When I get out, I text Danny. *Did you get to work okay?*

Yes, I'm bloody knackered though.

Sorry, my fault.

Best night I've had for years.

My heart leaps. Dances. I think of a quip about him needing to get out more. I'm thinking like Mrs Marriott though. The cool girl. Fun. Breezy. Light and uncomplicated.

Not like me, Hayley DaSilva. Hurt, tender. Damaged.

I say, *Me too.* And then, *X.*

CHAPTER THIRTY-EIGHT

Everyone watches Jackie on the news. Seb thinks how different she looks on the television. Smooth, calm and unruffled. All the things she hadn't been when she was spitting her frustrations out at him and Lucy. It was fair enough. They were a team; it was part of the job to vent. He, and probably Lucy, had felt fully hair-dryered, but Jackie wasn't mad at them. She was mad and frustrated at the situation. They all were. The leak, it turns out, had come from one of the girls in the admin office, got chatting to a bloke in a bar who, unbeknownst to her, was a journalist. Seb had had Mike Townend dig into where the story had originated, promising him anything new before anyone else got it. She was reprimanded by Jackie, and Seb didn't envy her. Plus, it was done. It was out there now.

'As the papers have already reported we no longer consider Leonard DaSilva to be guilty of the murders of Anita, Matthew and Ethan DaSilva, nor of Ryan Dudley.' She pauses. There are audible murmurs in the room.

Ken, next to Seb, shakes his head. They all feel sorry for her. No officer in that room would want to be in her shoes right now.

'We are working tirelessly to see the release of Leonard DaSilva happen quickly and smoothly. Mr DaSilva himself is being fully co-operative and has admitted his part in it, which was, of course, a full confession, received by the investigative team working then and taken in good faith. I have my best officers working tirelessly to solve this case. Thank you.'

Voices are raised. Jackie points at a reporter in the crowd who is hand-waving. 'Has Leonard DaSilva retracted his statement?'

'Yes.'

'Why did he confess in the first place?'

'I can't give details about that at the moment, but I can tell you that Mr DaSilva is co-operating with us, is keen to see the real culprit caught and bears no malice or ill will towards the police force.'

'Even though you locked him up for something he didn't do?'

Jackie's smile is tight, her eyes pinched. 'As you yourself said – he confessed. I was not part of the original team, nor were any of my serving colleagues, but we can assure you that that confession was taken in good faith.'

'What possible reason could he have had?'

Jackie shakes her head. 'New questions, please?'

The journalist can be heard mumbling something Seb assumes is less than appreciative. Jackie doesn't even blink.

'When will Leonard be released?'

'As soon as possible. We are working our way through masses of red tape.'

'What will happen to the officers who worked the original investigation?'

'Sadly, Mackenzie Arnold, who was the lead officer on the original case, is no longer with us, and as I have said, whilst we will, of course, be looking over the way everything was handled then, we had a confession made and received in good faith.'

'Would you have done anything differently?'

Jackie smiles her rage smile, and Seb finds himself flinching slightly at least ten miles away from her in the incident room. 'Not being able to time travel, I can't really answer that.' She's gathering up her notes. 'Thank you.' And leaving to the flash of bulbs and the high frenetic buzz of questions still being fired.

Seb turns to the team. Ken shakes his head. 'Bloody Mac, eh?' And Seb feels that relief again. Ken adds, 'We'll get everything down, guv.' He can't seem to bring himself to call him Seb. 'If anyone linked to this case farts and one of you mentions it, it will be written up, filed appropriately and easy to find.'

'Did you know Nigel, Ken? Nigel Baker?'

'Didn't know him well but always got the vibe that he was a corner cutter.'

'Oh?'

'Mac didn't run things like Jackie does. He was lax, and that's the kind of force he headed. No room for people like him but they used to be ten a penny.'

'Thanks, Ken.'

The older man smiles easily at him. 'No probs. I appreciate you might have got bored working the domestics and the bar brawls but what a case to take your first lead.' He laughs, but it's in good nature, Seb thinks, so he grins back.

Lucy says, 'Poor Jackie.'

Ken pats her shoulder. 'She'll be fine, love. Jackie might seem like she's always on the verge of a nervous breakdown, but she's made of steel, that one, you mark my words.'

–

It's almost lunchtime when one of the DCs comes back, half running into the incident room, cheeks red from the cold he'd been out in and excitement shining in his eyes. He scans the room and heads for Lucy. 'Lucy?'

She looks up from Diane Smart's original statement. 'Yes, Fin, isn't it?'

He nods.

'What is it?'

He's grinning. 'Okay, this from Hazel Munroe who was at the party that night, with Douglas Beattie, who she confirms lives with his mum on Lovelace. I think we knew that?'

'We did, and Seb and I will be going to see him.'

'Right. She also told me that Cat and Gabe were gone.'

'Gone?'

He nods. 'From the party, that night.'

Lucy frowns. 'For how long?'

'She's not sure but thinks after Hayley and Danny went and then back by the time the sun came up which I estimate to be about four fifty a.m. that time of year.'

'And she was watching that closely?'

'She had a crush on Gabe, she said, didn't like Cat much.'

Lucy nods. That makes some kind of sense. 'Good work, Fin.'

He beams. 'Thanks. In fairness, we've questioned about thirty people between us. We just lucked out finding one who remembered anything.'

'And what did she know about Douglas?'

'That he sold weed, a few pills and grams here and there. Nothing big time.'

'Good work, though it certainly shows yet another hole in this absolutely bungled investigation. Write it up with your name, give it to Harry and Ken, yeah?'

CHAPTER THIRTY-NINE

Seb heads back to his; he has blocked out an hour and a half for lunch to go home and check on Tilly.

As he gets in, Val gives him a quick hug and whispers, 'She's in the living room,' before getting out of the way.

He looks in at his daughter. She is wrapped in the awful fake-fur blanket she'd wanted for Christmas. It makes her look like the top of a strawberry ice cream cone with a head instead of a cherry on top. It also makes her look impossibly young. For a moment he just stands in the doorway looking at her, unsure whether he's angry – she has been suspended from school – or just very sorry. He's both, and sad too. She deserves the best of everything, and if it was up to him, that's what she'd have. But he can't control Charlie. Can't shape her into something she's not. Doesn't – he realised after a few soul-destroying years of trying – even want to.

'I guess I'm grounded.' She hasn't turned around, but they are familiar to each other. She'd have heard the door, his footsteps, sensed her father behind her.

He heads in. Sits in the armchair across from her. She looks at him from wide, damp eyes. 'I mean, you can't really go out during suspension.'

She half smiles, he smiles back, holds her gaze. He's not angry, actually. Any glimmer of it sinks away now as he looks at her. What a week it's been for them both.

He clears his throat, 'I'm… I'm sorry, Tills.'

'Really?'

He nods. 'I should have…' Should have what? So many things. 'You shouldn't have had to find out, like that.'

She looks out the window, Seb follows her gaze. There is a mother overseeing a toddler, his fat, short legs propelling a scooter, and a little girl, slightly older but not much, on a bike with stabilisers. It makes him think of years gone by and maybe her too because she tells him, 'You're a good dad.' And fear he didn't even know he'd been holding seems to release, just a little.

'You should have had a good mum too.'

She shrugs, that too grown-up half a smile on her face. 'One out of two isn't so bad, and I've got Nan.'

'She said she'd talked to you?'

Tilly nods. 'She said my granddad wasn't a nice man?'

Charlie had refused to see her father buried, refused to grieve. She'd been fourteen and full of a festering hate. Seb hadn't known her then. Then he'd been two towns over. But she'd told Seb about his death full of puffed-up bravado, and he'd seen the scared kid she must have been, still was even then by the time they met. It was something she'd not been able to get over. Part of the reason, he supposes, that she is where she is now.

'He wasn't, no. Your mother…' He swallows. 'Charlie didn't have it easy.'

'Neither did you.'

He shrugs. 'Me and my adopted parents didn't get on, and that wasn't great, but I had other things: a good education, a clean, safe house to come back to, physically at least.'

Her eyes widen. 'He was that bad?'

Seb nods, can picture Charlie flinching when he moved too quickly near her. Feels the familiar squeeze of pain clench his heart. Is momentarily amazed that after everything, he has soft feelings towards her. Still, the first thing he thinks when she springs to his mind is that he has to protect her. But you can't protect someone so intent on destroying themselves.

'Did she not love me?' Tilly's voice is so small the clench gets worse, an awful feeling running from his heart up and down the length of him.

'She loved you so much. The day you were born is the only time I saw her really, truly happy.' His voice is thin and cracked; his nose stings with tears rising to his eyes. He thought he'd had everything that day, won the lottery of life. Cut off from his family, separated from everything he knew, but he had her, and they had Tilly.

'Then why isn't she here?' His daughter's tears are painful enough to feel like his own.

'She's not well. I didn't lie about that.' His voice is barely a whisper. Not enough words to tell her, to explain something he doesn't fully understand himself. So many hard, twisted feelings in a big, wrecked heap. Tilly now looking at him, desperate for answers he doesn't have. He says, 'Whilst that's an imperfect answer, and I wish I had a better one, it's all I have.'

She's crying now, really crying. He goes over and holds her, the movement so natural, so well worn, he doesn't even think about it. They adjust to the familiar pattern of each other. Her pressed into the crook of his arm, his chin resting on her hair, soft and smelling of her Body Shop banana shampoo. He wills himself to be strong enough, tough enough, to withstand all of her pain, to remove as much as he can and at least be willing to bear witness to the rest, even as it cuts him up, because that's his job. He holds back his own tears. Finally, she pulls away, reaching for a tissue, wiping her face.

He says, 'Anger, Tilly, won't take you anywhere good.'

She nods. 'I know. I felt bad about the fight. It's not me.'

He smiles. 'It's not, no.'

'I have to apologise in the head's office.' Her face screwed up now.

'Okay.'

She sighs. 'She shouldn't have said it though, like that.' *Junkie bitch.* Words he himself flung at Charlie more than once. Awful words that mean awful things. Not everything; he can never tell Tilly everything.

'No. But two wrongs don't make a right.'

'I know.' She sighs. 'I know.' A pause, long but not unpleasant, some of the tension he's felt for the past twenty-four hours softens, then she asks, 'Do you know where she is now?'

The truth is a slippery thing. How much is too much? Especially now where there are so many shades of grey. But Tilly is looking at him like he has all the answers, the way she always did when she was learning to ride her bike and trusted him to keep her safe, her first day at school, getting left out at lunchtimes. It's been a while since she's looked at him like this. 'Last time I knew where she was, it was Catford, South London.' He still checks on her; he can't help it. He doesn't tell Tilly that her name came up on the system in conjunction with a soliciting charge. That her known abode was a vile crack den where there had been two fires and a multitude of violent altercations. That when he tries to picture Charlie there, lost, small and alone, he feels like his heart may break all over again.

His daughter nods. 'Not far then.'

He closes his eyes. Not far and yet she hasn't come here, hasn't visited. He says again, 'She's not well.'

Tilly nods, her lower lip sticking out, stubborn. He can almost see her hardening herself. The Charlie effect, you had to get tough, or she'd break you. He should know.

He takes Tilly's hand, squeezes it. 'Are we okay?'

She nods. 'Yes.'

'We can talk more… about her.' Heart hammering in his chest, bile bubbling in his gut. Talking about Charlie, like pouring vinegar in an open wound. The last thing he wants to do. But he'll do it for Tilly. He'll pick at old stitches and deal with it the best he can.

CHAPTER FORTY

I suppose I should feel something. Distraught, terrified, heartbroken. I don't though, not where Sean is concerned. Now I am here – my dad innocent, Danny exactly who I thought he'd grow up to be all those years ago, I find that I feel nothing but a sort of emptiness towards the man I'd married. When we were dating, I found the whole thing, him, intoxicating. The sex – new to me. The money. Dinners at lavish restaurants, beautiful hotel suites with extortionately priced lingerie laid out on four-poster beds alongside roses, chocolates, love notes.

He'll divorce me if I don't do it first, I suspect, and I wonder if he'll replace me with Sophie. I check my phone. No missed calls or text messages from him. He didn't ask yesterday how I was, which, despite my dishonesty, surely most husbands would. He didn't care. That was the truth. I am a shiny trinket and nothing more. He's used me as I suppose I've used him.

I did it under the belief that love hurt. Love killed. Look where it got my mother after all.

But Leonard is innocent. This crime isn't on him, and with that knowledge, maybe I am changing. Softening at the edges.

My doorbell rings, and I frown. I glance at myself in the mirror. I'm in jogging bottoms and a vest. I pick up the cashmere jumper I wore last night to meet Danny, pulling it on as I go.

I am hoping for him, I realise, even though I know he already said he'd be at work all day.

Instead, I get Cat. 'Oh, hi.'

'Hi.' She pulls off her shades. Her eyes look tired. Red-rimmed. The baby, perhaps. I've heard they never sleep. Thought about that too as Sean has pushed and pushed for years for us to have one of our own. He wouldn't be getting up. He'd likely be willing to employ staff, but is that what I want? So many things I hadn't considered at eighteen when I sleepwalked into our marriage. 'It's freezing. Can I come in?' Her voice is hard, clipped. She always sounded this way though; it was rarely an indicator of her mood.

'Sorry, yes, of course.' I swing the door open. 'Coffee?'

'Sure.'

She walks around the small but open-plan space, eyes searching every detail. I boil the kettle, fill the cafetiere and ask her, 'Milk, sugar?'

She shakes her head.

I bring the drinks to the low table and gesture for her to sit on the armchair. I take the L-shaped sofa in the spot I already think of as mine.

'It looks different in here.'

I nod. 'I actually had very little to do with it. I left everything to a management agency.'

'Fancy.'

I shrug. Not filling the space with the truth, which isn't fancy at all. I wasn't able to come back here. I owned the place outright as my mother had before me and for the first two and a half years whilst I camped out at Nancy's and worked various menial jobs, I hadn't been able to force myself to visit even the town. I'd wake in the night with ridiculous thoughts pounding around my mind: had I left the water on? A cooker? Were the bloodstained carpets clean yet? And the worst and most harrowing thought of all: had Ethan come back?

I'd visited only once, just before Sean and I left for America. It was then that I met with a decorator. I'd arrived early, having felt as though I might jump out of my skin at my own shadow the entire way. I'd opened the door, looked in and found I couldn't go any further. The decorating firm had turned up, and I'd remained standing in the small front garden. They didn't know the full story, I imagine, and by then the carpet in the living room had been ripped out, taken away. No one had been in the place for almost three years. The man and woman who'd come along to assess everything had to have the 'direction' about my requirements and money stuff agreed on the doorstep. Money was in fact no object. When Sean had found out I owned a house that wasn't in great condition, he shoved a platinum card into my hand and told me to sort it. So the decorators got free rein, the only requirement, 'minimalist' – ready for the rental market. When they finished, they dropped keys to a local estate agent who, despite what I've told Sean lately, I've still never met.

Right now, viewings are on hold, and I am starting to think perhaps there will be no more as it is looking increasingly like I'll need somewhere to live.

'Is it weird?'

'Being in the house?'

She nods, blows on her coffee, the thin skin under her eyes twitches. She is paler than I am. Sean and I had a break in Mexico not long ago. He is a fan of winter sun, and

I myself dislike the grey and the cold so don't complain about such trips.

'I hadn't stepped over the threshold since… you know.'

'Oh.'

I nod. 'Decorators have been in, letting agents and I've had five sets of tenants come and go, replaced the sofa recently. It doesn't feel the same, as it did.'

'I suppose not.'

'The estate wasn't here then either, was it? It's so much busier.'

'It is.'

'Plus, Gabe is no longer next door.'

She smiles at that, but it's faint. 'You two used to sit out there and get stoned.'

I laugh. 'We did, yes. My poor mum.' I can almost picture her concerned little face at the window. Watching out in her nightie as I stumbled in via the back door, eyes swollen, blood turned to sludge and the giggles threatening to escape. Her hissing, 'Smoking is bad for you.' Me pointing at her Marlboro Lights and her telling me to go to bed. It hadn't occurred to her, I don't think, that I would have been smoking dope, though she found out later when Matt blabbed. So normal, teenagers arguing with parents. So mundane really, and as if it never happened. Not to me anyway. That whole summer has a surreal vibe to it.

'I hated it.'

'I'm sorry?' Though I knew at the time. Know now what she is getting at.

'You and him.'

I sigh. 'There was no me and him.'

'We were happy.'

'You and Gabe?'

245

'All three of us. Danny, Gabe, me.'

'What, until I came along and ruined it all for you?'

'I was having a difficult time then. My parents had some money trouble.'

'I'm sorry. I didn't know.'

'No one did. Not everyone has to wear their problems so brazenly, Hayley.'

She drinks her coffee. Doesn't say anything else. I flop back on the sofa, her words stinging me. Was I brazen about my parents' split? I didn't think so, but I was fifteen and not made of stone. I am exhausted, not in the mood for this petty shit. I murmur, 'It's not like things turned out well for me, is it, and you got to marry him.'

'I got to marry Gabe.'

I frown. 'You can't mean...'

She puts the cup down. 'I'm meant to be at work.'

'Oh.'

'Or I thought I was.' She shrugs. 'I checked in and it seems I got my days off confused. I'm actually off today, on a late tomorrow.'

'Right.'

'I should go.' She stands, picking up her handbag. I follow her to the door, and she turns to face me as it opens, the cold whistling in behind her, and I shiver slightly. 'When are you leaving?'

'I don't know.' I don't add that I might not leave at all. The way she is looking at me, from eyes filled with hatred. Real molten dislike. I take a step forward, making to close the door, and her hand jumps out, propping it open. 'You have a habit of bringing problems with you, Hayley.'

I shut the door. Press myself to it. Imagine her pressed on the other side. I think of her back then. Beautiful, sulky, difficult. Danny *had* gone out with her a few times.

When I asked him what happened he said 'nothing'. She just wasn't for him. He called her 'high maintenance'. I suspect she is. I feel kind of sorry for Gabe. I imagine he never hears the end of it about his job.

My phone rings – an unknown number.

'Hello.'

'Hayley, it's Owen Talis.' Sean's solicitor.

'Oh?'

'I'm calling to inform you that your husband is filing for divorce.' The words come out on a sigh. His job, for which he'll be being paid handsomely, but this is still a shitty phone call to have to make. He clears his throat. 'Papers should be with you later today via courier.'

'Right.'

A pause.

'Thanks then, Owen.' He's saying something else, but I cut him off. I find I'm laughing as I hang up and once I start I can't stop. At some point the laughter turns to tears and they come in waves. My heart aching for the girl who'd married him, stupid and full of hope. For how disposable he considered me. That our almost eleven-year marriage isn't even worth a face-to-face meeting before dissolution.

CHAPTER FORTY-ONE

How Gabriel looks more than anything when Seb and Lucy arrive is nervous. He stands too quickly as they head in, door opened by the eyelashy receptionist, and as he does so, he knocks papers flying everywhere. He bends to start picking them up, so does Lucy and they almost bang heads.

She laughs, good-natured, and hands him the things she's managed to collect. He takes them from her with a murmured, 'Thanks.'

Then he stands there dumb and still. Eventually, Seb clears his throat. 'Shall we take a seat?'

'Sorry, yes. Yes, of course.' He gestures opposite, and they settle down. He grins at them. 'How can I help?'

'We'd like you to walk us through the night of the party again. Start to finish.'

Laughter now, slightly too high, feigning annoyance. 'I've done that, haven't I?'

Seb smiles.

Gabe adds, 'I'm sure my wife has as well.'

'From the beginning.'

He blunders his way through it. More pauses this time, ums and ahs. He is struggling for words. A thin film of sweat breaks out on his forehead.

When he is finished, Seb doesn't speak, nor does Lucy. Gabe laughs his on-edge laugh. They remain straight-faced, still not speaking.

Eventually, Gabe asks, 'Everything all right?' Voice small and unhappy.

'No. Not really.'

'Oh?'

'Why are you lying?'

'I… uh… What do you mean?'

'We have it on good information, Gabriel, that you weren't at the party the entire night. In fact, we heard you and Cat went missing, for almost as long as Hayley.'

He swallows. Seb can see his Adam's apple bobbing up and down. He reaches for a glass of water sitting on his desk, takes a sip. Rubs a hand across his face. 'Christ.'

Still they don't say anything. The quiet fizzes up and around them all. Nothing can be heard bar the faint hum of an air humidifier and Gabe's shallow breath.

'What happened, Gabe?'

'God. The thing is about Cat, my wife. She's the jealous type, you know?'

'Did she have reason to be?'

'Then?'

Obviously, Seb thinks, but just nods.

Gabe sighs. Glum. 'Not of me exactly. Hayley wouldn't have looked twice, but it wasn't me Cat wanted.' Bitterness makes those words sharp and hard-edged. He says 'wanted' like he's ridding his mouth of venom. Still the officers don't speak. Gabe sweats, fidgets.

Finally, Seb says, 'Danny?'

Gabe nods.

'And now?'

He laughs a bark like a seal coming up out of the water for glorious air. 'I'd say until recently she'd never regretted her choice, which is how I think she saw it.'

'You didn't see it that way?'

He shakes his head. 'Danny never wanted her. Only went out with her because she kept asking. Thought it would ruin their friendship, ours, if he didn't at least take her to the cinema once.'

'And that's what he did?'

He nods.

'Then you, what, changed her mind?'

'Then there was Hayley.'

'I imagine she was a real looker even then.'

Gabe nods. 'I mean, so is Cat and she was then, but Hayley, she's something else too.'

'Oh yeah?'

'When we met her, she was cross. At her parents, I guess. It made her sort of brittle, and she drank too much. That night at the party her being out of it wasn't an isolated incident.'

'She was off the rails?'

He shrugs. 'A bit. But underneath it you could tell she wasn't like that.'

'Like what?'

'I don't know, bad, for want of a better word, though that's too simplistic.'

'You're saying she's a nice person? She was a nice person then?'

He nods. 'Exactly.'

'And Cat wasn't?'

'Ha. Cat can be great. She's charming and all. And when it comes to Dylan, well, as a mother, she's special, giving. There's nothing she wouldn't do for that boy.'

'And you?'

'We were cool, until I lost my job.'

'And then?'

He looks at them evenly now, shoulders straightening, 'I remembered she could be spiteful.'

'She was spiteful fifteen years ago?'

'Look, until Hayley, me, her, Danny, Ryan, we'd been a pack of four, you know? One cute girl, three guys. Suddenly there's this super-hot chick, and she's from London. She's all angry and out of sorts and, just, cool in a way Cat never could be to us. We'd known her since we were toddlers, for god's sake.'

'Still, you married her.'

Sharp eyes narrow at Seb. 'I love my wife. I was half in love with her then, but I was also a fairly average teenage boy.' He shrugs.

'So Cat starts a thing with you?'

'Right, and she's the first girl I'd ever had a crush on, the first girl I kissed, touched, you know. I was fairly loved-up from the word go.'

'But she was still jealous of Hayley?'

'She was still jealous. We lived next door to each other and back then we all smoked dope, Hayley and I would smoke at the back of our gardens. That annoyed Cat.'

'Understandable,' Lucy murmurs.

Gabe nods. 'Probably was, and I didn't help by not getting that at all. But then, I got to be jealous of the way she looked at Danny all the time, only that wasn't allowed because I was "imagining it".' He makes quotation marks in the air. His words are full of pent-up frustration, and Seb wonders how much Gabe dislikes Cat and whether it is just resentment or something darker. He'd said she was a good mother, but he hadn't said she was a good wife, or a good girlfriend back then, and the picture he's painting isn't overly flattering.

'So that night?'

'Hayley argued with Matt. Poor sod was heartbroken. They were close. Like real close, being twins and all. I know she adored him and Ethan. She told me often enough. She loved her parents too, I reckon, though she was hurting over their split. You could see that a mile off.'

'So she argues with Matt?'

'Right.'

'What time?'

'Eleven.'

'You're sure?'

He nods. 'I had this shitty Casio watch, I checked.'

Seb thinks — finally, someone that night with a watch. 'So then what?'

'She storms off.'

'And Matt wants to go after her?'

Gabe nods. 'Right.'

'And you offered.'

A pause, a slight flush on his cheeks. Lucy says, 'Understandable, she was your friend.'

He looks at her, clearly relieved. 'Yes. But Cat got the hump.'

Lucy nods again, sympathetically 'So…?' she asks.

'So Danny goes. Which is probably what she'd have wanted anyway.'

Seb says, 'And then?'

'Danny came back in the morning. Early hours, like I said.'

'And where were you?'

'Wh… what?'

'Where were you? After Hayley went, then Danny went after her. Then Cat disappeared too.'

He pales visibly. 'Who said that?'

'Does it matter?'

He looks away. In the little Portakabin, there is a window to the outside. There's nothing happening there, but there are vans parked, and Seb has seen at least one man walk to one, take tools out, move on.

Gabe says, 'We didn't do anything wrong.'

'You didn't mention you left the party though either.'

His eyes turn back to them and seem almost to be pleading.

Lucy leans across. 'Gabe. Can I call you Gabe?' Her voice is treacle, a cold compress on a painful sprain. He nods. 'The best thing you can do, honestly, is tell us what happened. Okay?'

'Cat will go mad.'

'I'm sure she'll understand.'

He snorts. Lucy says, 'The truth will be easier all round.'

He sighs. 'Cat spiked her.'

Seb frowns. 'Hayley?'

'Yes.'

'What did Cat spike her with?'

He flinches. 'An E.'

Seb frowns. 'So she was fall-down drunk and Cat slipped her an E?'

'Yes.'

'Giving someone drugs without their knowledge is incredibly dangerous.'

Gabe groans. 'I know. If I'd have known what she was planning to do, I'd have stopped her.'

'When did you find out?'

'After Hayley went off. I tried to go after her. Cat and I, we argued about it. I said she looked worse for wear. By this point she and Matt had rowed and she really was off her head. Huge pupils, could hardly stand. She was... wild. Out of control. Cat told me what she'd done, I was shocked, but she made it sound... I don't know, like an innocent prank gone wrong. She was upset herself. I said to Cat we had to tell her, tell Danny at least so they knew what they were dealing with.'

'And then?'

He turns crimson.

'Mr Smart.' Seb's voice is stern.

'We, ah, started to go, walked off and she, Cat, we...' He looks down at his hands. 'Got distracted.'

Seb blinks. 'You knew Hayley had been spiked, had run off and you, what, stopped to have a quick shag?'

His eyes are damp. 'God, it was my first time. I was sixteen.'

Seb shakes his head.

'Then what?' Lucy says, soft, gentle.

'I... I fell asleep.'

'Where?'

'In the woods where we... you know.'

'When you woke up?'

'Cat was gone, I realised I had the beginnings of a hangover, and at first I couldn't get my bearings, work out where I was.'

'But you did?'

He nods. 'I did, yes.'

'And where were you?'

'Sorry.' He rubs a hand across his face. 'This isn't easy.'

Seb doesn't say anything. Doesn't point out that 'easy' would have been telling the truth at the time.

'I was near home, it turned out.'

'And Cat?'

'Well, that's the thing, when I couldn't see her, I figured she'd have gone back, to the party. I was going to go back, catch up with her, but by then I felt really shitty so I figured I'd nip home, get a glass of water, maybe a can of Coke or something, then find her.'

'Right, so you weren't worried?'

He frowns. 'Why would I have been worried?'

'You'd just had sex with your girlfriend, for the first time, according to you, and you wake up and she's gone.'

'Oh, I see. No. Cat does that, always has.'

'What specifically?'

'Wanders off, leaves me places.' It's said without pity, just stating a fact, and Seb thinks these two have an odd relationship, though who the hell is he to judge? He spent enough time chasing after Charlie, always hoping for a different result, never getting it.

'So you went home?'

'Well, I almost got there. I saw Cat.'

'Where?'

'Literally by our houses. Mine and Hayley's.'

'What time?'

'Three. My head was pounding.'

'How long had you been asleep?'

'I reckon about three hours.'

Three was an hour before Hayley got back to her house. She'd kissed Danny at the edge of the clearing where their houses were, gone in and had her life irrevocably ruined. At three the DaSilvas were already dead. But not by much. They would likely have been killed between the time Gabe fell asleep and when he woke up. If that was what he'd actually been doing.

'What was Cat doing?'

'She'd nipped back to mine, to get a change of clothes.'

Seb's frown deepens. 'She kept clothes at your place?'

'Yes, she was there a lot. My mum and dad would let her sleep in the spare room; she lived over the other side of town.' Adding, 'Her mum and dad knew. They were fine about it.' As though that is the issue here.

'And how did she seem?' Seb asks through clenched teeth.

'Irritated.'

'Why?'

'I don't know, She could be that way.'

'Even when you'd just been close.'

He shrugs. 'Women.' Then to Lucy, 'Sorry.'

'So what you're saying is that at some point, you're not sure when, but around the time the DaSilvas were being bludgeoned to death, your girlfriend nipped back to your house, next door to the crime scene, and changed her clothes.'

He nods and then, 'Oh, hang on a minute, I see what you're getting at, but surely you don't think…' His face is pale, the blood visibly draining from it now as he looks at them, stricken.

But Seb is standing, gesturing for Lucy to do the same. 'Where is your wife now, Mr Smart?'

'At work.' His voice is barely a whisper.

CHAPTER FORTY-TWO

Seb and Lucy arrive at the pub where Cat works. She's nowhere to be found. Seb was concerned that Gabe had called ahead and she'd done a runner, but that wasn't the case. Her work tells him there has been a mix-up with her shifts. Seb calls Gabe. He tells him with a sigh the same thing Cat's manager has just told him.

'She said she was shopping,' Gabe replies. 'I'll ask her to get in contact as soon as she's home.'

'Right.' He can't bring himself to say thank you. What Gabe should do is make his wife contact him now. There are pressing questions which need answering.

He and Lucy get back in the car. Lucy's phone rings. 'Hey.' He listens to her half of the conversation. She hangs up. 'Fin again.'

'Oh yeah?'

'Yep, says a few people have mentioned that Nathan Smart was the main supplier in the area.'

Seb lets out a low whistle.

Lucy nods. 'Right.'

'Whilst we're waiting for Cat to show her face, let's go give Mr Beattie a visit.'

—

As estates go, the Lovelace isn't so bad. The flats and houses at least are spacious and, whilst they have that industrial look of all social housing from the outside, Seb knows that there are far worse estates. This is where Charlie lived when he met her, living with a cousin after Val had left to move up north and Charlie had refused to go with her. He doesn't like the place, has too many sullied memories of it. Just being here he can almost picture Charlie grinning at him, waving from the balcony. Beautiful then.

Now there are gaggles of youths with hoods up loitering pointlessly around the shop. Two small boys are kicking a football at a *No ball games* sign, and the shops themselves – a newsagent, off-licence and tiny post office – have shutters on their fronts.

Douglas Beattie, the possible dealer from the party fifteen years ago, lives on the top floor of a nice block that Seb knows is mostly privately owned now. A lot of the people who live here are students. Landlords bought a load of flats as buy-to-lets when the council started selling off homes. It changed the landscape around here, but the core demographic has remained the same, and there are still pockets on this estate and the Old Oxford estate on the other side of town where you wouldn't want to walk alone after dark.

They knock on the door and a short, round woman with a pleasant face answers. 'Is Douglas Beattie here?'

She frowns. 'He's just in from work.'

'Can we speak to him?'

'You police?'

Seb nods, fishing his ID from his pocket as Lucy does the same.

The woman sighs. 'He's not been in trouble for years. He's a decorator.' As if that explains not being in trouble.

Seb smiles. 'Just a quick word, honest.'

'Wait here.'

The door is pushed in their faces. It's opened a moment later by a tall man who must be in his thirties if he's Doug Beattie, which is how he introduces himself, but he has an almost angelic face. All chubby cheeks surrounded by golden hair. He grins at them. 'Scared my poor ma half to death, come in, come in.'

They follow him through. Inside, the place is nice. Decorated well, homely.

Douglas sees them looking around and says, 'I bought it for her last year, figured we should do it up. Did it myself. Nice, isn't it?'

Lucy nods. 'It is, yeah.'

Seb asks, 'You're a decorator?'

He nods. 'Yup. Though I'm branching out into renovation, you know, buying dumps, doing them up, selling them on.'

'But you're still living with your mum?'

He laughs. 'Yeah, I know.' With a self-deprecating eye-roll. 'It was always just me and her. I will move out, but it makes sense for me to be here while I set up the business, and she likes having me around.'

Doug's mum pokes her head around the living room. 'Tea or anything?'

'We're good thanks, Mrs Beattie.'

'Miss, thank you very much.'

Doug says, 'My dad was a bit of a wanker, and they were never married.'

Lucy suppresses a grin, looking down at her notebook instead.

'You're not here for my life story though, are you?'

'No. You don't seem very worried.'

He grins. 'I've not done anything wrong.'

'Not lately.'

He leans his head in agreement. 'Very true, not lately, and I suspect you'll know I served a few years for dealing in my younger days.'

'We do know that.'

'That why you're here?'

'Hayley DaSilva?'

His face falls. 'That poor kid, eh? Jesus.'

'You remember her?'

He nods. 'Of course, yeah. Awful thing. I was at that party. Saw her, off her head she was.'

'Her friend, Cat Carter, spiked her, apparently.'

His eyes widen. 'What a cow! She'd been hassling me that night for a pill.'

'You sold her one, did you?'

He shakes his head. 'No way! She was fifteen for fuck's sake. We had a rule about under-sixteens. It was a kid I had on my payroll' – he looks at them evenly – 'whose details I won't be sharing, before you bother asking.'

Seb says, 'You were above selling to minors?'

'I was, as it happens, yeah, and the lad who broke the rule didn't work for me again.'

'Where is he now?'

Doug shrugs. 'I don't move in those circles any more.'

'Fair enough.' Seb believes him. Can see he's doing all right, but he's not rolling in it. This place is steady-job money, not fat-bundles-of-drug-cash-held-with-rubber-bands-and-passed-hand-to-hand money. 'Who supplied you?'

He frowns. 'You kidding?'

'You don't want to tell us?'

He shakes his head. 'You surely already know?'

'Why would we?'

He shrugs. 'Everyone did back then, you lot included.'

'Enlighten me.'

'Nathan Smart, mate, served the whole area far and wide. Was mates with at least one of you though.'

'Nigel Baker?'

'Yeah, that's it, slimy fucker thought he was the bee's knees. If he hadn't been Old Bill, I would have taken him down a peg or two myself, and the boss.'

Seb frowns, looks at Lucy. 'Mackenzie Arnold?'

'Right. They used to drink together at the Old Crow.'

'You're kidding?'

Doug laughs. 'I kid you not. It was part of the appeal of getting supply from him, Nate, you were likely to be left alone.'

'How come you got out of all that?'

He shrugs. 'Went to prison. Nearly broke my mum's heart, bless her. She had no idea.'

'Did Nathan approach you when you got out?'

He shakes his head. 'God, no. Far as I know he pulled the plug on all of that after the DaSilva girl's family got mullered.' Which is what Diane had said, what Nigel had hinted at.

Seb stands, Lucy follows suit, and he stretches his hand out to Doug. 'Thanks so much for your time.'

He shrugs. 'Sorry I couldn't help more. She okay? The kid?'

'Grown woman now.'

'You know what I mean.'

'She will be.'

He nods. 'Read you got the wrong fella.'

'We did, yeah.'

He shakes his head. 'Hope you sort it out.'

Seb says, 'Me too.'

Seb drops Lucy home, and his brain mulls everything over. Mackenzie Arnold and Nigel Baker had drunk together at the Old Crow. Nigel was in it up to his neck. Whichever way Seb looked at it, he was a bad cop. The kind of idiot who gave all police a bad name. No wonder he wanted a lawyer. No wonder he wanted all of this left behind him. He'd had too much money back then. Been half in love with the wife of a known drug dealer, and worse still, according to Douglas Beattie, that drug dealer had the protection of the local force. The whole thing stank. Rotten and fetid. But was it connected to these murders and, still, the main question that Seb keeps circling back to, why was Ethan so far away? Why not kill the boy and leave him with the other bodies? Back then there was nothing for miles around there. A few derelict cottages, from what he could work out, that had since been demolished. Taking Ethan somewhere else was the odd part of this case. Certainly, he wouldn't be here now looking into all of this if Ethan had been accounted for back then. In a strange way, this anomaly in the crime has made reopening the case possible. If Ethan had been killed at the same time, Seb and his team wouldn't be looking into this now. Leonard would be in prison until he died, and Hayley would have always wondered about her own involvement.

CHAPTER FORTY-THREE

After Cat left, I'd not done much of anything. My heart was thumping. My husband wanted to divorce me; my frenemy from yesteryear still hated my guts and seemed fairly intent on causing me at least mild pain with her bitchy comments, if not real problems. Though, really, what could she do?

I flicked through the TV channels, drank too much coffee. Eventually, I wrapped up warm, walked to the shops and bought a few groceries like a normal person. I like it here, I realise. I have started, with everything that has begun to unfold, to toy with the possibility of this being home. Even in the winter it is pretty. The walk from the little house takes me down a main road, and then I can slip off its track and wander to town along the river. The grass is sharp and jagged with frost and the whole scene is like a Christmas card.

I try and imagine flying back to the States, getting geared up for the endless, manic spinning wheel of entertaining and events that take up much of our time in December. So many functions. Will Sean do them alone, I wonder? Surely he can't walk in with Sophie just yet. In fact, I'm not sure he'll really go through with the divorce when it comes down to it. I feel like he's making a point rather than being serious, and, if I had to predict it, he'll be waiting for me to reach out, try and smooth things over. Promise to be better, do better. He won't want a divorce because that will look like failure. Right now he's humiliated. That's because of me, which I have to acknowledge. I've played my part in our crappy marriage just as he has his. The lawyer's call was an attempt to wound, the first strike in a wagered game of fisticuffs, a low blow for sure and one I hardly felt, which tells me all I need to know.

I get back to the cottage at three and my phone beeps. Sean. *I'm willing to listen if you want to talk.*

I text back: *Not really a lot to say.*

If you want to play it that way. But I'm not playing anything. For the first time in the entirety of our relationship, I'm being real. Honest.

I type, *I think divorce is the right option for us.*

I imagine him there. My never ruffled, always charmingly smiling husband will be puce-faced and venomous by now. He doesn't have an explosive temper, it simmers hot and long, and I can almost see any love he had for me curdling before my very eyes.

I write, *No hard feelings*. And then, *Maybe Sophie will be less damaged?* before I can resist.

You won't get anything you didn't come in with. The fact he doesn't even acknowledge the affair, or that I know about it solidifies what I already knew in my heart of hearts. I don't love my husband, and he doesn't seem even vaguely worried about me. Maybe I am nothing more than a thing. A replaceable object.

I type, *No problem*. I won't fight him for it either. I have my house and I'll find a job. My dad will be out soon; a matter of weeks, they think, if the case is solved and Locke seems fairly confident. Danny is here, and I realise that this is the first time since my family was snatched from me that I feel a glimmer of anything resembling hope. I tried to be what Sean wanted, needed, but I'm not her. I'm also not the same girl who went out to that party that night and came back to find everything smashed to pieces – but she isn't entirely gone. I muffled her for a while, the day I left here and arrived at Nancy's. It is almost as if I can picture old me still there, in Thamespark, having never left. London Hayley, Hayley Taylor, was like a holding email but in the form of a human body. I find as I'm moving round the kitchen putting away groceries that I'm singing along to the radio. The first time I've heard my voice in many years. I sing until the end of the song. Maybe I'll work in music. When I was a kid, I wanted to write musicals. Maybe I could do that.

It won't all be lightness and sweet, of course. There is a murderer to catch, and Cat Carter clearly hates me. We had a clingy, fraught friendship back then. I bent to her will, tried to mind her feelings, but she never offered the same in return. I hope it doesn't cause problems for Gabe or Danny, for that matter. I glance at the clock; he'll be home from work in an hour.

–

He picks up on the first ring, and I laugh. 'What, were you holding the phone?'

'I was literally just messaging you.'

'Oh yeah?'

'Yeah, to see if I could take you out for dinner again?'

'Why don't you come here? We'll get takeout.'

'Okay, even better. I'll see you in half an hour.'

By the time he arrives, I've changed my clothes twice. I'd spent the day in jeans, a T-shirt and a jumper and I changed that for a dress. Then, realising that was a bit over the top for a takeaway at mine, changed back into my jeans, tee and jumper. I do put on some make-up though, decent underwear and spray perfume. By the time the doorbell rings, I'm honestly a nervous wreck.

'Hi.'

He holds out a bottle of wine.

'Thanks.'

We order Chinese food, which arrives in half an hour. We both have half a glass of wine each. He shows no signs of wanting another one and I'm relieved at that. For obvious reasons, big drinkers don't attract me. I tell him about Cat as we eat, and he shakes his head. 'What's her problem?'

'Um, she's in love with you?'

His scowl deepens. 'She's married to my best friend, for god's sake.'

'I know.'

He murmurs, 'Shit.'

'Were you really that oblivious?'

He shrugs. 'Yes.'

I frown at that, putting the question into my facial expression.

He sighs. 'Okay, no. I don't know. When we were younger, I guess I knew. When she first got together with Gabe, I figured she was trying to get my attention.'

'You went out a few times, right?' My voice is light, but my heart is pounding as I wait for the answer, wondering if it will be different to the one I got back then when we were kids. Ridiculous of course to be jealous of anything that happened when he was a teenager, but Cat gets to me; she always has.

'We went to the cinema, Burger King. I kissed her once.'

I nod, relieved. More so than I have a right to be as I sit here, a married woman who is essentially on a date.

He says, 'I think I did know, like, more recently.' His voice is soft and his skin flashes red. I take his hand. 'There were a few times, early on in their marriage, where she was... too friendly.'

'Did you tell Gabe?'

He shakes his head. 'No, though I tried to avoid situations where she'd be there. Like, I went cycling with Gabe on my own and stuff. Then he started contracting. Money was coming in, just what Cat wanted for herself, and they seemed happy. Dylan came along, they asked me to be his godfather, or Gabe did. Everything was fine.' He shrugs. 'I know they've been fighting recently. Gabe's told me, poor sod. Her coming here like that though.'

I nod. 'I know.' I eat a chicken ball, dipping it in sweet and sour sauce.

Danny picks up the wine bottle to top us up when his phone rings. 'Shit, it's Gabe.'

'You'd better get it.'

'All right, mate?'

There are fast, garbled words from the other end of the line, which I can't quite make out, but Gabe's voice is raised.

Danny murmurs, 'Shit.' Then, 'Okay, okay. Stay put. I'm on my way.'

He's standing before he hangs up the call. I stand too. 'Danny?'

'It's Cat, she's not come home, and she wasn't there to pick up Dylan either.'

'Oh, my god.'

Danny's nodding. Heading out to the hallway grabbing his coat. I slip my feet into my shoes and say, 'I'm coming with you.'

CHAPTER FORTY-FOUR

Seb has just got home, managing to eat dinner with Tilly and Val, and finds himself starting to relax for the first time in… days? It's only been a few days. Tilly is in a good mood, more so than she's been for ages. Seb will take it while he can, and he's teasing her about her English home-work and she's giggling between bites of pizza which she 'made' herself. It has way too much cheese on, but he isn't complaining. He was starving, grateful to eat something that wasn't a soggy, sad sandwich from a garage in the car with Lucy. As the three of them sit around the table, it feels more like his life, theirs. He's barely been in at all this week. The kitchen is full of good odours. There is also a freshly baked cake on the side.

Val watches him eat, and he pauses, grinning. 'I was starving.'

She frowns. 'You've been living on sausage rolls and sandwiches, I suspect.'

He nods sheepishly.

'And are you nearly done?' she asks.

He shakes his head. 'I'm not sure. We might have a breakthrough.' She nods, not pressing for further detail. She knows he won't tell her anyway and also that he doesn't necessarily want to bring his outside life here, into the warm hub of their home.

Val says, 'Tilly, did you tell Dad about your report?'

She shakes her head. 'Not yet, no.'

Seb says, 'Well?'

Tilly grins. 'Mostly eights and nines, a few sevens.'

Seb is pleasantly surprised. Hard to believe she's put enough study in; every time he pokes his head around her door she's on her bloody phone. Despite her suspension and the dramas of the week, he feels a swell of pride. 'Way to go, Tills.'

She blushes, shrugs. They eat. Val cuts three slices of cake.

After dinner, Tilly says she's got calls to make and heads upstairs, stopping to squeeze Seb quickly on her way up. He inhales the scent of her, the banana shampoo from the Body Shop which she gets through by the gallon, and some sort of musky body spray. Teenage girl is what she smells like. It's almost as pungent as walking past Lush when the doors are open.

He says to Val, 'Calls to make, huh?'

She nods with an eye-roll. 'Honest to goodness, you'd think she hadn't seen those girls for years rather than a few days. It'll do her good to go back tomorrow.'

'It will. Hopefully, her and this girl will make up.'

Val smiles. 'I'm sure they will. Maybe not best of friends, but Tilly's life is currently her social circle; she'll make it right enough.'

Seb nods. 'Teenagers, hey?' Though that had hardly been him. He'd been bright, and in a very good fee-paying school. He'd also been sporty and good-looking, all things which should have gone in his favour and equalled popularity but never did. He had held himself separate really. He knows that. His rags-to-riches adoption and the clear and ongoing disappointment of the couple who'd taken him into their home with high hopes, higher sadly than his ambitions, always made him feel other. He was never picked on, his size guaranteed that, but he wasn't included either. Not everyone had mobiles back then of course, but if they had he doubted his would have rung off the hook as Tilly's did.

When they hear the door shut upstairs, Seb says, 'Clever little bugger – her report.'

'Just like you and her mum,' Val mumbles. 'For all the good it did my Charlie.'

Seb reaches across the table, squeezes her little hand, which disappears in his. 'Tilly will be fine.'

'I know; she's had a different start.'

'Charlie's had plenty of time to sort herself out. You gave her more chances than most would.'

She nods, sighing. But Seb feels for her. It pained him to turn his back on his ex-wife; he couldn't imagine having to do it with your own child. He suspects Val never would have stopped giving her money, a place to stay, which she'd invariably rob, or generally sacrificing her own sanity in a vain attempt to fix her daughter if it hadn't been for Tilly.

He stands, giving Val a kiss on the cheek and heading through to the living room.

He's sitting down to watch some mindless TV when his phone goes, and he groans.

'Locke.'

'It's Lucy.'

'Figured.' The station number had come up on his display.

'It's Cat Carter.'

He sits up at that. 'Oh yeah?'

'Yes, she's missing.'

Gabriel Smart is at least a little bit drunk. Whilst Seb understands the stressful and obviously frightening situation he finds himself in, it's probably one of the least helpful things he could have done right now. Hayley is in Gabriel's kitchen making a pot of coffee. Danny is sitting next to his long-term best friend, face screwed up in concern.

Seb asks, 'You're sure there's no one she could have gone to? Her parents?'

Gabe shakes his head. 'I've called them. They've not seen her since the weekend.' Adding, 'I'm not stupid.' As though someone had suggested he was.

'Friends then?'

Gabe laughs. 'She doesn't really have any.' Then that frown again. 'Oh, hang on, there's Jo something from our NCT group.'

'You have her number?'

'Yes.' He gets his phone out, fumbles with it, but eventually finds the contact. Seb nods at Lucy to make a note of it, which she does.

'So you last spoke to her when?'

'After you came round here accusing us of all sorts.'

Seb doesn't falter, doesn't blink. 'You told her what was said?'

He nods, miserable. He reminds Seb of a cartoon parody of a sad sack.

He pushes aside annoyance. 'And you mentioned she actually hadn't been at work today?'

'No. Her boss muddled her shifts.'

Hayley has brought the coffee in and a tray full of mugs. Seb takes one, so does Lucy. They are both tired, both frustrated, but also both hyper-aware that, dreadful though Cat's disappearance is, this may be the big break in this case. Certainly, it is the most worrying new development since Ethan's bones were uncovered. Seb's mind is whizzing by all the possibilities: Cat is guilty; she killed the DaSilvas and has fled at the first sign of the police knowing. She'd left the party, gone back to pretty much the scene of the crime, changed her clothes. Not mentioned it to anyone at the time, nor since. But Ethan was found far away. Her part in his burial had to be ruled out in the same way Leonard's was. So she couldn't have acted alone, unless she'd gone back, of course. Stashed his small body somewhere, revisited to bury him. Unlike Leonard, she wasn't sitting in a police cell the next day and night. But what was her motive? Obviously, she was jealous of Hayley, saw her friend as a threat rather than an ally. But why kill her family and not her? That was more the action of a psychopath, and Seb didn't think Cat fit that bill. Plus, she had been a teenage girl, statistically very unlikely to commit such a crime, and she would have been easily overpowered by Matt and Ryan. He accepts that she is probably selfish, manipulative even, but clearly she loves her son, has feelings of some kind for Danny. What is ringing alarm bells for Seb right now is that Cat hasn't picked up Dylan.

Gabe looks at him, damp-eyed, wobbly-lipped. 'You have to find her. Dylan will be beside himself.'

Seb and Lucy exchange a look. Gabe seems more concerned about his son missing his wife than his wife being missing.

Gabe stands and makes his way to the kitchen on wobbly legs.

This leaves Seb and Lucy with Danny and Hayley.

Seb asks Hayley, 'Okay?'

She shrugs. 'My husband wants a divorce, and I'm wondering if my old best friend killed my family.'

He murmurs, 'I'm sorry.' He's also sorry that he had to fill her in, as Gabe was in no fit state to.

She sighs. 'It's okay.' She says, 'Cat came to my house yesterday.'

'Tell me everything.'

CHAPTER FORTY-FIVE

Gabriel is an obnoxious drunk, and I see for the first time how he might have annoyed Cat. He is knee-deep in sanctimonious self-pity and currently veering between blaming her for everything and wailing with awful desperation about whether she's okay.

He's now calling his mum. He mutters things down the phone, his worry mainly. He has poured another ill-advised whisky, and I flinch as I listen to the slur in his words. In the end, I take the phone, gently and with a smile.

'Diane, hi, it's Hayley DaSilva.'

A sharp intake of breath. Not every day a blast from the past like me arrives. Not every day you have to confront the untimely and brutal death of your former neighbour, friend, and her children. 'Hayley.' The word comes out breathy and long.

I say, 'Gabriel's a little worse for wear.'

'He sounds it.'

'Dylan is there?'

'Yes, and he's fine. Nathan will be back soon.'

'Okay.' And then, 'Are you all right?' Which feels strange from me to her. I hadn't known her well. At that age, other people's parents were of even less interest than your own, but she'd been good to my mum. Had been there for coffee and chats when Mum had needed a friend. She was far nicer to her in those final months than I was.

'I am, love. Thank you for asking. This must be dreadful for you.'

I say, 'Yes.' Though I'm no longer sure if it's as dreadful as trying to live in a fairy tale that somehow became a claustrophobic horror story.

Diane says, 'Is he okay?' Gabriel is half-asleep on the sofa.

'He needs to sober up.'

She sighs. 'Always thought he was better than that. His dad used to like a drink.' I remember that. Hearing snippets of conversation between Diane and my mum about it. Whispered words I was meant to ignore but had learned to tuned into by then. Be on alert. Be vigilant. We'd learned to be that way because of my dad. My anger at him hadn't been without cause even before this. I'm surprised to find that I'm not only happy to have seen Leonard, I'm also looking forward to him being free. I've decided too that I am going to be here for it, for him. Us. But we have a lot of repair to undertake. He broke my heart. Then it was shattered even more that terrible morning and it's never been pieced back together.

I say, 'I'm sure it's just the stress.'

'I hope you're right, love.'

I squeeze my eyes shut. Imagine my mum, who would have been Diane's age, saying that to me. How I've missed it, how I've missed so much and been so fragile, I could never risk replacing it. Danny puts a hand on my shoulder, mouths: 'Okay?'

I nod, tell Diane we'll let her know if we find anything out, and she agrees to do the same.

Gabe is snoring now and Danny looks at him with a sigh. 'Silly bugger.'

I say, 'I'll go and find him a blanket.'

I look in their bedroom, feeling like an intruder. Nothing here other than the duvet, which feels like overkill. Then I see an airing cupboard in the hallway. Bingo. I work my way through sheets and pillowcases, duvet covers folded and ironed so neatly I wonder if Cat outsources her domestic duties. Probably not, in light of their money troubles.

I find a blue fleece blanket which will do, and I'm pulling it out when a box tumbles along with it.

It's one of those wooden hippy sort of things and I recognise it at once. The memory makes me smile. Gabe used to keep dope, Rizlas, half-cigarettes and a plastic weed grinder in here. I open it up and almost laugh to see a small bag of weed, a packet of Silk Cut and several Rizlas housed in a torn packet. Maybe it was Gabe that folded the sheets so well. I can't imagine Cat still getting high. I pull out the baggie, opening it up and inhaling. As I do so a thin silver chain with a guitar pendant catches on my little finger. It takes me a second to work out why it fills me with horror, and when I do, the box drops from my hand.

The hallway is carpeted in plush dove grey. The whole house is so spotless it's hard to believe a baby lives here. When Ethan was small, he mucked up everything. It didn't annoy me at the time, but I have clear recollections of my mother prising sucked lollipops from his fine hair, wiping fingerprints from drawers, tabletops and objects. There had been child graffiti on the walls of our London flat, little doodles of faces with something resembling petals coming out the sides, watercolour splurges on the kitchen wall, which, it turned out, were far more permanent than you'd have hoped. There is nothing like this here. The out-of-place dope box makes a muffled sound on impact, the weed falling from the baggie and scattering across the landing, Rizla papers following suit, grinder, fags.

My mother's necklace slipping from my fingers, me dropping to my knees, my hands grasping desperately for it.

I looked and looked for this chain that my father had given her on the day Matt and I had been born and that hadn't been seen since she died. I sort of assumed my dad had taken it, perhaps that it had gone wherever Ethan ended up. She'd been wearing it when I left, I was sure. She never took it off. A silver guitar on a silver chain.

I scrabble for it now, my hand coming back up with it wrapped around my fingers. I hold its familiar weight.

I am a little girl in my mother's lap. She smells of coconut shampoo and soap. Her hair is long and soft and tickles my face. My little hands twist around this very chain. This shiny, lovely object that is so small but seems somehow to represent all of the love between my mum and dad. Something, I thought then, I will have when I grow up.

I feel the scratch, scratch of my own necklace, a large set of angel wings covered in a thin and expensive spattering of diamonds. Sean had put it around my neck the night of my fairy tale wedding, which had been a lavish party. It had everything, things my mum and dad couldn't have dared dream of – chocolate fountains, champagne, a few minor celebrities. But no love. Not really.

No ceremony full of people who loved me, no father to hold my arm and pass me to the man who'd cherish me. No mother to fuss over what hat she'd wear.

No Matt. No Ethan.

At some point Danny must have come up, quiet steps on the thick carpet, and he kneels, wraps me in his arms and I let it all out. When I am finished, I tell him in a whisper about the chain, and he looks at me and says, 'Gabe's still sparko.'

'I need to get out of here.'

CHAPTER FORTY-SIX

Seb is tired. Looking over at Lucy, he thinks she seems shattered too. It's been a long week and they aren't even at the end of it. He asks her, 'Okay?'

She nods, yawning. 'Sorry about interrupting your dinner.'

'We'd eaten. You've not been home, have you?'

'Nope, I wouldn't mind a shower.'

He smiles acknowledgement. This is how it goes sometimes in this job. He says, 'I don't think we're going to find her tonight.'

'Really?'

'I don't think she wants to be found, do you?'

Lucy sighs. 'No.'

'She wouldn't have left the boy unless she felt she had to.'

'I agree, and in light of what Hayley said, about her jealousy, she's not coming off looking good, is she?'

'She's not, no, though I'm more concerned with her being at the house that night, changing her clothes.' He shakes his head. 'And not mentioning it. I can't help thinking it's all got to have something to do with Nathan's dealing.'

'No smoke without fire?'

'Something like that.'

'I guess we'll be able to see what he's like, if nothing else.' She pulls up outside of the address for the Smarts.

The door is answered by a man, and Seb asks, 'Nathan Smart?'

'Old Bill, eh?'

Seb starts to take out his ID.

'No need. Can spot you lot a mile off. Hopefully, you're here to find my daughter-in-law rather than give me any aggro?'

'We very much want to find her, yes.'

'Come in then, take off your shoes. She can't stand the mess.'

'Your wife?'

'Right.'

In the living room, Diane is on a striped armchair. Again, Seb is taken aback by the strong and overwhelming array of patterns on everything. The sheer volume of colour in the room is distracting. Diane looks small and delicate, perched as she is, wine glass in hand. She holds it up. 'After all the stress.'

Seb nods – sympathetically, he hopes. 'Who could blame you?'

She sighs, waves to the sofa. He and Lucy sink into it. Nathan takes the chair next to his wife and says, 'Little 'un went down no probs.'

'He stays here often?'

Nathan nods. 'Has done of late anyway. I've been away so not seen much of him.'

'Anywhere nice?'

Nathan shrugs. 'Work stuff, trying to adjust to changes in supply, that sort of thing.'

Seb nods. He knows a few people in the building trade who were badly affected by Brexit. He says, 'Actually, Mr Smart, we had been hoping to speak to you.'

Diane makes an outraged sound like a snort. 'Surely your focus is on finding Cat?'

He smiles at her. 'It is, of course, but working out what happened then might help us find her now.'

Diane shakes her head. 'You don't mean...' She looks at Nathan and his face softens. Even now in her later middle years she is a beauty, anyone can see that, and Nathan still seems charmed by his wife.

He pats her hand, turns to Seb. 'You can't think she had anything to do with it, surely?'

'Did you hear her enter your house?'

He frowns. 'What?'

'The night of the killings?'

He laughs, realises Seb is serious and stops. 'Why would she have come to ours? The kids were all at a party.' He looks at Diane who nods agreement.

She says, 'I was asleep. Nate came back late, didn't you, love?'

He grins sheepishly. 'I'd had a few, had to get a cab back. You know how it is.'

Seb smiles. 'Which cab firm did you use?'

Nate's face looks less benevolent. 'The one in town. Tony's. They are still in business if you want to check.'

'It wasn't checked at the time?'

Nate frowns. 'I wasn't asked.'

'By your mate Nigel?'

His face screws up for a moment like a crumpled piece of paper then it breaks into a grin, and he chuckles. 'Diane's number one fan.' He's grinning at his wife who glares at him now.

She murmurs, 'Just as well he was.'

Nate's face takes on a more serious expression, and he looks from his wife, suitably chastised, to Seb, 'I, uh, had a bit of bother.'

'So we heard.'

Nate sighs. 'You can't think it's anything to do with Cat.'

'I think Cat's links to this case are the reason she's missing now.'

Nate shakes his head. 'She was a kid.'

'You liked her?'

'Well...' He looks at his wife.

Diane sits up straighter, patting her hair. 'Cat is the mother of our grandchild and will always be special to us.'

'And did you like her?'

'Then?' Diane.

Seb nods.

'Not at first, no, in the name of honesty. Which doesn't detract at all from the fact that we have made our peace over the years, and I want her home. For Dylan as much as Gabe.'

Lucy says, 'You tolerate her.'

Nate firmly now: 'No, we love her. She's family.' He puts an arm out across the back of the sofa encompassing his wife's shoulders, and she squeezes his hand.

Seb's phone rings, and he looks at it. 'Excuse me.'

He heads to the hallway to take the call. Lucy says, 'What was she like then?'

Diane sighs. 'Moody, really. Stayed at our house more than she did her own. I didn't hear her come in that night, but I'm not surprised. She was always leaving things at ours.'

'Did she not like her own house?'

Diane shrugs. 'She's close with her mum now, but that woman didn't have a lot of rules – three kids, her dad was a travelling salesman so they were given quite a bit of free rein.'

'And you didn't mind her staying with you?'

'Well, she slept in the spare room.'

Nate chuckles at that, and Diane swats him.

Seb comes back in. Lucy looks at him, questions in her eyes. He says, 'We need to go, but very quickly can you talk me through your last conversation with Anita? I believe she called you that night.'

'Oh. Yes, she did. I was worried.'

'Because you knew Leonard was going over?'

Diane nods. 'She was pretty messed up about the whole thing.'

'The separation?'

'I got the impression he'd been a good husband before his breakdown or whatever. She was a bit overprotective of me.'

'About Nathan?'

Diane nods, patting her husband's hand again. 'Sorry, love.'

He shrugs. 'I was a bit of a handful, the drugs thing...'

'You were dealing.'

He snorts. 'Bit of a stretch, some personal, a bit for a few pals.'

'You didn't supply Douglas Beattie?'

'Who?' His face is the expression of bewilderment.

Seb smiles tightly. 'The dealer at the party your son was at, his junior sold an Ecstasy tablet to Cat, which she slipped into Hayley's drink.'

His stunned face is real this time. As is Diane's, who presses a hand to her mouth. 'Jesus.'

'So Anita called, after Leonard had left.'

'Right.'

'And how was she?'

'Not great. I couldn't make sense of it, but she said they'd argued, something to do with the kids.'

'The kids or Hayley specifically?'

'The kids, she said.'

'So she was upset?'

'Yes.'

'Was she frightened?'

'I... I don't know. She was upset, just upset. She'd been hoping for things to go well. Instead, there'd been some sort of row.'

Seb wonders if Leonard and Anita fought about Hayley. He'd need to ask Leonard.

Diane says, 'I wasn't worried for her safety, if I had been...' The words trail off.

Seb says, 'But you knew he'd hit her before, and you got the impression they argued that night, but details were unclear.'

Her eyes fill with tears. She looks down at her lap. 'It was late.'

'How late?'

'Getting close to midnight, after even, I'd say.'

'That's quite late to get a phone call?'

'She knew I tended to turn in quite late. I think I said at the time I struggled with insomnia.'

'Yes,' Seb says. Diane had told them, according to her original statements, that she'd taken a sleeping tablet just after the phone call, which wasn't an unusual occurrence for her then.

Cat and Gabe were in the woods. So was Hayley, dangerously out of her head, but with Danny at least to calm her down. Leonard had gone back to the Travelodge. Matt would arrive home one hour later and walk in to his death. Two hours after that, Gabe would bump into Cat in new clothes. They'd go back to the party. Someone had taken Ethan away. Cat? Had she left him out in the woodland, come back later and buried him? The next day? Why? Where has she gone now, and why run if she isn't guilty?

'Then?'

'Then I went to bed.' Her voice is barely a whisper.

Nate says, 'Diane had trouble sleeping back then. I'd got her a few Valiums, she took two after Anita called.' That was documented and given as the reason she'd slept through everything.

'And you got in at what time?'

'Half-three, I'd say. Passed out next to her.'

His neighbours had been dead. His one-day-to-be daughter-in-law had been in and out. Hayley was making her way home from the woods with Danny. Gabe and Cat had gone back to the party. Hazel Munroe, who said they'd gone missing, verified that: said they'd been back drinking, laughing, having fun before the sun came up at least. She'd left at six. They were still there. They left with Danny, who'd come back, walked part of the way with him but had headed back home to Gabe's place, not Cat's, at six-thirty. Hayley had already been taken to the police station. Leonard had already been arrested. The house was cordoned off; the boys would have realised something was amiss.

Nathan says, 'I woke up when the police came, made a right ruckus, as you can imagine.'

'And Diane's fan Nigel took statements from you?'

'He did, yes.'

'And Gabe and Cat?'

'Arrived back later.'

'How did they seem to you?'

'Shifty at first, I'd say they were stoned, so had every right to be. I'd not have stood for that.'

'Though you sold harder drugs?'

Nate looks at him like he's very stupid. 'Not to kids, and not sold, passed on to a few mates. You make me sound like Don Corleone.'

Seb smiles. 'So, they were shifty?'

'Because they were stoned.' He says the words, trailing off as he gets what Seb is implying. 'Now hang on.'

Diane puts a hand on his arm. 'They're doing their job.'

Nate looks at her, back to Seb, settles again. 'Right.'

'We need to go. But we'll be in touch.'

–

They get outside. It's really dark now, the only light coming from a single street lamp at the end of the Smarts' drive. The house is secluded, and whilst Seb can certainly see the appeal of a detached property, this is too far out, too on its own and isolated for him. You'd have to drive everywhere. As he and Lucy get back in the car, she asks, 'Where to?'

'Hayley's place. She's found her mum's necklace.'

Lucy glances over as she pulls away. 'The one she asked about at the time?'

'The very same.'

'Are you going to tell me where?'

'Gabe and Cat Smart's airing cupboard.'

Lucy shakes her head. 'You're kidding.'

'I kid you not.'

CHAPTER FORTY-SEVEN

We should have stayed at Gabriel's. I realise that by the frown the detective can't quite conceal and so does Danny seemingly because he says to Locke, 'We should have waited for you there?'

'It would have been best to stay put. But don't worry. Lucy here will call the station, send a uniform round to pick him up.'

I murmur thanks at her. She squeezes my shoulder and says, 'I'll nip into the hallway, make the call then make us all a cuppa, yeah?'

I nod again. 'Thanks.' I had to get out of there. I had to run. I had felt pricklings of… what exactly? Fear, confusion. A swell of nausea and a pounding in my head. It's hard to try and explain to someone how physical heightened emotion is. I've always felt my feelings in my body, found it hard to put them into words. Now I am thrumming with it all. On high alert and ready to snap at the next provocation.

Danny looks drawn; his jaw is tight, shoulders hunched. This can't be easy for him. His best friend. His best friend's wife. Whichever one is responsible, whichever one took that necklace and hid it with their stash. I take his hand, squeeze it. The detective's eyes flick to the gesture and away. Lucy pokes her head around the door. 'Harry's sending someone out.'

He nods. 'Great. Thanks.'

The kettle whistles, and she goes to the small kitchenette. The sound takes me back to my mum. She always liked one that made a sound for her endless cups of tea. She never drank coffee, said it was too bitter. My eyes travel to her necklace, now in a zip lock bag from the kitchen.

Locke asks me, 'Do you remember any of the conversation with your parents that night?' Me shouting, what, I hate you? Leave me alone? Classic favourites probably utilised by every teenager for the whole of history. So much worse when they are the last things you might have said to the woman who loved you, sang you to sleep. Who you adored really and never told. Maybe I don't want to remember. Maybe it isn't just the dubious possibility that I killed them all, which I don't think I ever believed. Not really.

Maybe I just don't want to think of the last things I said.

I shake my head. 'No, not exactly. I shouted I think. What, I'm not sure. I was angry.'

'Because your dad was there?'

I nod. 'And they were laughing, I remember that, when I walked in.' The sharp annoyance of it. The split second where I'd looked at them and thought it might be okay before I remembered. And the staggering, heart-thumping fear from the booze racing round my system. I say, 'I was so out of it.'

Danny nods. 'She was.' Then to me, 'I was so scared. I'd never seen you like that.'

I smile. 'It scared the shit out of me.' Twisted, lost hours; weird, disjointed images.

Lucy has come in with steaming mugs of tea, one for me and one for Danny, which she places in front of us.

The police officers exchange a look, and I snap, 'What?'

'We think...' He clears his throat, pauses.

She leans in, soft eyes, hand tapping mine. 'We've reason to believe Cat Carter spiked you.'

My mouth opens in a stupid, wide O. That feeling I'd had of going from drunk to absolutely smashed. I say, 'I'd smoked a bit of weed.' And had reacted badly to it. Normally, getting stoned chilled me out. That night it made my frayed nerves more jangly. I'd felt disorientated, disconnected. The whole evening is flashes of fast images which don't make sense.

Danny's frowning. 'Spiked with what?'

'Ecstasy, we think.'

He murmurs, 'Jesus.'

My voice is stuck and faltering. 'Why?'

But Danny says, 'You know why, to try and humiliate you. I knew she was jealous, but god.'

'It can't have been her...'

Lucy is walking towards us with mugs in hand for her and Locke. They both look tired. It's late. I wonder how many hours they've worked today, how exhausting this case is and whether Cat's disappearance might make things easier to discover. I try and push that unkind thought away, but it protrudes nonetheless. I do want her to be okay. I want Dylan to get his mother back, and I want her to be innocent, but, I realise, I also would be glad never to see her again.

Lucy has her mug in her hand and almost at her lips when her phone goes. She puts the cup down. 'Hey.' Her face seems to fall, and Locke looks up with a frown. 'Okay, thanks, bye.' She looks at Seb, then to us. 'Gabriel isn't home.'

I blink at her stupidly. Then I look at Danny.

Locke says, 'Where was he exactly when you left?'

'Passed out on the sofa. He was in no state to drive.'

Lucy says, 'His car's still there.'

Locke: 'Any sign of a break-in?'

She shakes her head.

He stands. 'We'll need to go. You'll be here?'

I nod, panic rising again, pushing heat to my cheeks and a tremor to my hands. I put down the tea I've been grasping, its heat no longer comforting, more dangerous in my unreliable, shaky fingers.

He pauses. 'You make sure you stay here, okay? I cannot stress this enough.'

He's worried. That I am in danger, which would make sense. Is Cat clearing up the wreckage of that night? How far would she go? Would she hurt Gabriel, or is he in cahoots with her? Are they both guilty of not just lying but also murder? I think of us standing at the back of our gardens high and giggling. I liked him, considered him my friend. Matt liked him, said he thought he and Danny were all right. Never warmed to Cat, said she had sly eyes. I laughed, rolled *my* eyes, but she did. Does. Always watching, weighing up everything anyone ever says. She used to repeat things I'd told her, stupid white lies about my family usually, my dad in particular, who, even then, I was still keen to paint as some kind of hero. I stole a bracelet from a shop in town. The only thing I'd ever taken, and I remember telling them my dad had sent it for me. Cat had listened, then, one day, when we were walking around the shops, she pointed out the same ones and laughed because the little shop was unique to

Thamespark. 'I didn't know your dad had been down.' Gabriel knew that I'd lied, so did Danny, and I remember Gabe telling her to shut up. I can still feel the embarrassment of it as though it was yesterday. A warm flush on my face, as painful as if she'd slapped me.

I took it back to the shop in the end anyway. Left it on the side. Worn twice. I hadn't been comfortable with my theft any more than I was comfortable making sarcastic comments to my mum, fighting with Matt or drinking. I was lost underneath my bravado. Cat had seen that hurt and tapped into it, using it to make me feel small.

I nod, then Locke says to Danny, 'Can you stay as well?'

'Yes, of course.'

'Don't answer the door to anyone. Ring me directly if anything else happens.'

And they are gone, leaving two steaming mugs of untouched tea. I stand, pick up and empty them, rinsing them in the sink. I wipe the sides, and then Danny is behind me, hands on my shoulders, and I turn round, bury my face in his chest. I can hear his heart hammering as fast as my own.

CHAPTER FORTY-EIGHT

They drive over to Gabriel Smart's and speak to Harry, who apologises as though it's his fault the man isn't there. Obviously, it's not. The NCT friend hasn't spoken to her for months, and Cat Carter's parents are currently on holiday. Seb and Lucy drive to their house anyway. Knock on the door just in case. No answer and there are no lights on. Lucy says, 'She has an older sibling who lives in Scotland. Even if they headed up there, they wouldn't arrive until tomorrow.'

Seb says, 'No point calling them now, or her parents.'

'No, probably not. Hopefully, she'll show up before they get back?' Her voice rises in a question, though it's one he obviously doesn't have the answer for.

Seb is shaking his head as he gets into the car. A glance at the clock on his dashboard tells him it's almost ten. 'Where the hell are they?'

'I don't know.'

'If it wasn't for the fact they've left Dylan behind, I'd have assumed they'd done a runner and guilt on both parts.'

'It might still mean that.'

'It might. She struck me as a hard sort of woman, but seeing her with the kid, that felt real.'

'Maybe it was, and they still ran.'

He sighs. 'Maybe. Whatever the case, she's got some serious explaining to do, and now so has Gabriel.'

Lucy nods agreement. 'If he'd just stayed put he could have denied knowledge and shunted the blame onto Cat.'

'Which suggests whatever they are in, they are in it together.' He sighs. 'Let's go to the Smarts senior, then we'll call it a night?'

Lucy nods, stifling a yawn. She is, she realises, exhausted. She'd stay if she was needed, but, like Seb says, without any specific leads as to their whereabouts, they've nowhere left to go.

–

Diane Smart answers the door, bleary-eyed and in a dressing gown. 'You've found her?'

'No, I'm afraid not, Mrs Smart, and now we can't find Gabriel.'

She frowns. 'What are you talking about?'

'He's not home.'

'He'll be looking for Cat?' But her voice doesn't sound sure.

Seb tells her, 'Hayley said he was still a bit drunk.'

She groans.

'Sorry to bring bad news.'

'What can I do now?'

'Nothing, just keep your phone on and listen out in case they come here.'

She says, 'They will. Dylan's here.' Her voice so sure, it's bordering on denial.

They are about to leave when Seb notices the empty driveway. He says, 'Is Nate out?'

She sighs. 'Silly sod is scouring the streets for Cat. Told me to try and get some kip, though slim chance of that.

I guess I'll call him and add Gabe to his search now too.' She presses a hand to her lips.

Lucy says, 'I'm so sorry, this must be very frightening.'

Diane nods.

Lucy adds, 'It's extremely rare for adults to go missing without a reasonable cause. My guess is they'll show up of their own accord. Okay?'

Diane nods. 'Thank you.'

Seb says, 'If Nate finds anything.' He hands her another card with his details. She must have two at least already, but she takes it, and he sees the slight tremor in her hand.

'I'll call.'

'Thank you.'

Lucy again, 'And do try and get some rest. I'm sure your grandson will be up early and raring to go.'

She smiles faintly, nods.

As they leave, Seb says to Lucy, 'We need to get some rest too. If anything else happens tonight, I'll call you.'

'Maybe Nate will find them?'

Seb shakes his head. 'I don't think they want to be found.'

Lucy says, 'You didn't tell Diane about the necklace?'

'Never give the family too much info, Lucy. The last thing we need is armchair detectives.'

CHAPTER FORTY-NINE

We don't really sleep, but we do get into bed. I find myself undressing shyly, aware that he is watching me whilst pretending not to. I slip under the covers fast in knickers and my T-shirt. He does the same and reaches out for me. I snuggle into the crook of his arm and inhale. Back then he'd smelt of Brut, Nag Champa incense and dope. Now he smells clean, fresh and lemony. But he feels the same, and I rest there, eyes shut, listening to the faint thud of his heart underneath my ear. Feeling the muscles on his arms hard-pressed along my back. His fingers run light circles just beneath my shoulder blades. A fiercely intimate and completely comfortable feeling.

We lie there, not speaking, pressed together for minutes, and I find I'm starting to doze when my phone rings, shrill and intrusive. I lunge for it, sitting up too quickly, pressing it to my ear and managing, 'Hello.' A breathy exhalation.

I am so sure it will be one of the detectives that when Sean's voice cuts in like a knife, I find myself cringing into my own body.

'Did I wake you?'

'No, actually.'

'Oh yeah, been out partying?'

'I came here because my little brother's remains were found, Sean. What kind of trip do you think I'm on?'

'I don't know. I don't even know what kind of person you are.'

'Not one who's likely to party, as you put it, whilst I'm embroiled in an active murder investigation.'

'I read that the case had been reopened. Another thing it would have been nice to have heard from you.'

I close my eyes, inhale and open them again. Extremely aware of my husband's voice in my ear and the heat emanating from Danny's half-naked body beside me. How quaint that even as I plan my divorce, even as I have solid proof, and no denial from him, that my husband is cheating on me, I still feel the discomfort of my muddied vows.

He has a point, and I say, 'I should have told you.'

'Why didn't you?'

'I wanted to pretend it never happened.' I don't stop before I speak. I don't need to. 'I wanted to be someone else entirely. I couldn't go back to being who I'd been before.'

There is a pause then. The first time I've been really honest with him, and he's speechless. I am too. 'I liked the girl I met.'

'I know. I made sure you did.'

'What does that mean?'

'I don't know. I just, I was dazzled by you.'

'And all of my charm.'

I smile and am surprised to find a sharp stab of sympathy for him and perhaps for me too. I say, 'What I did, not telling you, wasn't right and I'm sorry.'

He sighs. 'Everyone's talking about it.'

'Oh god. Are they?'

'Of course. There's not going to be anything juicier, is there?'

I say again, 'I'm so sorry.'

'Were you ever in love with me?'

'I don't know.' Quiet. Whilst we both think our own thoughts. I ask him, 'Were you? In love with me?'

'I'd never planned to marry for love. My father didn't; none of the men I knew had. I wanted you badly. I thought you were very sweet, and you were so...'

'Amenable?'

He laughs. 'God, yes. Probably. That makes me a bit of an asshole, doesn't it?'

I say, 'I don't know.' And mean it. 'Do you love Sophie?'

He sighs. 'How long have you known?'

'A while.'

'Shit.'

'Do you?'

'I don't know. I'm very fond of her.'

'I guess you two will be able to find out now.'

He snorts. 'I don't think me publicly starting up with her whilst you're there making headlines would be a good look. I suspect Len wouldn't like it.'

I giggle. He does too, then says, 'Bloody hell, as you Brits say.'

'I know, right?'

'You're not coming back, are you?'

'No.'

'Okay.'

'I'm sorry, Sean.'

'Hey, as you've pointed out, I've hardly been the best husband.'

'No.'

'I'll see you right in the divorce.'

'You don't need to.'

'I know.'

'Feel bad about Sophie?'

'Ha. I do a bit, yes.' A pause and then, 'And for you, you know, what happened to you. I, uh, I can't imagine.'

'No.'

'Must have been pretty shit.'

'It wasn't the best.'

'You probably deserve better than me.'

'Same.'

Another snorty laugh. 'And all I get is Sophie?'

'She seems very sweet.'

'She's too young for me.'

'There is that.'

'I'm sorry I got my lawyer to call.'

'I'm sorry I'm not who I said I was.'

As I hang up, Danny looks at me. 'Your ah...'

'Husband?'

He flinches.

I say, 'We're getting a divorce.'

And he grins, then tries to stop. 'Shit. Sorry.'

I smile. 'That's all right.'

'It's not really cool that I'm happy about it, is it?'

'It is, actually.'

'Really?'

I nod. 'Really. But...' – I wriggle around in his arms – 'and it seems silly saying this since we're in bed together right now...'

'You need to take it slow?'

I nod.

He shrugs. 'I've only waited fifteen years. What's more time?'

CHAPTER FIFTY

Jackie honestly looks like she's suffering from apoplexy and Seb genuinely feels bad for her as he lays out the latest unexpected, shitty twist in this case.

'So now you're...?'

'Waiting for Nigel Baker.'

'And his lawyer.'

'And his lawyer.'

'Great.'

'So the baby is still with the Smart seniors?'

'He is.' Seb called in this morning on his way to the station. Nate was asleep; Diane murmured that he'd been out looking all night. She didn't look like she'd slept much and the baby, on the verge of toddlerhood, sounded in fine voice, full of energy and with no respect for the fact that his carers were exhausted.

Jackie says, 'At least the baby's not missing.'

'I suppose.'

'That's what's bugging you, isn't it?'

He nods.

'So come on then, you don't think Cat Carter is guilty, and all we have to do is catch up to her?'

He shakes his head.

'Brilliant.' Her voice is heavy with sarcasm.

He says, 'If she was guilty, a woman like that, she'd have had a get-out plan that included the kid.'

'You reckon?'

'I do, yes. How hard would it have been for her to go and collect him and get away before anyone noticed?'

A knock at the door, Ken. Jackie shouts, 'What?'

He pokes his head round. 'Sorry.' Nods at Seb, 'You'd better come check this out.'

Jackie stands and follows Seb.

Ken looks at her, slightly askew. 'Might be nothing.'

'Which is all we have so far,' she snaps. Seb cringes slightly, and Ken shoots him a sympathetic look.

Lucy is talking to two of the constables. They are scattered around a small table. They all sit up a bit straighter as Seb and Jackie approach. Lucy stands.

Seb says, 'Well?'

'Three things.'

'Right. Start with the first.'

'Cab company at the time and the only one operating in the area back then, no record of dropping Nathan Smart home at four a.m.'

Seb shrugs. 'They can't be expected to remember every customer from fifteen years ago, nor to have the same drivers.'

Lucy's shaking her head. 'Yes, we thought of that.' Her jaw tenses and Seb wonders if she's close to rolling her eyes. She wouldn't have sent Ken to get them if it wasn't something.

He says, 'Sorry, go on.'

'The guy who manages that firm managed it then, and he said he gave a statement at the time saying no one had driven Nathan home.'

'Who to?'

'Ben Green.'

'Ah.'

'Right, and I've checked with Ben.'

Seb swears. Jackie says, 'Ben took the statement?'

Lucy nods at her. 'He did, yes.'

'Is it in the book?'

She shakes her head. 'Nope.'

Jackie murmurs an obscenity now. Then to Seb, 'This Ben... you believe him?'

'Definitely.'

'Then you need to pressure Baker.'

Seb says, 'Who's coming in lawyered up.' Then to Lucy, 'The second thing?'

'This one is weird.'

'Okay.'

'The phone records from the DaSilvas are in the file.'

Jackie makes a derisive sound. 'Suppose they had to pad it out somehow.'

'And?' Seb says.

'Anita didn't make any calls that evening.'

He frowns. 'Diane said they spoke. Specifically, that Anita called her.'

Lucy nods. 'She did, yeah.'

Seb's brain is whirring. 'She had a mobile?'

'She did, found up in her bedroom, switched off.'

'Doesn't mean she didn't use it.'

'No, it doesn't.'

'We'll go ask Diane later.'

Lucy shakes her head. 'Diane took the call on her landline, no caller ID. I already checked over the notes.'

'Oh.'

'But, I am on to BT to find the records for incoming calls at the Smarts.'

Seb grins. 'Even better.'

She nods. Jackie says, 'The third thing?'

Ken gets out a piece of paper. It's an evidence docket. Seb and Jackie lean over to look, Ken points to the names involved, and Seb lets out a low whistle. 'Bloody hell.'

Nigel Baker's face is held so tight that it looks almost painful. His mouth is drawn to a thin line, eyes stare straight ahead, his shoulders ride high.

Seb takes a few moments longer than he needs to settling himself and Lucy in, then, eventually, he grins. 'Hey, Nigel.'

Nigel nods but doesn't meet his eyes. The lawyer introduces himself, inserting his unwelcome presence between Seb and Nigel. He refers to his client as 'Mr Baker'. Seb's going to stick to Nigel. Is even toying with 'Nige'.

'Do you know where Cat and Gabe Smart are?'

A flash of surprise, stiff jaw opening slack. 'Wh… what are you talking about?'

'Cat or Catherine, Gabe or Gabriel, Smart. The Smarts junior as we've come to tag them, haven't we, Lucy?'

She nods. 'We have.'

'Maybe ask Diane and Nate?'

'Your good pals?'

He cringes. 'We went to school together.'

'All of you?'

He flashes a glance to his lawyer, who is inscrutable. 'Diane, I told you.'

'Oh yes, and that you'd dated, a couple of times.'

'That's right.'

'But you got over it?'

He laughs a nervous laugh. 'We were kids.'

'Still, you liked her enough to get charges dropped against her husband.'

303

He turns an appalling shade of crimson. His lawyer says, 'I believe my client has already told you this?'

'He has, yes, though he downplayed it. Nathan Smart himself mentioned it.' Seb looks down at his notes, written in shorthand, the best thing he had from his short-lived journalism career. '*A bit of Percy and a bit for his pals.*'

Nigel shrugs. 'Well, there you are.'

Seb smiles. Lucy thinks it's the sort of smile that could freeze entire lakes. 'Would you consider two hundred Ecstasy tablets and a kilo of cocaine "Percy for me and a few mates"?'

Nigel turns visibly paler, makes a sort of spluttering sound like a car struggling to start 'I...' He looks at the lawyer, who pauses, removing a piece of imaginary lint from his suit.

'That's a big accusation.'

Seb nods. 'It is, yeah.' He slides over the evidence docket that Ben Green had been clever enough to keep to himself all those years ago when it became apparent his boss wasn't interested. Better still, Ken went looking for it after Ben emailed his copy, and he found the original, which is what they are all staring at now. They hadn't charged Nathan, but they had confiscated the drugs. Mac's team were slapdash even in their borderline criminality.

Seb says, 'My problem is, aside from the obvious...' He grins at the lawyer, whose lips tighten. 'You are a liar. Proven now.'

'I didn't lie.'

'Misrepresented then?'

Nigel nods. 'I guess.' Voice glum, head low like a repentant schoolboy. But his sorrow is not for any wrong-doing on his part. He is sad to have been caught.

Seb says, 'Nice guy, that Ben.'

And Nigel looks up, frowning. 'Never said he wasn't.'

'Doesn't like you though.'

Nigel flushes again. 'Can't be everyone's cup of tea.'

'He didn't like Mac either. Left the force because of your bumbling ineptitude.'

'Mind yourself.' The lawyer.

Seb holds up his hands. 'I apologise.'

'So when Ben tells me you were half in love with Diane Smart, and I see this docket here, which took more than turning a blind eye, more like covering for what to me looks like the iceberg tip of a big operation.'

Nigel's shaking his head. The lawyer says, 'You can't know that.'

'I know it wasn't personal use and a little extra for a few pals.'

'But running an empire is a bit of a stretch.'

Seb turns dark eyes on him, and he's not smiling any more. 'Is it?'

Nigel looks like he's going to throw up.

Seb says, 'Your house is nice.'

Nigel looks bewildered.

Seb adds, 'Where did your wife get her cash from?'

'Um, family.'

'And you didn't mention she was wife number two.'

'His wife's financial affairs are nothing to do with this case.'

'I disagree. Nigel, which wife was it? With the money?'

'Kate.'

'Number two?'

His skin is letting him down; his whole face is lit up like Rudolph's nose on Christmas Eve. He nods.

'But you left the force at least a year before you met Kate, right?'

'I told you the job wasn't for me.'

'Fair enough, and I can't honestly say it was our loss.'

'Mind.'

Seb holds a calming hand to the lawyer, who himself is starting to look less than comfortable. 'I apologise. That was rude.'

Nigel leans his head in a sort of nodding relent.

Seb says, 'You wouldn't want us being rude in the midst of a murder investigation you'd screwed up.' The lawyer opens his mouth. 'Anyway, what we'd like to know is where you got your cash before Kate?'

'Wh… what?'

'Well, costly divorce, speaking to wife number one.'

Nigel groans.

Seb grins his wide, benevolent grin, 'Nice lass, Angela.'

He slumps over the table, placing his bright red head in his hands.

'According to Angela, your child maintenance payments were nothing short of generous, and she tells us you paid off the mortgage and managed school fees for the kids.'

'I, uh, was dating Kate.'

Seb nods. 'You started dating her shortly after she moved to this area from Devon, right?'

'Right.'

'That was well after you started making those generous payments to Angela.'

The colour drains away from his face, then he looks at his lawyer, who smiles tightly and says, 'I'd like to speak with my client.'

Seb stands grinning, Lucy rising next to him. 'I bet you would.'

CHAPTER FIFTY-ONE

Seb gets into a quiet house. Just the cat who hears him come in and slips out of Tilly's room down the stairs, looking at him closely, hope gleaming in her eye.

'Come on then, or you won't give me any peace.'

She worms around his legs as he opens a sachet of vile-smelling miscellaneous meat chunks and only stops when he puts her bowl on the floor.

He is shattered but still wired from the day, his head busy with all the ruinous puzzle pieces that almost but don't quite yet fit together. He is pondering Hayley, her sudden, jolting return to this life she thought was a million miles away, and marvelling that she and Danny seem to have reconnected as if no time has passed.

He goes up and slips into Tilly's room, knocking softly first, just in case. No answer. Her star lamp is on. A blue IKEA thing that she's had since she was tiny. It throws small, delicate white stars across her walls, bed and her sleeping face. He kneels down next to her, taking her in. Always she's been like this for him. A cleanse at the end of what could be brutal days in his job. A reminder when he is so often faced with the world's appalling horrors that good exists, great things happen. Mundane normal stuff, like your child growing up right under your nose.

She looks younger now, asleep, her hand flung off the bed. He moves it back on, and she shifts slightly then starts to snore gently. He's about to leave when he sees a sharp corner of something poking out from under her pillow. He tugs at it and looks down in his hand to a photo of him and Charlie. Her belly out, too big and too much for her young, skinny frame. He, a boy still, in a man's body. Both of them grinning. His hand is pressed on her stomach, on Tilly.

It captures so many things: trepidation, the youth of these soon-to-be parents, and also joy and love. He is grinning down at her, and she is looking up at him as though he is everything she ever needed.

He can't catch his breath, can hardly see for the wet sting of tears in his eyes. He hasn't seen this picture for years. Tilly must have been through the albums he keeps of pictures from then. There is one photo of Charlie up in the house, in a magnet on their fridge, her holding Tilly when she was about eighteen months old. He sees it every time he gets food but never registers it, really.

This hits him in every place he has feelings. He presses one hand to his mouth, uses the other to slide it back under her pillow.

He goes back downstairs, makes his cup of decaf Earl Grey. Pets the cat, watches some TV and wonders if he and Charlie would be like Danny and Hayley if they were reunited. If things were different. If she was well.

But she isn't, and he does his best to push it away, remembers Tilly's tearful face the last time Charlie hadn't shown up. How it felt to pull her latest rap sheet.

Charlie was like a tornado, spinning up everything she came into contact with, pulling it up high into the air and ripping it apart as she left, all the stuff she'd touched smashing into a thousand pieces.

And yet still, all it takes is one damn picture for his heart to spin with a loss he genuinely thought he was over.

He goes to bed, radio on in an attempt to keep his thoughts at bay and at least succumb to a few hours' rest.

CHAPTER FIFTY-TWO

Locke calls. I put him on speaker, and he addresses both me and Danny. Passing no judgement on a married woman having a prolonged sleepover with her ex. Or maybe he's just not voicing it. Either way, I find I'm relieved. I hardly know myself what I think of this whole thing. I doubt Sean would mind. He sounded... reasonable on the phone, and it occurred to me that he isn't a terrible guy. He isn't a great guy either, or even a good guy, but he isn't the worst. I'll get my divorce, and it sounds like I'll get more than the prenup suggested too, so that's good. I was prepared to come out of it broke, but obviously I'd rather not.

Locke tells us that he suspects Nigel Baker knew full well that Nathan Smart was dealing in the area, adding, 'To a large group of people.'

Danny murmurs, 'Bloody hell.' Then, 'Didn't Matt say something about him?'

I screw my eyes up and look at him. Locke says, 'What did he say, Danny?'

'That night, he asked you, Hayley, if you'd bought drugs off of him.'

I shake my head. 'I wish I could remember.' Then, 'I'm so sorry.' I'm not sure exactly who to.

Seb says, 'Doug Beattie said Cat asked him before the party if he could get her anything and he said no.'

Danny says, 'I know Doug. He's a good guy.'

'He said he absolutely wouldn't have sold to a "kid",' as he put it.'

Danny agrees. 'He wouldn't have. I mean, I bought puff off of him back in the day, and I still know him to say hi to; he's a decent bloke.'

'Do you still smoke?'

'Like, my job, you know?'

Locke says, 'Okay, don't answer that.'

Danny is looking at me, sheepish and slightly pink. I shrug.

Locke says, 'Hypothetically, and considering we found some dope at Gabe and Cat's, who would you buy it off around here?'

Danny wipes a hand across his face. 'Hypothetically, if you, ah, dabbled occasionally, maybe your best mate would be able to hook you up with the odd eighth here and there.'

'Gabriel Smart.'

'I mean, I had no idea it would be relevant to anything.'

'It's fine. I'll call you later.'

And Locke's gone, leaving an awkward silence in his absence. Danny says, 'I'm not a stoner.'

I laugh. 'Danny, it's cool.'

'Hasn't put you off?'

I shake my head. 'No, but you probably should have said when we found Gabe's weed.'

He nods. 'Agreed. Do you think the detective…?'

'I think he's got things other than you to be worried about.'

CHAPTER FIFTY-THREE

Locke is in a funny mood this morning. He doesn't give much away about anything outside of work, but Lucy is learning his ways, and she thinks he is distracted by something – and he looks tired.

Locke is now sitting so still and is so quiet that Lucy almost asks if he's okay. Then he moves as if startled and looks at her. 'Ryan's mum…'

Lucy frowns. 'What?'

He's got his notepad out and is whipping back pages. 'Here it is.'

'What?'

'Mrs Dudley said, "Matt was concerned about his sister smoking weed and also thought he knew who was responsible. Not long after Anita told me herself, she also said it was a bit awkward because I think he suggested to Anita that Nathan might be into it, which meant possibly Gabe."'

He looks at Lucy, who frowns and says, 'She was worried for her friend.'

Seb nods. 'Diane was her best mate and she also, I think, saw some of herself in her. What if Anita confronted Nathan?'

Lucy nods. 'Or, the two women looked alike, right?'

'Diane and Anita?'

'Yes.'

'What if Nathan was in trouble for, say, losing an enormous amount of saleable narcotics to the police?'

Locke nods now, enjoying the zinging of ideas, seeing Lucy get into her investigative stride. 'What are you thinking, mistaken identity?'

Lucy shrugs. 'Maybe. Like, someone wanted to teach Nathan a lesson so targeted his wife?'

'And Matt, Ryan and Ethan were just incidental.'

'It's possible.' But she's more doubtful now. 'Bit far-fetched?'

He frowns at her. 'Not at all. It's as good a theory as any.'

'Okay.' She releases a relieved breath.

'But it doesn't explain where Cat is or Gabriel.'

'No.'

'They are either guilty or they know more than they are letting on.'

'Yes.'

He looks at his watch. 'Let's finish up with Nigel.' He'd ended up leaving with his lawyer claiming he hadn't felt well but had agreed to come back in today.

'Do you think we'll get anything more?'

'Nope, but I think we've got enough. Unless I'm very much mistaken, and I don't think I am, he was running something with Nathan and associates.'

She sighs. 'I think you're right. Which is bad, isn't it?'

He grins. 'Oh god, yeah, going to make an absolute ball-ache for Jackie.'

She groans. 'She's going to shout.'

'Yup. I'd say so. Especially when you factor in that Mac was probably in on it too.'

Her eyes widen. 'Fucking hell.'

They don't get anything more, though Nigel does break down, tears and everything, and admits he had been in love with Diane Smart. He is, however, adamant that that is no longer the case. When Seb pushes him as to his reasons for letting Nathan Smart get away with what was clearly a serious crime, all he says is, 'I didn't want to ruin Diane's life.' With a sniff added for noble effect. It doesn't work.

Seb doesn't buy it at all. He believes Nigel thought he was in love with Diane though he's not convinced snivelling little toads like him do love like the rest of the human race. He can, however, accept he was enamoured and had been for years. He knows the power of those intense youthful feelings. Especially when they follow you persistently into your adult life, but he doesn't believe for a second that Nigel Baker was so utterly selfless that he'd see the husband of the woman he claimed to adore go free just to protect her feelings.

If anything, he thinks that Nigel would have relished an opportunity to be rid of Nathan Smart. There are two motivating factors at play for corrupt little numpties like Baker: the money and the honey. Seb bought his crush on Diane, but he firmly believes that it was completely overridden by Nigel's desire to be rich.

It takes a strong man to turn down unearned, un-grafted-for cash. Seb would; he knows that without having to think about it. He could have been far wealthier than he is if he'd been willing to play his adopted parents' game, but at his very core, he isn't that way. It's how he is built; corruption isn't for him. It wasn't for Ben Green either, which is why, Seb thinks, he was pushed out by his colleagues.

Most officers he knows wouldn't stray like that. Most officers are good. It's always the few bad pennies that ruin it for everyone else.

Nigel Baker is a disgrace, and no matter how this case plays out (and Seb strongly suspects they'll be arresting Nathan Smart soon), he'll also have Baker, and he'll make it hurt too. This is about justice for the DaSilvas, for a little boy no one bothered to look for.

CHAPTER FIFTY-FOUR

Leonard is frowning at Seb. 'Is Hayley in danger?'

'We don't think so.'

'It sounds like she is.'

Seb cannot lie, cannot bullshit this man colleagues of his threw in here without a second thought. He is due to be released in the next week or so, but that doesn't matter; what matters is he isn't out there to protect his daughter now. If Tilly was in trouble and Seb couldn't be there, it would eat him alive.

'I'm in close contact with her and will remain that way.'

'She's all alone? At the house?'

'She… ah… Danny Morgan is with her, actually.'

Leonard manages the glimmer of a smile. 'She said her husband was a bit of a dick.'

Seb nods for want of anything else. Tries to imagine Tilly being married to a dick, or being married at all. It sends a tremor of panic through him, and he pushes it away.

Leonard asks, 'Do you have children?'

'A daughter. Tilly.'

Leonard nods. 'Then maybe you understand my concern…'

'I do, and I also appreciate that your behaviour during this has been exemplary.'

Leonard raises an eyebrow.

Seb says, 'The local police force was corrupt.'

'You don't say?' He's grinning.

Seb frowns. 'You suspected it?'

He shrugs. 'I don't know. Suspect is too strong a word; at the time, all I wanted was for my daughter to have a fighting chance. If she had done an awful thing while she was drunk or even if she was just in with druggies or whatever, I didn't want that to define her. The thought of her sitting in a cell, being questioned even, whilst having no one.' His voice cracks a bit. He leans forward. 'Do you have a big family?'

'It's just me and my daughter, and my mother-in-law.'

'Oh yeah?'

'Yes. Tilly's mother… it wasn't for her.'

Leonard nods. 'Sorry to hear that. Anita and I, if we'd had more money, we'd have had a bigger family. As it was, I was delighted we got twins. Then when Ethan came along it all felt complete, you know? I was young, yes, but determined to be better than my own dad.'

Seb says, 'I'm sorry.' And finds he is. Really, genuinely.

Leonard sighs. 'I blew it, but I don't think it was beyond repair.'

'You don't strike me as a quitter.'

'No, the booze had me licked though. Honestly, I was pretty smashed to pieces.'

'And the police?'

'Well, I confessed, but it was more like your man, big fellow?'

'Mackenzie Arnold, detective superintendent.'

Leonard nods. 'Right. He spoon-fed me the words; all I had to do was nod and sign it.'

'Which made you think…?'

'Well, I thought, and the policeman suggested, that there may be a drug element to the whole thing, which made me think of the trouble Hayley was getting in.'

'Aside from that night, what made you think Hayley was in trouble?'

He looks surprised. 'Anita. She found a torn Rizla packet in Hayley's room. Called me in a right panic.'

'When?'

'She'd suspected it for a while but was really upset by it all about a week before I came down. It was the prompt I needed. I had a month clean time which sounds like nothing, but I hadn't managed twenty-four hours or even twelve all year.'

Seb thinks of Charlie, the numerous times she'd insisted with full sincerity that she'd sort herself out, clean up, how firm she could be about it in the morning and still be wasted by lunchtime. 'A month doesn't sound insignificant.'

'I think the split was hardest on Hayley. She was acting out. But smoking dope? At fifteen?' He shakes his head. 'Man.'

'A worrying development.'

'Right, but, as I said to you before, not the worst. Then Anita starts needling Matt about it, not in a bad way but because those two were inseparable.' He shrugs. 'People make this thing about twins being separate people, and they are, course they are, but they are uniquely close. When they were born, they'd cry unless they were bang next to the other.' His eyes sparkle with tears. He takes a breath in, and it shudders.

Seb looks away, allows him this moment of unbearable grief. He can't imagine the loss of a child. But he had grieved for Charlie, could still twist his insides into painful knots at the very thought of her, and she wasn't even dead.

Leonard sighs. 'Matt didn't want to rat on his sister. I imagine he'd have gone, tried to talk to her.'

'He did at the party. Danny said they argued.'

Leonard nods. 'I suspect it wasn't the first row. He'd told Anita that he was convinced she'd been getting the drugs from their neighbour.'

'Gabriel Smart?'

'Right. But Anita liked the kid, said it wouldn't be his fault. His dad, she said, was a wrong 'un, but she was good friends with his mum.'

'So what was she going to do?'

'Talk to her friend.'

Seb sits back. The phone call that Diane spoke about, but she said she'd been checking up on her mate. Maybe Anita went round there? But surely Diane would have said. Was she so scared of Nathan that she'd lie? For all these years? Or did she just not know or suspect?

They needed to get Nathan Smart to talk, and they needed to do it now.

CHAPTER FIFTY-FIVE

Danny has to go to work. He offers more than once to take the day off, and each time I tell him I'll be fine. And I will. It's fairly busy round here in the daytime.

After he leaves, I find I don't really feel fine at all. I feel jittery and disjointed. Leonard, my dad, is now allowed to take calls from me. While we are wading through paperwork, he still has to stay put. But in leniency they have given him a phone.

He is an innocent man, in that he did not kill my mother, Matt, Ethan or Ryan. He is guilty of other things, as I am too. I hadn't grown up properly, not the way I should. In some ways, neither had he and my mum. They'd been young when they had us. She'd lost her parents over their relationship, his had never cared anyway. It was amazing they hadn't imploded before they did. Buckled under the pressure. I'm not cool with how he acted, but, I find, I forgive him. The feeling is perverse almost, like a tiny glance at how freedom might look for me. For him. I hate the way I was towards my mum, Matt, my anger lashing out at them so often like a whip with a sharp end taking tiny chunks from their skin. I hadn't wanted to be that way, wished so many times since that I'd been a better daughter, sister. Maybe this is my chance as much as Leonard's. I don't know how to rebuild our relationship, no idea where to start, but I find, for the first time in fifteen years, I want to try.

He picks up on the first ring. 'Hay Hay.' I am flooded with relief and something else, something buried so far... Love. It is sharp and consuming and almost unbearable. 'Sweetheart?'

'Sorry. I'm here... it's just... your voice.'

'I know. I feel the same.' Quiet while maybe we both contemplate how many phone calls have been missed. I know I do. I've had many chats with him in my mind, ones where I screamed and hollered. This isn't how I imagined it. I'm about to tell him I don't know what to say when he says, 'The detective tells me you've been hanging out with that stoner kid.'

I laugh. I'd forgotten, under the weight of everything else, that Leonard could be funny. I tell him, 'He's a youth worker.'

'Was a stoner kid back then.'

'The one time you met him.'

He chuckles, a rueful sound. 'He seemed all right.'

'He is.'

'Better than the dick husband?'

'Much better. We're getting divorced.'

'That okay for you?'

'Oh yes, and for him.'

'All right then. So you won't be rushing back to America?'

'No. Actually, I was going to suggest that, when you're free, you'll come here.' I hadn't been going to suggest that until the words were out, but I realise I mean it.

'Until I get back on my feet.'

'Maybe we can do that together.'

'Maybe we can.' My heart fizzes. I am hit by so much feeling it takes me a second to unpick it and realise it's… happiness.

I say, 'The house is only small, but…'

'It's the last place they were in.'

I shut my eyes. No one else could have got that, understood it. I know that people — Cat, Gabe, probably the police — think it was morbid of me to come back here, but when I got that call, when I knew Ethan was waiting for me, there was nowhere else to go. I could have sold it. Probably should have sold it. I could have bought two flats for the same price and made plenty more money than I had. But I hadn't. Even if I couldn't visit, couldn't step over the threshold knowing it was here, it being mine felt safer than it being someone else's. Now the thought of me and Dad here makes sense of everything.

He says, 'Do you remember us all squeezed into that flat?'

I think of that too-small place where I invariably ended up with Ethan in my bed, a place where there was no such thing as privacy. It used to drive me mad on Sunday mornings when I'd wake up to the hubbub of them all. Ethan racing up and down the hallway floorboards that he loved to slide along in his socked feet. Matt who'd get up, shovel cereal in his face and then start playing video games in his room. My dad, radio on, singing along, often better than the pros who'd landed record deals. My mum eventually bringing me a tea with a stern, 'It's midday. The whole day is gone.' Me groaning but taking it.

My mum.

I say, 'We were happy once, weren't we?'

'We were. There was a lot of love in that little place.' His voice is thick and cuts off halfway through the word 'place'. 'We'll make a home again, okay? I've got lots of years to make up for.'

'Me too.'

'The policeman was asking about you taking drugs.'

My stomach chills in the way you'd expect it to if your parent mentions your recreational drug use. 'I mean, I smoked a bit of weed back then, but I don't now. I hardly even drink. I haven't since...'

'I'm not mad at you, Hayley, jeez. I was drunk for almost a whole year.'

'Okay.'

'Your mum, she'd been pestering Matt.'

'About me?'

'Yes.'

'And what did he tell her?'

'He thought it was your neighbour you smoked with. Gabe.'

I sigh. 'Yes.' I feel a terrible shame that she had found out and, worse, hadn't said anything to me. I say, 'I didn't think she knew.' If she'd confronted me, what would I have said? That I was scared all the time and that the dope took the edge off, that I liked drinking too, that it made me feel brave when I wasn't?

That night had scared me because I'd lost so much time. Been so out of it. I didn't even know Cat had spiked me. I frown. Cat. A thought tremors there, like I can almost grab at it, then it's gone. Even if the booze wasn't to blame, I had no interest in picking it up with that kind of gusto again. I never had more than one drink, hated having my senses dulled.

'She did. That's what we were talking about that night. She liked Gabe though, she said. Was adamant it'd be the boy's father; she'd never liked him.'

'No, she thought he was mean, and rumour had it he ran around behind Diane's back.'

'Would your mum have confronted him?'

I frown, then see where he's going, where I suppose the police must have arrived at.

And then it hits me in a blinding flash. Little things start pinging, and slotting into place. Even things from this week. 'I'm not sure.' I should tell him what I'm thinking, say something, but what can he do from there?

He says, 'Okay, well, the police are on it. I think they'll have gone to pick him up by now.'

'Probably.'

'I'll be there soon.'

'I can't wait.'

I hang up and dial Locke. His phone goes to voicemail. Lucy's does the same. They'll be picking up Nate, as Dad had said. I think about calling Danny, but he's at work. It's not something I want to put in a text, and I may be wrong. If I'm wrong, it won't matter. If I'm not, then at least I'll know.

I head out, hit by the cold but somehow immune to its effects. My blood feels like it's on fire, and my determined anger seems to keep me moving one step at a time.

CHAPTER FIFTY-SIX

Nathan Smart is sitting in his office looking... vacant... if Seb had to describe it. On the desk in front of him is an open bottle of whisky and an empty tumbler. He looks up when Seb and Lucy walk in and offers a faint smile that collapses before it reaches his eyes.

'Not going to ask us if we've found your son or daughter-in-law?'

'Have you?'

'We were hoping you might be able to help with that.'

''Fraid not.'

'Two kilos of cocaine. Two hundred Ecstasy tablets.'

Nathan frowns at him. 'Excuse me?'

'That's what Nigel Baker caught you with.'

He shakes his head. 'Wasn't Nigel who caught me. He'd have just told me to get on my way.'

'It's his name on the cover sheet.'

He nods. 'Yes, he took over once I arrived. Had to confiscate the drugs obviously, because they were already on their way down to evidence.'

'Who picked you up?'

He shrugs. 'Can't remember his name, but he wasn't one of Mac's.'

'You knew Mac?'

Another nod, weary. Everything about him smacks of defeat. Seb doesn't know what he'd been expecting.

Defiance? Denial? Certainly not this. Nathan says, 'I think you know I did.'

Seb sits opposite him, and Lucy takes the chair beside. Seb feels his phone vibrate in his pocket and ignores it. He is nearly there. Can feel the truth just within grasp.

'They were in on it?'

'Yes. Started off with Nigel.'

'A mate of yours?'

'No. In love with my wife though.'

'And you didn't mind?'

He frowns. 'I didn't like it, but Diane…' He shrugs.

'So you and Nigel become pally?'

'I was dealing, small time, mind. Back then it really was just to look big in the pub, nothing more. I liked to have a good time, liked to make sure everyone else was too. Nigel suggested he could get me larger amounts and make sure I had safe passage when it came to shifting the merchandise.'

Seb shakes his head at that. Nigel was the instigator of all of this. Worse even than just being pulled into what seemed an irresistible opportunity.

'Mac found out.' Nathan smirks at the memory. 'Gave Nigel a right old bollocking, told him to wait twenty-four hours while he had a think about what to do.'

'Was Nigel worried?'

Nathan laughs. 'He was absolutely shitting himself. He's a coward, isn't he. It's what they do.' He looks misty-eyed, unfocused.

Seb wonders how much of that whisky he's drunk. Whether he should take him to the station, breathalyse him. But things feel on the verge. Now isn't the time to interrupt.

Nathan says, 'He needn't have worried though. Mac was close to retiring, and it turned out that he hadn't put by as much cash as he'd hoped and had also accrued a few, yet to be paid, costs along the way.'

'He wanted in?'

Nathan nods. 'Yup, he wanted in. So he came to see me, with Nigel, and we struck a deal.'

'More than looking big down the pub?'

He shrugs. 'More in a month than I could earn in a year.'

'Your arrest happened after that?'

'It did, yes, and like I said, if it had been Nigel who'd picked me up, all would have been fine. It was fine anyway, so I thought, but I guess the fact you know what was confiscated suggests it wasn't really?'

'Nigel made the charge sheet disappear, wrote it up as a minor offence, slap on the wrists, quick chat and on your way, but as you said, the evidence was there. Buried, admittedly, but still there. It took some digging, but the trail led back to it, yeah.'

'Right.'

'So after that?'

'I cut the loss, had to pay my man from my own pocket. That annoyed me. I felt like Nigel and Mac should have dipped into theirs, but...' – he shrugs – 'they were the law. They could stitch me up anytime they saw fit. Rock and a hard place.'

'But you were a drug dealer,' states Seb, not wanting this man, whom he strongly suspects murdered the DaSilvas, painting himself as a victim.

'I was an idiot who liked to be able to hand out treats like sweeties in the pub. I'd never thought of making it a business thing. I never had big plans for anything. It was Diane wanted us to 'do well', which essentially meant being rich. How's a man like me meant to do that without a bit of skulduggery?'

'You run a successful business now.'

'Yeah, and how do you think I found the capital to start it up? No one would have given me a loan, would they?'

'They might have.'

He shrugs. 'It was meant to be enough to get us started. Nigel and Mac got bloody greedy though, so did she.'

'Your wife?'

He nods. 'I didn't want anything to do with sodding Nigel, didn't like him at all.'

Seb frowns. 'She knew what you were doing, your wife?'

He nods. 'Pretended not to, like, turned a blind eye, but she knew, of course. Nigel approached her about expanding first, not me.'

'And you didn't want to?'

'No. Didn't want the risk.'

'What changed?'

He smiles, a rueful expression that seems tired and worn. 'When I met Diane, I thought all my luck had come in at once. Beautiful she was, as well as that she seemed to be easy-going, cheerful. My other mates got nagged by their wives a lot. Where you going? When will you be in? None of that from Diane. If anything, sometimes I wondered if she cared what I did. Then Nigel started hanging out more.' His lips tighten. 'I got the hump, and she pointed out she didn't restrict me, I had nothing to worry about, yada yada. Couldn't fault her logic, but I didn't like it. Anyone could see the bloke was in love with her. Then Gabe got into my stash, took a bit of weed, not a lot, just a bit, but I was worried about it. He smoked puff with his mates, I knew that, but I didn't want him going wrong, you know, and branching out meant... well, other things.'

'Understandable.' Lucy's soft voice. Seb keeps his mouth shut, keeping inside the long lecture he could give on drugs around children. He'd thrown Charlie out to avoid the same fate for Tilly. You always thought you hid stuff from them, but they knew, kids. Even as a toddler Tilly had been unsettled and getting more so as Charlie got worse. Drugs and kids are an accident waiting to happen. Things that ought never be combined.

Nathan says, 'I told her, that's it. And that was when she sprang the idea of working with Nigel.' He shakes his head. 'It seems such a stupid thing to have agreed to now, looking back, but... the money. The amount I'd have to shift. What you got was nothing, the tip of the iceberg. And with local law turning a blind eye, it was like a ticket to print cash.'

'Irresistible.' Lucy again.

'Right. All me and Di wanted was enough. Gabe, he was bright, and we could see him going to uni, doing well. We wanted for him to have a good start, you know?'

'How long were you planning to keep it up?' Seb keeps his voice even, removing judgement from it. Speaking to idiots with hare-brained schemes is the norm for him, but he never fails to be amazed how daft money can make people. Still, until you found yourself with not enough, it was hard to know the lengths you'd go to yourself.

'She grew up poor.'

'Diane?'

He nods. 'Yeah, then we had Gabe young. We had plans, wanted to get ahead, and we always seemed just about on the brink, then a big bill might come in and we'd be back to square one. We were renting that house then. Never would have been able to buy, expand the business.'

'How long did it take you to meet your goals?'

'A year. That's all. I got a wedge, so did Nigel, so did Mac. Obviously, the cash had to be handled delicately. Laughably, we had the most success with that. Nigel threw it about like water. Bought my wife a pair of diamond fucking earrings.' He shakes his head.

'Were they having an affair?'

Silence.

'Nate?'

'She said no.'

'You didn't believe her?'

'Nigel was an idiot, but he was a plodding sort of idiot. It wouldn't have occurred to him to do what we did on his own.'

'She slept with him as persuasion.'

Nate's head hangs forward, a flush of red creeps up his neck. 'Probably.'

'We heard you were running around town with other women?'

'Trying to get her attention. Never went anywhere.' Defence in his voice.

'Did it get her attention?'

A sigh now. 'It did when Anita started worrying about her.' He leans over the desk, presses his head into his hands.

Seb's mind is racing. 'Anita asked her if she was all right?'

He nods, his face glum, his whole body sagging inwards. 'They were friends, you know. I was so pleased. Anita was a soft soul. I thought she'd be good for Diane.' He shakes his head, breathes in and it catches like a gasp.

'What did she tell Anita?'

He looks at them now, clear eyes shining with unshed tears. 'That we had problems we were trying to work on. She sobbed on her friend's shoulder.'

'And Anita bought it?'

'Everyone always buys it.'

'Tell us what happened, Nate. That night.'

Another head shake. 'I love her. I've always loved her. I thought we could put it all behind us, and we did. We had. Gabe did well, didn't he?' His voice has a tinge of desperation, and since it's not really a question, no one answers him. 'And Dylan, we have Dylan, and we love him. We're good grandparents...'

Lucy asks, 'Where's Dylan now?'

Nate looks at her, half-dazed. 'Nursery. Diane dropped him there a few hours ago.'

Seb exchanges a look with his young DC. Relief.

'Tell us what happened, Nate.'

CHAPTER FIFTY-SEVEN

It takes me almost half an hour to get there. The cold biting at my ungloved hands as I go. By the time I ring the bell on the Smarts' large front door out here in the middle of nowhere, I can hardly feel my fingers and the skin looks dry and wrinkly. The thought of a winter holiday flashes through my mind. When this is over... I can imagine sitting on a beach somewhere, in stunned shock, with my dad maybe? Or Danny?

She answers with a smile, and I feel a funny sort of unfurling within me. I say, 'You look so like my mum.'

'We could have been sisters.' Her words are careful, her voice steady. I look at her straight; she looks right back. 'I suppose you'd better come in.'

I follow her through a busy hallway. The walls are filled with photographs that boast the trappings of their success. Gabriel's school photos. His graduation. His wedding day. Cat stunning and serene. Diane and Nathan, impeccable, smiling, the perfect in-laws.

'Is Dylan here?'

'No, he's at nursery.'

'And you haven't asked me if I've come about Cat or Gabe.'

She gestures to a seat at her kitchen table. 'Sit. Drink?'

'No, thank you.'

She takes the chair opposite. On the table in between us is a perfect Victoria sponge under a lacy cake cover. Alongside it is a sharp knife. Not the same one that sliced into my mother's throat or slashed Matt's arteries. But it feels symbolic somehow. She sees me looking. 'Your mother gave me that recipe.'

'She loved to cook.'

'She did.' Said on a sigh escaping from her body like trapped birds leaving a restrictive cage. 'Do you want a slice?' She reaches for the cover, turns the tray towards her, the knife now on her side. Her fingers a small movement away from its handle.

'No, thank you.'

A shrug. 'Well.'

I don't say anything. I look at her and remember that summer. Their friendship. My mother's joy in it. Ever the optimist.

I tell Diane, 'She loved you.'

She smiles. 'How did you know?'

'I was asked today if my mother would have confronted Nathan.'

'About his dealing?'

I nod and say, 'I don't think she would have. The first thing she would have done is try and talk to you.'

'Always keen to help.'

'She was a good person.'

Diane laughs. 'She was, yes, deserved better than a daughter causing all kinds of trouble. Getting in the midst of things better left alone. And Matt, your mother's little spy.' She shakes her head as though she is terribly sorry. Like she has done a tiny, wrong thing that, sadly, couldn't be helped and, perhaps, was my fault anyway.

'Did you do it yourself?'

CHAPTER FIFTY-EIGHT

'Diane had been a bit concerned about Anita, but reckoned she could rein her in. If it hadn't been for Hayley keeping a stash of Rizlas of all things,' Nathan says. He shakes his head; his face is blank. His eyes looking past Lucy and Seb at distant horrors from yesteryear. 'They met in the day. Had a coffee. Anita was worrying about her kids, Hayley specifically, and nervous because her husband was due up here. Then she told Diane about me. Dealing, rumours of other women.'

There is a second whilst Seb considers the distortion of this. Not untrue, but also not the full story. He says, 'Go on, Nathan.'

'She came back at me, livid she was. When she got like that... she was unreasonable and, honestly, she frightened me.'

'What were you frightened of?'

'I don't know. I know it must sound stupid, me being twice her size.'

Lucy says, 'It doesn't.'

And he smiles at her. 'She's smarter than me, always has been, and she has this way of... I don't know... making me feel confused. Like, things happen, and I think they went down one way, but she says it was something else entirely. I'm never sure what's right. Often I'm wrong, or I... I can't remember whether her version or mine...' He trails off. Then more firmly, 'But I remember that night. I wish I didn't.'

Seb's mind flicks back to the photos. Anita on her living room floor, a wide pool of blood fanning out around her. Matt, his hand stretched towards his mother. And Ryan. Nothing to do with anything. But dead nonetheless. Seb says, 'She was friends with Ryan's mum too.'

Nathan nods. 'People always like her, at first anyway. She doesn't have close friends though, not long-term ones.'

'She and Nigel?'

'They stayed in touch, but he didn't want anything to do with us more than he had to. He got to escape it all.' His voice is bitter, like sharp lemon at the end of your tongue.

'Did Anita call her after Leonard came round?'

'No. Diane waited though. Heard him leave, then she went in. She told Anita she was checking she was okay but what she wanted to know was what she'd told him and what she'd decided to do. She'd suggested to me... well.'

'What did she suggest?'

'Killing Anita before she saw Leonard. She didn't want her to tell him anything. Said I could hit her with the car, knew what time she was going to the shops and everything.'

'What did you do?'

His eyes focus now, zeroing in on Seb. 'Told her to leave off, that she was mad. She said we'd go to prison, or more to the point, I would if we didn't do something, if Anita got hold of the wrong Old Bill, or realised the police didn't want to help. I didn't think it would happen, because of Nigel and Mac, but I was prepared for it. Rather that than killing a woman. A mother of three.'

'You said no?'

'Course I said no.'

'Where were you, when she went in to see Anita?'

'Out, at the pub. I went to cool off.'

'So she's in with Anita and…?'

'Anita said she'd told Leonard she was worried about Hayley and that she was also worried about Diane, and she was, you know. That's the worst of it.'

Lucy nods sympathetically, though that is obviously not the worst of it at all.

'Diane asked if she'd said anything to her husband about me. She said she'd mentioned it but no detail. Diane said she'd go and make them a tea. When she came back, Anita was at the window, looking out, expecting Matt back. He'd messaged her, it turned out. Diane didn't know that though. Anita didn't stand a chance.'

'Diane stabbed her then?'

He nods. 'In the throat.' Which Seb knew. He'd seen the photos. The large, gaping hole. She must have turned and faced her attacker before she fell, onto her back.

'How did she think she'd get away with it?'

'I don't think she'd thought that far ahead, just assumed she'd find a way; she always does, and she did, didn't she?'

No one could argue with that.

'That's when she called me, said I needed to get back ASAP and to call Nigel for a lift. Matt and Ryan must have arrived just before we did.'

He's crying now, openly sobbing.

Lucy says, 'She killed the boys?'

He nods. 'Said they walked in, and Matt asked her what had happened, was she okay, before he saw the knife in her hand and realised.'

Seb murmurs, 'God.'

Nathan is slumped, head low, a defeated man.

Seb says, 'What about Ethan?'

He breathes in. 'Nigel took it all in, told Diane she'd need to go and clean herself up, and she did. That must have been when Cat came back.' He shakes his head. 'Her dad owed me money.'

'Cat's dad?' Seb frowns.

Nate nods. 'A lot.'

'For drugs?'

Nate shook his head. 'No, he had a gambling problem. We were in a card game at the pub. He should never have been involved. A few guys I dealt with, heavies, you know. I could afford to lose a bit; he couldn't. I fronted him some cash. The idiot went and did the same thing again though, with the same guys.'

Seb's mind is whirring, the vague mention from Gabe that Cat's parents had been having financial problems.

'Diane knew?'

Nate nods. 'Told Cat to keep her mouth shut and things would get better for her parents. We'd pay the debt.'

'My god.'

Nate smiles. It is a sad look. 'Worse than that, Diane had Cat take the bloody clothes, go off and burn them. Diane held that over the girl too. She was an accomplice, she said.'

Seb shakes his head. She'd been a kid then, probably scared, but she still could have come forward after the fact. 'Did she know? What Diane had done?'

Nate shrugs. 'She figured it out.'

337

'She never said anything.'

Nate says, 'She and Diane aren't so different. Not really. Cat was glad her parents were okay, glad there was money in her house again.'

'Hayley was her friend.' Lucy sounds shocked. Nate sighs.

Seb will get back on to Gabe and Cat in a second. First, he needs to know. 'Ethan…'

'He came down. His little voice.' Nathan pauses, a hand pressed to his mouth, head shaking as if it is happening all over again right in front of him.

Seb says, 'Go on, Nate…'

'Nigel and I were frozen, standing there. For ages, it felt like. Nothing was real, do you know what I mean? I kept thinking they'd get up in a minute.'

'You were in shock.'

He nods. 'I think, I reckon Nigel was too. Anyway, Ethan pulled us out of it, came in, said, "Mummy?" I almost fell to the ground. But Nigel was there. In uniform, and he said, "It's okay, come with me."' A thick swallow. They all hear the sound of Nathan almost gagging as if he's trying to eat and store away this information. This awful, terrible secret that has sat there in his bowels for fifteen years, festering like cancer. 'Thing was, he'd seen them. On the floor.' His voice nothing more than a whisper. 'But I couldn't… I wouldn't have…'

CHAPTER FIFTY-NINE

I watch Diane talk as calmly as if she were describing a mild inconvenience. She has adopted the soothing tone of a mum, perhaps, relaying a nasty but not-so-bad incident between children who'd fallen out.

She says, 'Nathan should have been more careful. Leaving stuff around for people to find, Gabe nicking his dope. And Anita, well, she should have kept her nose out of it.'

'What about Matt and Ryan?'

She sighs that weird sigh. My heart hammers. *Badada-boom badadaboom.* Everything inside me slips and slides. I'd liked Diane. Matt had liked her. Why had we? Because she looked so like our mother, the one person in the world who'd take care of us, love us even when we were unlovable. Also, because she hadn't given us reason not to, she was Gabe's mum, our neighbour. A monster hiding in the house next door.

'And Ethan?' My voice hardly makes it out of me. It releases like a poisonous puff of noxious gas.

She stares at me from glassy eyes. 'The thing is, Hayley, I had a terrible time of it as a child. My stupid parents produced more children than they could ever afford. Nate and I had Gabe, not planned, and I wasn't proud of that, but it didn't happen again. I needed to ensure he had a better start than I had. This was our way out of mediocrity.

We'd put so much effort in already, risked so much. I couldn't just... lose it.' She smiles. 'You'll understand yourself when you're a mother.'

She is completely and utterly mad.

CHAPTER SIXTY

'He went, the little one, holding Nigel's hand, me a step behind, and they bumped straight into Diane coming back in. She looked from me to Nigel, whispered, "*What did he see?*" I said nothing at the exact same moment Nigel told her, "All of it'"

The terror. The absolute horror of it. Seb closes his eyes for a second. Small white bones laid out on a cold metal table. The bright nylon of his superhero pyjamas. Hands pressed around his neck, a snap. And then...

'Did he hear what was said? Ethan?'

Nathan nods. 'But he didn't understand. He still thought it was okay. Grown-ups were there, and we were going to help him.'

'Jesus.'

But Nathan doesn't hear Lucy, doesn't register anything. His mind is elsewhere; it is fifteen years ago on a warm summer's night turning into an unforgettable summer's morning. All this time he hasn't spoken, and now he can't stop. Words run from him, a river with its own fierce current racing towards the sea. They have eaten away at him. Taking every second of joy, tinging all good moments with deep regret: watching Gabe graduate, get married. Playing with his beautiful grandson. It was always there in the background, making everything that should be good stink. A fetid poison over the layer of his life.

Not for Diane. She was fine. He honestly didn't think she'd even have considered it if it wasn't for him. His nightmares. Waking in a cold sweat, crying. She'd moved him into the spare room a decade ago, because it was 'so annoying'.

'What happened next, Nathan?'

'They took him. Nigel and Diane. In her car. She said she'd speak to him, sort out his story.'

'Where did they go?'

'Out past the park, there was an old empty cottage close by, but we'd been using it, for storage.'

'Drugs?'

Nate nods. 'A place to hold them that wasn't linked to any of us. Was up and running. We had electricity, furniture. People who'd come and transport. I wondered if it was maybe where Diane and Nigel went…' He trails off. Shakes his head. One of the derelict cottages.

'It's not there now?'

'No, it was flattened, to make way for the new development.'

'They took Ethan there?'

He nods. 'He was still alive the next morning.'

Seb's heart is hammering. The half-arsed search, they hadn't looked that far. Hadn't searched those buildings. The search that was done under Mac's guidance. A DSI not just hiding money. Covering up murders, condemning a little boy. 'How do you know?'

'I made Diane take me there. Saw him through the window, sitting on the sofa watching TV.'

'And what did you do?'

'Told Diane she had to bring him back. He'd go wherever Hayley was being sent to. The police had been by then, officially. Nigel came back, responded to the 999

342

call, would you believe? Hayley had come home. It was unreal.' And all the time Ethan had been alive. A mere forty minutes away. Nate says, 'She promised she wouldn't hurt him.'

Seb says, 'When did you realise? That Ethan was dead?'

Nate presses a hand to his mouth, shakes his head.

Lucy says, 'Were you trying to pretend it hadn't happened?'

'God help me, but yes.' In that admission, the anger in the room deflates a bit. For Lucy, at least, whose eyes are damp with it all. Seb is older, has seen a few more horrors than this, but still, he feels the crack in his heart. All this loss. For money.

'Why are you telling us now, Nate?'

'My son, I was never sure if he knew. Always hoped perhaps he didn't.'

'He had Anita's necklace.'

'What?'

Seb nods. 'In a box full of dope. We thought they were guilty.' He adds, 'Of the murders.' Because Cat may not have committed any actual crime herself, but she was complicit in her silence. If she'd spoken up straight away, Ethan might still be alive.

'Diane said you would suspect them.' He shakes his head. 'She took that necklace, kept it in our room in her jewellery box. Said it reminded her of her friend. She was upset when it went missing. It was her only reminder of Anita. That's messed up, isn't it?'

No one needs to confirm that. It's obvious to them all, though Seb thinks how insidious these things can be, how abuse within the home can normalise even the most awful, the most unacceptable of things.

Nate says, 'She's not right.' His voice is forceful, strong.

'You just noticed?' Not even meant cruelly, a genuine question, seeking a genuine answer.

'No, I don't know. She is my wife. What she did was wrong, awful, but in her head, she was doing it for us and Gabe. And she has this way of putting things so you lose track of what is normal and what's not. She gets in your head.' He pokes his forefinger hard at his temple as he speaks. 'I wobbled, so often. Each time, she talked me round. Then Dylan came along, and we haven't talked about it since. It was the first time I thought maybe I really could forget. That boy.'

'You love your grandson.'

'And my son and Cat. That's the problem, you see.'

Seb says, 'She's planning to let them take the fall?'

'Yes. She says Dylan is our focus now. That it's a shame, but...'

'Has she killed them?'

He shakes his head. 'She doesn't know where they are. But I do.'

CHAPTER SIXTY-ONE

'Do you love me?'

Cat appraises him coolly. 'Of course. I married you, didn't I? Do you love me?'

'Yes.' He doesn't hesitate.

She smiles. 'I'm not sure if it matters anyway.'

What can he say to that? What does she mean by it? Always an enigma to him. He was seventeen when he toyed with his feelings for Hayley. Almost the opposite of Cat, he'd wondered what it would be like to be with her. He wonders now how different his life might have been if that had been the case. So many ifs. If only Cat hadn't gone back to get changed. If only he hadn't known. If only he'd grown up to be a better man. Stronger. 'We should have said something.'

'Really? My family would have been ruined. My dad owed Nate and those card-playing thugs hundreds of thousands; we'd have lost our house, probably my parents would have split up. Who knows where I'd have ended up? What would have happened to you, an only child, both your parents in prison?' This is the sort of thing that worries him about Cat. When he'd asked Danny why it hadn't worked out with her, he'd kind of shuddered. Gabe had pushed it and Danny had told him, 'She has weird views, and she's the kind of girl who will never let you breathe.'

That's exactly what it's like with her. Like fucking suffocating slowly. She makes the decisions for you. Her view is always your view. That's how it goes.

He suspects that's how it went for his dad too. He still doesn't know the details of that night. He doesn't want to, is the truth. He'd seen Cat coming from his house, and she'd grabbed him, pulled him into the woods and told him about the bloodied clothes. His mum in the shower, the card game and the money her father owed.

Gabe had seen his mother cause his dad pain and turmoil. She'd ignored him for close to a month once. Just quietly gone about her business. Speaking to Gabe and acting as if his dad wasn't even in the room. Gabe had been a little boy. He'd laughed, thinking maybe they were playing a game. It never looked fun for his dad though.

The next morning, after the party, when he was still a bit stoned and high on being with Cat, really being with her, they had arrived home to it all. He'd turned to her and said, 'What do we do?' and she'd said nothing.

His parents *had* carried on as if nothing had changed, and after Hayley had gone and they'd moved, he managed to convince himself from time to time that that was the case. Even when he found Anita's necklace in his mum's jewellery box. He recognised it instantly. Why he took it, he didn't know, and he didn't tell Cat about it either.

He was surprised when Dylan came along that Cat could just hand him over to his mother. He asked once, 'Aren't you worried?'

She shrugged. 'Diane was protecting you guys, you and your dad.'

He frowned.

Cat went on. 'You were flush after it all happened, right?'

346

He nodded.

'So it had something to do with money, setting you all up. Setting us up. She was looking after her own. She won't hurt Dylan.' That worried him. That Cat could think there was anything to rationalise here. Any justification for it.

He supposes, in some ways, her dislike of Hayley helped. She wasn't really sad for her friend; he isn't sure he's ever seen Cat sad for anyone other than Cat. He realises glumly now that he's married someone just like his mum.

He says, 'You said she'd never hurt us.'

Cat sighs. 'I guess I was wrong.' Tears spring to her eyes. 'I'll never see him again, will I?' They are locked in here, in one of Nate's new developments. Men aren't due on-site for hours, and who knows where their son will be by then, or what fate awaits them?

Just then, there is a banging at the door.

CHAPTER SIXTY-TWO

I say to her, 'Do you think you'll get away with this?'

'They think it's Cat or Gabe.'

'And if I go missing?'

'Yes, you have thrown a spanner in the works.' She smiles a pretty but dangerous smile. White even teeth.

'What are you planning to do?'

'Well, Nathan has made sure that Gabe and Cat are indisposed for a while. They will be that policeman's main suspects by now.' Said casually, as if framing your son for a murder he didn't commit is in any way normal. 'I have our passports good to go, and we've an overseas account we'll be able to access. I'm going to go and collect Dylan, meet my husband and then we'll be off.'

I say, 'They'll realise, that it wasn't Gabe and Cat, that it was you.'

A shrug. 'I won't be around for that, will I, and they'll never find us.'

She stands, picking up the knife quite calmly, walking round the table. I get to my feet; my hands held out in front of me.

She laughs. 'I'll give you a choice. I'll kill you now, or you can give me your phone, I'll lock you in my cellar and leave you alive. Think of it as an apology.'

'For killing my family?'

'Right.'

She means it. I say, 'Okay.'

'Take your phone from your pocket, put it on the table. The last thing I need is them coming after us too soon. There must be enough time for us to get going.'

'Get going', as if they are nipping off on holiday rather than framing their only child and kidnapping their grandson. I put my phone down between us, thinking blankly that there is some way to set an alarm off on it and I have no idea what that is. I should. I wish I knew. I let her lead me to the door at the top of the stairs; as I walk, I feel my anger rising. Dylan is a small, innocent baby. Just like Ethan had been not so many years before this evil woman ended him. She was calmly discussing having arranged for her husband to kidnap and frame her own son and daughter-in-law. What would she do to Dylan?

At the last moment I turn to face her and swing my leg out, sweeping it under hers. She collapses on the floor, the knife bouncing softly on her hideous patterned shagpile. I get on her before she can move, and we tussle. She is strong for a woman her age. I should have the instant upper hand, but she gets a swift blow into my jaw with a closed fist which hurts like hell and makes me loosen my grip for just a second. It's long enough, and she is scuttling towards the knife like a demented, crawling infant. I am dizzy from her punch, but I am also aware that I have broken the terms of our agreement and she's likely to try and kill me now and I don't want to die. I want to live and hurt and heal. I want to take the chances *they* never got and try and make the best of things. I push myself up and manage to get a foot to the knife kicking it away and then I grab her by the hair.

Fights on TV look cool. We must look insane. Arms, legs writhing in and out, bodies pressed together as we roll around on the floor. It's strangely exhausting, and I'm wondering, behind the pain that hits various parts of me, how long I can keep it up, how long she can.

A voice breaks in, a battering at the door, the detective calling Diane's name, and I scream. 'Help, we're in here…'

CHAPTER SIXTY-THREE

Seb walks into the living room, and Tilly switches tabs on the computer. He pretends not to notice, and she leaves for school, giving him a quick hug and Val a kiss on the cheek. Her friend Claire is waiting at the end of the path, and Seb watches from behind net curtains as the girls head off. Things are mostly back to normal. They've had some door slamming, and oddly Seb felt relieved after a few days where it had felt almost as if they were treading too carefully around each other. He hasn't mentioned the photo; she hasn't either. They are yet to have that chat, but Tilly has asked him and Val a few things about her mother, and he knows it's coming.

He heads to the PC to shut it off. She never remembers, and he can't resist pulling up the tab she'd last been looking at, but the history is blank. When he checks, she's deleted the last twenty-four hours. There are ways around it, of course, and part of the reason the computer is here is to keep her safe. His head visits every worst-case scenario, and he thinks about taking the PC into work. Getting one of the geeks there to have a go. But where do you draw the line? She'll be fourteen this year.

Fourteen.

She has some right to secrets, privacy. Her life is online, and just because his wasn't, he doesn't want to fall into the camp of 'it's all bad there'.

He's spoken to her frankly, told her hard facts. He trusts her. She's a good kid.

A car beeps out front. It'll be Lucy. His phone pings as he's stepping outside *Hope it goes okay today. Let's talk later. X.* Faye Doyle. Who'd been so persistent he ended up going for that drink, and it turned out she did consider it a date. She was also quite adamant it ought to be the first of many. They are taking things slowly, stupidly slowly. It is the only way he can do it, but he finds her easy company. Tilly and Val like her, and he is, for the first time since Charlie, open to new possibilities. He sends back a *Thanks* and then a *x*.

He pulls at the collar of his suit, sweating under the shirt, feeling strangled by the tie. Lucy says, 'Hot, isn't it?'

'It is.'

CHAPTER SIXTY-FOUR

The day we bury him, it is boiling. The kind of heat that illuminates England in all her glory. It's easy to forget during the long grey winters that they are setting the scene for this lushness yet to come. Without those cold, wet months, we couldn't have this fresh, alive green. It is as if the plants themselves are breathing. Birds chirp in the distance, and the priest – because my mum would have wanted it that way – says things that I don't fully take in, but his tone is soft and soothing. Sean has sent a beautiful floral arrangement. Extravagant and over the top. It takes up almost all of the space. It makes me think of him, and I do so with fondness. We speak occasionally on the phone, and our divorce is almost finalised. He's going to ask Sophie to marry him because, as he puts it, he's not getting any younger and needs a few kids to boss around.

I feel my dad take my hand in his. He stands next to me, tall and proud. His hair is so long it is halfway down his back and it's held together with a dark leather thong, a feather at its end. His skin against mine feels like things I'd longed for for so long it can be hard to believe they are real and happening to me.

I am not alone.

Tears stream down his face as they do mine. This is a sad day as we put my baby brother to rest alongside my mother and Matt.

In the small house where my mother grew up, we have redecorated. We've filled it with pictures of us all together, and me, my dad and Danny are adding more all the time.

Leonard is teaching music to ex–offenders, and I started helping out one weekend when they were short-staffed and found I enjoyed it. I'm about to start that degree in music. I don't know exactly what I'll do with it, but suddenly I have a hunger to learn and create. I hadn't been living, not really. I'd been going through the motions and adamantly refused to even consider killing myself, though the numbness threatened to swamp me more than once. I could not justify my death when they hadn't got to live.

Now I find I cannot justify wasting time when their years were cut so cruelly short.

Diane will spend the rest of hers in prison. Nathan has been sentenced as well; he'll serve at least seven, they say. Nigel was charged with various things and has a court date coming up soon. It looks like he'll do at least some time. I asked Cat and Gabe not to attend today. Gabe phoned, and I took the call, but there was nothing to say. I am appalled that Cat is still free, going about her business, but her crime was silence, and she was a child in the eyes of the law – she won't be convicted for it. She, to my mind, is as sick as Diane, and I want nothing to do with her ever again. Gabe is weak, not evil, I understand that, but it was Nathan's and Gabe's weakness that laid the ground for everything that happened, and meant the wrong person paid for so long. Danny will never speak to him again either, I don't think.

I don't know if I can ever forgive any of them; certainly, it is not something Leonard or I can ever forget, but I don't want to feel angry and hard done by.

Diane was scared of being poor, of not having enough, so was Cat. Nathan was scared of upsetting her. Gabe was scared of not managing without his parents' help, and I don't think he would have either.

I will not live my life in fear. I will accept that some things are frightening, and I will try to do them anyway. For years I was so risk-averse it became a perversion. Now I promise to let myself love, laugh, get hurt, pick myself up and try again. Life isn't fair. I know that in a way other people still get to be cushioned from. It can turn in a second from one thing into another entirely.

The priest gestures to me, and I step forward, pick up the first handful of dirt and throw it in. We stand for a long time whilst the small group gathered here starts to leave. Leonard holds me close, it is too warm for the embrace, but I need it, so does he. Finally, we break apart. I say goodbye to them. Not just little Ethan but also Matt and my mum. I wasn't the perfect daughter or sister, but I loved them, and I say that now. As we walk away, I finger the solid silver wings that sit around my neck, all that's left of the marriage that wasn't meant to be, all that's left of Mrs Marriott. A reminder... because she served me well when I needed her. I touch the guitar at the end of the chain. Leonard and I walk towards Danny and the other mourners. Ready to open our door to them. Ready to open the door to far more than we've been able to for a long time.

A letter from Niki

I first wrote Sebastian Locke as a secondary character in my standalone thriller *Found Her*. Readers were very divided about my protagonist but pretty much everyone loved Locke. He's a young detective in his early thirties who became a father at eighteen. He ended up with sole custody of his daughter Tilly and lives with her and his ex mother-in-law Val.

The idea for the mystery itself came about from an episode of Crime Girl Gang, a true crime podcast I used to host. It is loosely based on a real case in America which we covered. An entire family was wiped out in one night, one family member was missing and their remains were discovered years later.

It got me thinking… which is generally how my stories begin. As with most of my books it touches on themes of family, guilt, belonging and addiction. It is my first detective series and I'm really excited to have it published. I've always liked series and long form storytelling in books and on TV. I am a huge fan of American crime writers like Lisa Gardner, Harlan Coben and Karin Slaughter who always seem to seamlessly blend the psychological and procedural elements involved in a good whodunit and, I guess the Locke books take a lot from that format.

I hope you enjoy the book, I hope you like Sebastian Locke as much as I do and if you do perhaps you might visit him again…

I'm very responsive on social media so do feel free to get in touch and tell me what you think…

https://twitter.com/NikiMackayBooks
https://www.facebook.com/MadisonAttalleebooks
https://www.instagram.com/nikimackaywriter/?hl=en
https://www.tiktok.com/@nikimackayauthor

Acknowledgements

Thank you so much to my fantastic editor Keshini Naidoo at Hera books. I've long admired Hera and their commercial spirit and I am delighted that we found a project to work on together. Also a huge thank you to the wider team at Canelo and Hera. Copy edits and proof reads for this book were an absolute joy so thank you to Ross Greenwood and Lynne Walker, the cover is gorgeous, thank you, Ghost Design.

Thank you to the sales marketing and publicity team at Canelo and Hera, Jennie, Thanhmai, Claudine and Kate.

Thank you to my lovely agent Hattie Grünewald for editing, deal making, hand holding and so on. Thanks to the criminal minds group for the chat that never ends, and to my husband, the teen, the little loon and the over-sized cats for making home the very best place to be.